DELUGE

DELUGE

ALBERTINE STRONG

HARMONY BOOKS
NEW YORK

Published by Harmony Books, a division of Crown
Publishers, Inc., 201 East 50th Street, New York, New
York 10022. Member of the Crown Publishing Group.

Random House, Inc. New York, Toronto, London,
Sydney, Auckland
http://www.randomhouse.com/

Harmony and colophon are trademarks of Crown
Publishers, Inc.

Printed in the United States of America
Book design by DEBORAH KERNER

Library of Congress Cataloging-in-Publication Data
Strong, Albertine.
Deluge / Albertine Strong.—1st ed.
1. Ojibwa Indians—Fiction. I. Title.
PS3569.T69748D45   1997
813'.54—dc21   97-1563
CIP

ISBN 0-517-70621-0

10 9 8 7 6 5 4 3 2 1
First Edition

For L. WING,

> companion,
> life-mate,
> wonder—
> with all my love

ACKNOWLEDGMENTS

I WISH TO THANK THE FOLLOWING individuals for their help: Eric Vrooman, for his keen insights; Leslie Meredith and Sherri Rifkin, for their sharp and rigorous editorial work; my friend Bear Who Guards the Cave, for his wisdom, time, and investment in our future. And as always, I acknowledge the workings of the spirit in its infinite manifestations, whatever its name may be, or as it is said, *Anindi abigwen Manido? Mioma abigwen.* (Where is the dwelling of the Spirit? *Here* is my dwelling.)

Baba'maciyan' gicigun'

I am carried by great winds
across the sky

Prologue

In 1909 my grandfather boarded a train outside Prentice, Wisconsin, in what was to become one of the heaviest rainfalls in Lake Superior history. During a three-hour period that day nearly fifteen inches fell. Bridges collapsed. Roads were washed out. Trees toppled. But my grandfather, then nineteen, knew nothing of the hard rains to come, nor did the others boarding the train.

He brought with him an old trunk, bound in leather straps, a penknife, a sandwich—in his jacket pocket—and reading glasses.

In a photograph of him taken that morning, he has a startled look in his eyes, as though the camera were a rifle—*click! click!*—dry-firing.

The photograph has a certain timeless quality to it. Papekewis, or Peke, as he was called, was looking down the barrel of extinction. Supposedly he was to fire back. Out of the entire male population at Lac du Flambeau, he had been chosen to attend Grinnell College in Grinnell, Iowa, as an honor student. Already he spoke three languages: Ojibwaymowin, French, and English. His math work was outstanding, and he had a ferocious interest in the sciences. He tested in the extraordinary range and wasn't even trying.

In the photograph, the collar of his newly bought shirt rides the sides of his neck so tight the skin bulges. His temples are shiny with sweat. Knots of muscle run in stiff lines from his jaw. The wings on either side of his nose are flared, and his lips are set in a harsh, unwavering line.

No doubt this thing he was doing had not been his idea.

Back then the trains had steam whistles, and they sounded that whistle, pulling out of Prentice, two or three long toots. By then the sky was green with dense clouds, and a far-off rolling sound signaled the coming of more severe weather. A light rain was falling.

The train was to pass through Saint Paul, then jog southwest, through Mankato to Des Moines. From there my grandfather was to take a buggy.

The train headed out into the approaching thunderheads. *Toot! Toot-toot!* My grandfather's car was filled with businessmen from Chicago, cigars and suits and card-playing. My grandfather sat near the rear of his car, rain washing down the window. He could see this was no ordinary rain. He was thinking of Trickster in his incarnation as Wenebojo. He was always thinking of Wenebojo, and he thought perhaps there was to be a big trick played on them all.

He told me, *Aja, I could just see him dancing in that rain.*

Only this time blue pants and hat. What a smile! Raindrops big as your teeth! You look out for him, that Wenebojo. He'll surprise you.

But the train. It began to rock in the wind. Clouds hung low and heavy up ahead. The businessmen worried themselves with cards. Some tried to read. Others, the most fearful, faked sleep. The car pitched and rasped. A conductor came through, said they'd make it to Saint Paul. The rain went on for an eternity.

My grandfather tried to break into one of the card games.

"Let the gent in," someone said. They looked him over.

My grandfather was big, six-two, two hundred and forty-some pounds. He did not have the nose Indians are famous for; rather, he had a ruler-straight, flat-bridged nose, high cheekbones, and broad, deep sockets for eyes.

There was a grunt of approval. They were playing pontoon, a version of blackjack. They were not too good, but then, how does anyone play against someone who can memorize the whole deck? Peke could do that, keep track of what cards had been played. It gave him an advantage, one that looked like luck.

Cards flashed like spokes in a wheel. Wenebojo danced there in the windows, grinning and making faces. The roof began to leak in the car. "Put something under that," one of the men said, "anything."

The *plit, plit, plit* of the water on the empty seats at the rear of the car went on.

The game was in a fury, all bristling hair, humphs of indignation, and sighs at lost wagers. My grandfather, having realized his overzealousness might win him more than a few dollars, was in the middle of trying to give some back. One bad hand after another now. Again suspicious.

The train rocked and shuddered. The wind howled and whistled. Fistfuls of rain hammered the windows. A pint was passed around, and things got worse.

One of the men, a plumbing salesman, bet his stake in Saint Paul against my grandfather in a pick-and-draw, a kind of thimblerig, or shell game, played with cards. The salesman prided himself on his memory. And, no doubt, he, too, had a good one, but not as good as my grandfather's.

Imagine my grandfather's confusion.

He was to show them what a Chippewa could do. Self-sufficiency, honesty, and integrity were the highest virtues. And generosity. But in what order?

Were he to win, he reasoned, he would not be dependent on his sponsors up at Lac du Flambeau, or his family, the Dibikamigs. Not for some time, anyway. And if he were to have an unfair advantage, was he not to use it? Did that constitute dishonesty? Could he use it without lying about it? Weren't these inequities always present, as in a footrace? he reasoned. Someone had to be the fastest runner. Would it be generosity or stupidity to pass up such an offer?

The storm had reached fever pitch. They could not now distinguish the wind from the noise of the engine—and they were two cars behind it. The men were sweating profusely, and it was cold.

My grandfather wanted to tell them about old Wenebojo. "It's a joke on us!" he wanted to say about the storm. Had he been able to open a window, he'd have tossed tobacco to the Winds to appease them. Still, even thinking such respectful thoughts, he was terrified.

Look, one of the men said, pointing out the window. The rain did not fall, but hurled itself horizontally.

My grandfather was considering the salesman's proposal. He struggled with the virtues. A desire to win was powerful against them. (Generosity, the first of the virtues, did not befit the occasion.)

And, too, there were things he did not know, things beyond his power.

For example, my grandfather did not know that this plumbing salesman had embezzled a considerable sum of money from the company he represented and was on the run. He also didn't know the train would soon reach Saint Paul and the High Bridge—a span of intricate steel a hundred and more feet over the Mississippi. And he did not know that he could fly.

"Pick," the plumbing salesman said.

He fanned the cards. My grandfather could see just enough of them in the salesman's glasses to follow their movement, aided by memory. A woman up the aisle retched onto the floor. Rain oozed in around the windows, trickled in a thin stream from a hole in the roof.

My grandfather considered.

There was something in the moment he recognized: the card he would pull was like a lever. Sometimes it only took a little one. A tiny one. A card.

Pick, the cards said.

Perhaps it was a foregone development, what happened.

The car smelled of vomit and rain and damp wool and cigars. The clouds had bundled themselves in. Lightning flashed. The conductor clung to the brake handle at the end of the compartment. The lightning flashed again, and Peke decided what to do. He reached into the cards, the plumbing salesman having earlier pulled a king.

"Aces high?" he said.

The train was headed onto the High Bridge, into the Saint Paul station, and had just reached the first trestle. It was now or never, Peke thought.

"An ace!" my grandfather said. "How about that?"

The train swayed violently. They set upon him.

The businessmen, furious, beat my grandfather. Rock-hard fists and pointed jabs. He protested—in French—and they beat him all the worse. The plumbing representative walloped Peke over the head with his sample case, and Peke wrestled it from him, using it to block the punches about his middle. His feet were kicked out from under him, and he felt himself lifted.

"Liar! Cheat!" one of the men shouted, while another opened the window there. The glass slid up and out of the way, cold, damp air pummeling in.

To my grandfather's good fortune, the wind was with him, blowing over the train and away from the bridge. He gripped that sample case, and as if he were a battering ram, they hurled him at the window.

One, two, three!

And again, One, two, three!

The rain spewed in around the window casings and sash. Peke's shoulders hurt terribly. His shoulders were too wide to go through head on, so they turned him sideways.

One, two, three! They ran him at that window again. Only this time he went through, cleared the bridge, and, carried by the wind, tumbled end over end high above the wide, wide Mississippi, that sample case clutched to his chest. Somehow, at the right moment, he straightened up, went into the water feet first, and only broke his arm.

Keeeee-whap! he told me, slapping his hands together. *Hitting that water was like hitting cement.*

A little way off, his trunk came down with a final indignant splash.

The train went on across the bridge. My grandfather, dazed, dog-paddling, turned to watch the train clear the high sandstone bank opposite, where it should have jogged north again and disappeared into the trees. But what he saw instead was a funnel nosing down, taking the train and tossing it like a dog would toss an old shoe.

It was magnificent, and awful, my grandfather told me.

And like that, Peke rode the waves in to shore on that salesman's sample case.

(1909) ON THE FOLLOWING BRIGHT
spring morning, a girl stood high on the east
bank of the Mississippi. A damp breeze came up the river, and the
sun shone warmly; the sky was that achingly storm-clean blue. Still,
the girl was hesitant and vacillated between the shore and the big
stone house up the hill. It was a hobby of hers, collecting bottles and
bits of things from the river's edge. She had been told not to go
down alone, and the maid, who usually accompanied her, was ill.

Now she had stopped to consider which would be the greater of
two evils: following her parents' admonitions and returning to the
house empty-handed or . . .

The girl smiled to herself.
Who would know?

∿∿∿

Isabel Rose Olsen. She was a quiet, strong-willed girl, the daughter
of Swedish immigrants who had started a successful grain business.
She took her hobbies seriously. She was a great reader of newspapers and books, and pried into things, refused to be put off, and was
oftentimes at cross-purposes with her parents, who still spoke
Swedish at home and lauded the virtues of the old country.

Isabel, like most second-generation children, tried to hide her for-
eignness; she loathed the idea of Sweden. She wanted to get on in
the New World. The other children in her neighborhood were all
German and seemed to suffer the same predicament. And as if they
had agreed upon it, they studiously avoided each other, all lonely.

I have a picture of her, from around that time. Or, I should say,
pictures. Isabel was an only child, and her parents doted on her, so
they had her frozen in photographs at regular intervals.

Here is Isabel as a toddler: pantaloons and ribbons and hair as
shiny and light as flax. Here, Isabel at four: toy in hand, smiling, almost. Here, Isabel at ten: long-limbed, beside a pony somewhere,
her outfit tinticolored blue, a certain wary yet defiant shadow hanging around her otherwise light eyes.

In each, her face emerges more angular, her eyes big with bits of
white in her irises. A determined, but surprised look, and each year
sharper, as though life were cutting her down to size, even as she
grew.

And at last, Isabel at seventeen.

This photograph, greasy around the corners, I have handled
overmuch. In it, Isabel looks out at the camera—or was it the pho-
tographer?—with an undeniable melancholy. Her features are fine
and sharp, even fragile.

I have held this, Isabel's high school graduation portrait, alongside the photograph I have of my grandfather, taken the day he boarded the train. The resemblance is striking, down to the inbreath that must have caused the flare of wings on either side of the nose.

They had been, both of them, my grandfather and grandmother, photographed on the same day: May 27, 1909.

～～～

Yes, Isabel thought, and lifting her skirt, descended to the brush-tangled shoreline. There, newspapers and magazines had wrapped around the red willow in intriguing lumpy clots. A bloated dog lay on its side further up on a hummock of sand. She had the sudden conviction she was being watched.

That maid, she thought. The dirty snitch!

Then, just back from the river's edge, she saw what looked to be a trunk and a pile of muddy clothes.

It was just like Isabel to step closer, to see for herself what lay there.

～～～

A *Pioneer Press* newspaper headline from that week reads: "Salesman Thrown from Bridge in Railway Tragedy Found by Errant Girl." The article stated that a playing card, the ace of spades, was found in Mr. Broussard's shirt pocket.

My grandmother kept that story, and others, in a leather-bound album. The stories speculated whether or not Mr. Broussard had tumbled from the train as it crossed the High Bridge or had been carried to the river by the tornado. Mr. Broussard, it turned out, was the only survivor of the wreck. At the hospital he confounded the staff by speaking French. Isabel visited him there, under the auspices of goodwill and charity.

Isabel was fascinated, though not for the reason her parents thought:

Grain markets were good and times prosperous, and Isabel had been promised a trip to Paris. She had studied with Madame LeFleur, a private tutor, and had leafed through numerous volumes on Parisian life. All was in a state of readiness for her departure. This Frenchman, her parents thought, was just the icing on the cake.

But Isabel knew otherwise.

This Mr. Broussard, with his big dark eyes and coal-black hair, was not a Frenchman. Nor was his name Benjamin, nor was he a salesman, though he'd said as much, delirious, before Isabel went for help that morning.

He was, however, the most beautiful man she had ever seen, and was going to be her husband.

And that was that.

"Believe me," she told me, "you'll know."

~~~

Isabel told me, *Oh, how long I waited for him to call! And then I answered the bell one day, and there he was. Big, rawboned, his arm in a sling, straight out of the hospital. His eyes were the color of . . . chestnuts and chocolate, all dark and full of mischief.*

"Mama," I said. "It's Mr. Broussard. The Frenchman."

My mother blushed. She was wearing an apron and a blue shirt with yellow piping. I was wearing an embroidered sweater and skirt.

The kitchen was dusty with flour. We'd been baking. The trip was off, temporarily—I'd begged my parents to let me go in August, to escape the heat, I'd said—and my mother was happy to have me around. A pot of coffee was on the sideboard.

While my mother busied herself with the cups and saucers, this

Frenchman and I glanced at each other. Each time I looked up, he did too. Did he know then that I knew? I think so. His skin was the color of chicory, a deep reddish brown.

He spoke French with a guttural backwoods accent.

"How lovely," my mother said, handing him a cup of coffee. "I just love to hear French."

I winked at him.

A high red color came out in his forehead.

"I'm sorry," my mother said, "I didn't mean to embarrass you."

~~~~

They began seeing each other, escorted by Isabel's mother, Margaret. Margaret was chatty and tried to draw Peke out on issues pertaining to Parisian life, thus keeping the interaction on an educational plane. During those first few meetings, Margaret said things that so amused Isabel she had to pinch herself to keep from laughing.

One afternoon Margaret asked why she was always seeing pictures of workers tinkering with the Eiffel Tower. Monsieur Broussard replied that the Eiffel Tower had been damaged by woodpeckers and termites. "The wood, you see," he explained, "is reedled weet holes."

"I didn't know there were woodpeckers in Paris," Margaret replied.

~~~~

Isabel was like a vision, my grandfather told me. Like a gull. All bright and swooping down out of nowhere.

Wenebojo, he said, put me in that river bottom. Gitchi' manido sent your grandmother.

He always winked then.

"But what was I to do?" he asked.

He had left Prentice with enough money to tide him over until he reached Grinnell. The money, what of it there was, could do one of two things: keep his rented room, or buy food.

I had to look good, so it was the room, he told me, chuckling.

But the situation was not as funny as that. In truth, Peke was slowly starving, and he had no intention of getting on the train for Grinnell. "Not without your grandmother," he told me. Scholarship or no scholarship.

Thinking about school put some ideas in his head. He had a calling card, a name, and a brochure of vitreous china the former Mr. Broussard had sold. He had the sample case and order forms. Standard—it was a good name for sinks and toilets. There was some connection there, so he roamed the university in downtown Minneapolis, overwhelmed by the size of the stone buildings, trying to figure it out.

One afternoon he went into the library. His stomach churned. He had to make water. Downstairs, he was told. He went through the doors, and there, under the newly installed electric lights, he saw his salvation and nearly wept. "Toilets!" he told me. All old fixtures. Cracked, rusted. With old-style seals and gaskets! Earlier he'd leafed through page after page of Benjamin Broussard's sale-case brochures. He saw that tiled room come to life! New sinks! New commodes! New plumbing!

He went from building to building.

Nickel plating and chrome and china whirled and spun, sparked him. He went windigo with toilets!

He tallied fixtures, worked the computation sheets. When he'd come up with a conservative figure, he nearly halved it, then arranged to see the building inspector. He saw them all. He talked fluid flow, spit equations at them, some real, some fictitious, showed them the fixtures in the sample case. The administration argued over this newcomer.

He showed them pictures of work his company had done in Chicago, in Milwaukee, in Green Bay.

His offer was too good to refuse.

∿∿∿

Isabel thought likewise.

At the end of the month my grandfather made his intentions public, and Isabel's parents were delighted. A *businessman!* Little did they know their daughter was marrying a man who, in the plumbing business, had overnight become known as Mr. Potty.

What's in a name? my grandfather teased when I was little. Would you ever forget a name like Mr. Potty?

No, I told him, and he was right.

∿∿∿

But things were not to be so easy.

My grandfather suffered over what to do about his family. He knew they must think him dead. And Standard had sent him a curious telegram: "Confine area of operations to Saint Paul Stop."

And here, he told me, Wenebojo tricked us.

That story I heard while we were huddled around the table in Peke and Isabel's tiny kitchen.

"*Don't* fill her head with that nonsense," Isabel warned.

But he did, anyway.

He said, *One day Wenebojo was standing by a maple tree, and all of a sudden it started to rain. The thunders threw down bucketfuls, and he tried to hide under that tree. He was supposed to get married that evening. He didn't want his clothes messed up, see? The tree got tired of him leaning against there and threw him out. His buckskins got drenched.*

I've had it, he was thinking, and then the sun came out. That buckskin shrank so bad Wenebojo lay there, strangling. A dog came up the path.

"I'll fix it," the dog said, "if you give me your buckskins."

Wenebojo agreed to that, and the dog bit off the laces. Wenebojo had kicked this dog a few times: he was a camp robber, made off with whatever wasn't tied down. Wenebojo couldn't figure out why the dog was doing him this favor.

"Here," the dog said, and he messed around in the brush there.

Pretty soon Wenebojo was all dressed up again, only now in a red coat.

"You'll want this for your wedding," the dog said, and gave him a fancy hat with a feather in it.

Wenebojo promised never to kick that dog again.

The two parted, and Wenebojo hiked up to the wedding lodge. He was a little late and everyone was waiting. Tens of them. The chief and everybody. Wenebojo strode out into the clearing, proud as could be, and everyone stared. His bride, Omackwe, was staring too.

"What have you got that turd on your head for?" she asked. "And why don't you cover yourself?"

Sure enough, his hat was a dog turd with a feather in it, his jacket and breeches sumac leaves with his thing pokin' through.

Isabel's eyes got glassy. "Oh, Pop," she said, and he waved her off.

He said, *And Omackwe, she takes a chunk of that turd off his head and puts it on her own. Plucks a feather from her gown and sticks it in.*

"Nice hat," she said.

The dog was long gone, but I'm sure he was havin' a laugh.

"What?" Peke asked. "What's wrong now?"

"You forgot part of it," Isabel said.

"Oh," he says. He's got a big grin on.

Everybody set on Wenebojo.

But Omackwe, she kissed him, and they turned into partridges and flew away.

He lifted his hands over the table.

And that's why partridges have that black cap and tuft on their heads. It's that turd and feather the dog gave 'em.

~~~~

In Isabel's telling, their wedding day was clear, sunny, and cool. (Records, however, attest to temperatures in the nineties and high humidity. A developing cloud front indicated storms by that evening.)

The wedding was held at Isabel's parents' home.

Relations traveled from as far as South Platte, Nebraska, and Spokane, Washington. Since Isabel had not taken her summer abroad, the wedding refinements were all the more lavish—a beautiful gown, enormous flower arrangements, attendants to pour punch. The house was a beehive, Isabel told me. From the turret window on the third floor she watched people arrive. Some came in motorcars, the men in goggles and leather hats, the women windblown and flustered. Some came in carriages towed by fancy horses.

Isabel was frightened and bored.

Peke was late. The wedding party assembled downstairs, and Isabel waited in back of the parlor, her father beside her. He was not much taller than Isabel, but he had an aggressive, commanding demeanor. He was uneasy now, however. He pressed her arm. Three largish men sat on wooden folding chairs at the back of the room.

"Who are those men?" Isabel asked.

Isabel's father expressed surprise.

And at that moment, Papekewis, alias Monsieur Broussard, came striding up Summit Street, proud as a peacock.

Isabel watched through the open door.

He very nearly danced up the walk, then skipped over the threshold. He had bought himself a new hat and rented a tuxedo. He wore a red boutonniere over his heart.

He smiled at Isabel.

"Ma chérie!"

The three men in back stood. Two went around and blocked the door. The one remaining reached for Peke's hand as if to shake it and, pulling him forward, jerked up and around, pinning him.

"We know who you are," he said.

"A thief!" Isabel's mother said, tearing through the house. "A common criminal!"

Isabel, thinking she would right the situation, led the police to Peke's tenement and to the trunk he'd salvaged from the river bottom, a hope chest of sorts, and established his rightful identity.

"A heathen!" Isabel's mother cried, truly shocked now. "How could you!"

I liked that part. It made me want to pound my chest and dance in half steps around the table. "How, how, how, how!"

Her father would not speak to her.

∿∿∿

Down in Grinnell they told my grandfather he could not have his scholarship back. After all, he'd been dead for over three months.

They had, however, held his mail.

I have since been down to Grinnell and sat on the steps of the old administration building.

I imagine them there, Peke and Isabel, the cold marble, storm clouds rolling in from the north. The clouds, Isabel told me, very nearly followed the train down.

"Your grandfather has always attracted lightning," she told me.

The letter is water-stained, and the ink runs in places.

Was it raining? Or did the two of them huddle there on the administration steps and cry?

Lac du Flambeau
Aug. 20, 1909
My dear Peke,

We are all waiting to hear how things are down at that school. You were never away from home so long before were you? I don't believe you miss us much anyway. Your sister has been out to the country since Monday. Just think of it we only had four in the family all week. I thought of you a good deal during that awful spell of rain and your brother Herman on the ice wagon nearly got washed away. If you don't come home soon you won't know the place two large buildings they put up last week just back from the pond. Zo'zed and his wife and boys are on a visit from up north. We had them out to the boathouse last night. I hope we will see you soon and that you keep quite well let us know when you are coming and we will have a couple of nice chickens our calf is a dandy. I see by the papers the Mayor of Prentice is having quite a time of it.

Well, goodbye for now but write soon we are glad to get a letter and then I'll know you are all right.

With love,
Mama

P.S. You're always welcome here at home.

Time and again, I dig down through my box of keepsakes and find that letter. Isabel gave it to me one dreary winter afternoon when I'd reached what seemed to be yet another impasse in my life.

You think about it, she said, pressing the letter into my hands.

I handle that letter with care.

(1987) I LIVE IN A CITY NOW AND DRIVE a car. Use the telephone, where I run Little Red School, a nonprofit institution in downtown Minneapolis, like a weapon.

"Cough it up," I tell our sponsors. "We need the money, and *now.*"

My mother, when she visits, is amazed. She will never leave the reserve, she says. She does not have a telephone or electricity.

"I don't want it," she tells me.

We drink coffee by the pot in my kitchen at the Fair Oaks, an older apartment complex. My mother, Isabel's daughter, is adamantly Anishinabe: Chippewa. She talks reserve politics, a real radical. I sample her maple candies, listening, a lump in my throat.

"That Governor Carlson's got his head up," my mother says. "There's a new group fighting his legislation, the Anishinabe Ankeeng. How come you don't throw your oar in? Have you gone apple on us?"

It is a constant thread in our conversation.

At times I am tempted to tell her that from the standpoint of blood, I am the more Indian of the two of us. But I don't.

"You're distracted," my mother says.

I'm half asleep, half reclining, my head making a slow descent to the Formica countertop.

I'm exhausted.

My mother fills me in on the latest reserve gossip, gives me bits of history, tells stories. Her voice soothes, rambles. It is a kind of umbilical cord, but I will never tell her that.

"How come you're so tired?" she'll say.

And I will reply, yes or uh-huh, falling into a deeper sleep than I've had in months.

ᗯᗯᗯ

Daily I drive from what I think of as my quiet space, on Twenty-fourth and Third, into the thrum and grind of east Minneapolis, what some people in the Twin Cities call Tonto Town. In the middle of it, there I am.

A target.

The walls of Little Red outside are neon-bright with slogans; the lot is a battlefield of decrepit cars. McDonald's soft drink cups tumble by end over end. Out on Franklin, traffic hurtles downtown, to the IDS tower or the Foshay or one of the newer insurance company buildings.

I take one long, last sip of my third cup of coffee and tentatively step from my car. Already someone is dashing across the lot.

"Aja! The boiler died last night! The pipes are frozen and there's water all over the place."

"Aja! The shipment of pizzas didn't come in."

"Aja! The electricity's off!"

It has gotten so I lumber. My head is a chessboard of moves and countermoves. Do I need to call the police? Talk to parents? Calm my office staff or teachers? And always there is damage control.

I am a weak person, I know, but something in me won't sit down.

"Now, be calm," I coach. "It isn't the end of the world. That happened when Columbus got here. You know?"

"Custer's in the ground, girl. Relax."

"Sit," I coax. "Your mother does *too* love you. She just shows it in a strange way. She just hits so hard 'cause she loves so hard. All right?"

"I know, darling," I say. "I know."

Outside, fifty below with windchill, Thomas Tall Buffalo and I confront the latest indignity.

"Go home, timber niggers," someone has painted on the west wall.

Thom and I spray in large, uncompromising letters under it, "We *are* home."

Paint. Plaster. Wrench.

My hair a mess, my makeup smudged. Coffee boiling in my veins, I'm talking with teachers, badgering sponsors, trying to make ends meet. A woman in army fatigues brings in her brother's boy.

"I've got a tail," he says, kicking the legs of his chair.

"Like mine?"

"You're not Indian," he says. "Only Indians have tails."

And I've got to explain. Again. My name, for example, is not Aja, really, but A'jawac', meaning "Carried Across."

And Indians do not have prehensile tails.

Sometimes I'm not home until nine. A message will be on my machine from some collection agency. An invitation from someone, or several someones, I've met during the day—a man, or men. A threat from Tuesday Motors on Lake Street, where I bought my car, a lemon.

Pay up.

I pace my apartment in my grandfather's moose-hide slippers. I eat yogurt, listening to the machine. My dinner bubbles in the microwave. Even at home I am making plans for Little Red.

I'm going to go after Betty Crocker and General Mills while I'm at it.

On the couch I nurse a cup of Ovaltine. I rehearse my spiel. My head is awhirl with fantasies of simple solutions and quick fixes. Uneasy sleep comes on. I twist and turn in my nightgown, shivering.

Always in my dreams it is raining.

I'm forever wearing that crown of turds, a gaily colored feather cocked in it at some humiliating angle. My skin is blue with cold.

Tonight, though, I'm interrupted in my dreaming. There's a rude knocking at my door.

It's my mother. Visiting again.

So I'm up, my hand knotted in my hair, torn between the kitchen and the living room. No putting away the microwaved haute cuisine, no hiding the Old Dutch potato chips, no straightening the ragged orange throw on the couch or making sense of the dishes in the sink.

"Wait a minute!" I shout, making a panicked circuit of the apartment.

Kisses. The pot on the stove, whistling. I have had too much coffee already, but can't be empty-handed with Nina in the house. I chain-smoke from a pack of Marlboros. A man, whose name I can't remember, left them on my mantel. I blow a smoke ring.

"Got one for me?" my mother asks.

I offer her a cigarette. I'd rather she scolded me for smoking, said "When did you take *that* up?" She's subtle, my mother, without even knowing it.

"Are you coming up sometime?" she asks, and I can only roll my eyes. That eternal question.

"That old life, that's not for me," I tell her, which is far from the truth.

Even now, the smell of woodsmoke can make me cry.

In the fall, when people burn leaves, I am overwhelmed and visit my mother often. Her cabin, just thirty miles south of White Earth, has a loft window overlooking Lake Ketchigama. Around the shore, migrating blackbirds sway on ripe cattails; the air is thick with their reedy cries.

I am sick with nostalgia.

I fill myself with fry bread in my mother's kitchen. I cannot get enough pike and muskie. My mother's boyfriend tells me I should move back to the reserve if I'm so homesick. "After all," he says, "you're an Indian, aren't you?"

"So?" Nina asks.

I tell her I'll think about it, which makes her anxious. She throws out a few tidbits to draw me back in. Some are outright lies, some amalgams of the truth and fantasy, some embroiderings on things I've known since I was a child.

All bribes, these bits and pieces.

Did I know Isabel played the violin? she'll ask. Did I know Peke had a motorcycle at one time, an Excelsior, with a sidecar?

I try to play indifferent, but I am hungry for these stories.

His half brother, Herman, crashed it, she'll say. *I used to love riding on the back, Isabel in the sidecar, and there was a big root beer stand we'd stop at, in the middle of a cornfield, lights all around, and when it was dark the moths would come out and it was almost like it was snowing sometimes. Back then you could always hear the railroad going through, only they had steam whistles then and they made a kind of lonely sound.*

Your grandfather was the first to have a motorcycle up there. Did you know that?

Did I? "No," I reply.

"Tell me about Peke," I tell her. "About Isabel. Was she happy up there? Did you really almost starve one winter?"

My mother strings me along, testing me.

I am surprised, at times, to find that what makes up my memory is real.

Sometimes I say, enough.

"Betty," she says now, blowing a wobbly smoke ring, "Betty's thinking of starting a branch of the Tomahawk down here. Around the U."

Nina has been in my apartment all of ten minutes and still smells of snow.

"She is?" I ask.

"Sure, she says it would go over now. Says it would be retro to the kids."

"Retro?"

I am trying to shake myself awake. My mother is a night owl. It is slightly after eleven, and I've got to be up at five. I can't understand why she's talking about Betty, my aunt from my father's side, who has been a sore point between us for years.

The Tomahawk is Betty's restaurant up at White Earth, which she's decorated in buzzing neon, orange vinyl upholstery, and tacky warrior motifs.

"Cold out there?" I ask, changing the subject.

"A little."

My mother straightens herself on my sofa. Her face goes through a number of transformations—grim, cheerful, stricken. She's fishing for something.

"Now, wait one minute," I say.

I'm beginning to get the picture. Betty and my mother have gotten it into their heads for me to manage a Tomahawk in the Twin Cities, neon mess and all.

"No," I say.

"No what?"

"I'm not going to manage some *low*-rent, em*barr*assing, sleazo—"

"Aja."

"What?"

Pacing, my hands balled at my sides, I cannot tell who I'm most angry with—my mother, Betty, or myself.

"What?"

"Just listen, can you?" she says.

"No." It is more an experiment than a response. It is something I've promised myself. To try saying no. Just once.

"Why?"

"Because."

"*Why* because?"

Why? *Why?* Because you'll say, Just do it for us, and I'll say yes. Because you'll say, It's just till things get started, and I'll say, Sure, why not? Because I sleep like shit, work all day, have fuckers pissin' me off noon till night, and what do I get for it? A Tomahawk Burger, Inc., right in the forehead!

"Listen," I say.

But now my mother is off the couch, snapping her handbag shut.

"We're both upset," she says at the door, and like that, I let her go.

∿∿∿

For a week my mother does not call. Daily, at Little Red, I distract myself. I bend paper clips into clever shapes. Organize files. Make unnecessary inspections of the cafeteria.

A free five minutes stretches miserably.

"All right," I say when I finally call her. "I was unreasonable. But it wasn't fair to ask me what you did, and I'm *not* giving in and *that's that.*"

There is a long-distance hum on the line.

"Giving in to what?" Nina asks.

"Any of it."

"Good," she tells me. "Don't. We need you down there at that school." And then, as if telling me the time of day or something about the weather, she says, "Oh, I meant to tell you, Peke's brother Herman died."

I get a queasy feeling.

It is as if a fruit, one I'm not too sure of, has fallen into my lap.

"When did that happen?"

"Day before I visited you," Nina says.

Later I pace in my apartment. I alternately feel hot washes of shame, then cool disinterest. Herman, gone. In bed, I toss and turn. Sweat. I knot myself in my comforter, and when I'm exhausted, I sleep.

I dream of a lake of blood.

My feet, roots, travel deep, deep down into it.

It is not red or white or black or yellow.

It is pure, clear, and beautiful.

(1920) IN THE FALL OF 1920 A MEET-
ing of the church was held across the lake
against the wishes of the new priest, Father Eddie. Herman Oshogay, never one to be badgered by clergy, took his wife and boy with
him, though with a certain trepidation.

As they paddled across Turtle Lake, the clouds parted and a big
beam of sunlight shone through, like on a postcard or an illustra-
tion in a Bible.

Right there Herman got the uneasy feeling that something had
changed and that the change was for the good, but somehow he
knew it wasn't something he wanted. He dipped his paddle in and,

pulling back, feathered it around. It was a long way across, and he thought to take it slow, but really what he was thinking was that he could turn back. He studied the clouds to the north, boiling high and white in the last of the sun. He could turn around and say the weather had kept them from coming.

But no.

Those angry clouds made him think of the grain agent, Kluney, and the game they'd been playing. Herman didn't want to be around when Kluney got to the bottom of that sack. Kluney had been cheating Herman and his brother Del all season; to balance things out, they'd been augmenting their yields with pop bottles and rocks.

Every fall for the last few years it had been the same, but for one small difference: the value of the wild rice, or manomen, had risen, and with it had risen the grain agent's propensity to cheat them at the scales. A smut had wiped out one crop, wind had ruined another, so it was a strange blessing that the demand, caused by disaster, would lift prices, promising the most profitable harvest in decades.

Still, to point out Kluney's cheating would have been to lose their business. It was a tough spot to be in: they could not sell the rice to groceries and restaurants themselves—feelings ran too high, both ways, for that—so they had to rely on these middlemen.

And to make things worse, where the women had established shares by tying the rice in sheaves just offshore and marking with stakes the shares to be harvested, they could see the evidence of poaching.

Herman knew the offender to be Kluney or, if not Kluney himself, then Kluney's so-called partners.

There was big money in that rice. People's lives depended on it.

So, like that, the discrepancy at the scales became absurd. Herman and his brother, seeing the direction things were going, decided to bring it all out in the open, set things right.

People around for the weighing that afternoon had been shocked, their bags were so lumpy.

And Herman had put a note in the bottom of his: "Quit cheating us and we'll quit cheating you." And Del, in his inimitable fashion, had signed at the bottom, "Yours, Willy."

"What is it?" Louisa, Herman's wife, asked now.

Herman drew the paddle back and around, heading them off to the left.

"Nothing," he said.

Sam was sleeping in Louisa's lap, a look on his face that Herman, for no reason he could imagine, suddenly thought of as beatific.

That was a Father Eddie word.

Paddling, Herman tried to forget Father Eddie and the rice agent and his scales and his brother wanting to right things out in the woods. We don't have to kill him, Del had said, just shake him up a bit.

There was something like a hum in the air.

To the east was a logging camp and a road out to Farnsworth and the Union Pacific line. Now the train made a far-off, sad whistling.

"You hear that?"

"What is it?" Louisa asked.

He wanted to say, I don't know, but said, "It's the train."

"No, the other thing."

Herman shrugged.

"Father Eddie told me we shouldn't go," Louisa said.

Herman's wife was caught between two churches, Father Eddie's and this one.

"Don't go, then," Herman said.

"Maybe I won't."

"You do what you want," Herman said. "But it might rain again. And you never know—the point's not a good place to wait. Lightning and all."

"I want to go. If *you* go," she said.

"I *am* going," Herman said. "I told you that."

The island came to a point, a bare stretch of sand and rickety dock there. Herman spun the canoe around, stroking in powerfully.

Sand crunched under the hull.

"All right," Herman said, reaching for the boy.

They went up the hillside through a stand of white pine, following the path. It was nearly dark. The front boiled in from the north, putting a cap on the sun. They traversed a wooded sink, and the cabin came clear, green roof and log sides. The sun gave one last wink from under those clouds and the birch shone white and dappled, and then came a chill breeze.

Louisa reached for Herman's hand.

ᴧᴧᴧᴧ

It was dark in the cabin, just a couple candles going. They stumbled finding a place to sit, twenty or so of them in that small room, huddled side by side. The room smelled of pine and camphor and cedar smoke. They were late, and the service was under way. Herman nodded to his half brother, Peke, in front. Del, Herman's younger brother, was slouched against the wall in back, chewing on a matchstick. He made that circling gesture, palm down, as if he were opening a bottle.

Gotta talk.

Herman shook his head and, turning to the front, tried to keep his mind on the service. He didn't listen to Father Eddie as his wife did. "It's the work of Satan," the priest had told them. "You're risking eternal damnation." (Who was he, after all, but a boy, really, smooth pink cheeks and those piercing milk-blue eyes, sent up from the diocese in Saint Paul?) "I'll do something," he'd warned, but that was just nonsense. Still, Herman had been raised Catholic, and suffered anyway.

Kluney was on Herman's mind like a rotten tooth he couldn't stop poking with his tongue.

Herman shook himself.

People were reading Bible verses and humming. Cedar smoke twined out of an urn to the right, purifying, pungent. His eyes adjusted to the dark. A drum beat slowly, the room seeming to breathe in and out. Up front, Clarence Fisher, road chief for the night, prayed: "Great Spirit, Our Savior, thank you for permittin' us to carry on this meetin'. We still have a long way on the path to go. . . ."

Del smiled from across the room. It was an odd, twisted sort of smile, and Herman looked away. That *idiot!* Herman thought. He'd done something else now, and Herman could only guess at it.

A striped bag came around, and Herman reached in. Louisa waited to see what Herman would do. He sat with those peyote buttons burning in his palm. He was reminded of that feeling he'd gotten coming over. He thought about Father Eddie and the grain agent, and slipped the buttons into his pocket.

He had to keep his wits about him.

It was raining again. The rain splashed and pattered in a puddle outside the door. Lightning lit the room in powerful flashes. Clarence Fisher sang in a high, warbling voice. The room rocked with singing: *"Ina'kone',* the flame goes up, *awinegi'cig,* beautiful as a star."

The rhythm was hypnotic, the image warming.

Herman felt sick and melancholy; he hadn't heard it since he was a boy. And just like that, he thought, *Del,* and looking across the room, couldn't see him.

Candlelit silhouettes. Smoke twining from twin urns. But no Del. Herman stepped out under the eaves and, trying not to be rained on, went to the window on the east side and looked in. He swallowed hard, trying not to panic. It was nothing, after all. What made him think it was something other than Del going out to relieve himself? So he waited under the eaves.

The pines sagged dark and glossy under the weight of the rain. Herman's feet were cold, his back sopping. He cursed his brother. *Idiot! Fool!* All this time he'd had to watch out for Del. The wind gusting, Herman grinned, slapping his arms. He remembered the time Del had sent for a kite advertised in a dry goods catalog. When the kite came, in a cardboard box the length of a coffin, Herman asked Del if he'd neglected to tell his older brother something about this kite.

But I told you it was gigantic, Del said.

Later he'd insisted on flying it from a nearby bluff, and when the wind picked up, Herman found Del had tied the heavy line around his wrist. Herman had had to hold Del down by the ankles while getting his jackknife out of his pocket to cut the line, the kite threatening all the while to lift both of them right over the edge.

"But I want to *fly!*" Del had shouted.

Herman thought about that, trying to cheer himself. But this was not funny now. He shifted from side to side, shuddering with the cold. When he could stand it no longer, he headed out into the rain, tugging his collar up around his neck.

The path was slippery and, where the dirt gave way to stone, nearly impassable because it was so slick. He gripped the low-growing elderberry and red willow and slid and skidded in the direction of the point. He was moving faster now, letting his fear carry him. Over a small rise, he swung off the path and onto the spine of the point, skidding to a stop.

There was his canoe, and standing in the rain, his back to a large birch, was Del.

A strangely tall Del.

He was hanging from a spike, a burlap ricing bag stuffed into his mouth. His eyes stared dully at nothing. They'd cut off his braids and jammed them into his ears with a sharp stick. Herman circled the tree, thinking how to get him down. He reached up and pulled at Del's feet and Del's body slid queerly on the spike.

"*Nikan,*" he said. "Brother, forgive me."

Herman tried again, but the obscene sliding made him sick. He climbed the tree, finally, and embracing the body, jerked it loose, falling the distance to the path, the body knocking the wind out of him.

He got Del's arms around his neck and lifted, turning up the path.

On a spur off to the east, there were signs. Broken grasses. The stub of a cigar. A cleated print. Lightning flashed. The lake was dappled and dark, rain whipping across it in blue-black patterns.

Herman settled Del on his back. He would not go after them, he promised himself.

He carried Del to the cabin and stood under the eaves. He prayed a little there. Then he went in, carrying his brother. A brief commotion followed, after which Herman assured them he would go for the police. No one should get involved, he would see to things.

Clarence Fisher started another set of prayers; the others joined him.

Herman went back out into the rain.

He was not thinking right, so he decided to go to Del's cabin, just up from the lumber camp. He wanted to get a jacket, he told himself, and some rain gear, for the hike into Farnsworth. He was cold, that was all.

The ground was uneven and the going difficult. He did not think at all, really, just kept moving, one step after another. At Del's cabin the windows had been broken and the rain had been pouring in, making the floor slick. Here was Del's jacket, the sleeves ripped off, his medicine bag rent down the side, broken plates strewn across the floor, a lamp left burning in the corner.

Herman sank to his knees.

Paper was everywhere. There were pamphlets on travel to the Far East, sampans and paper lanterns. A brochure reading, "See the Great Pyramid!" with a photograph of someone looking natty in a pith helmet on the front. There was a catalog of strange electrical gadgets. And wrapped in twine, every letter Herman had sent Del from Saint Paul when he'd been down in the Cities doing steelwork.

Herman held his fists to his head and, something like steam coming out of him, remembered.

Revolver. His brother had always kept a revolver under a floorboard.

No, something told him. To move at all now would start it. He was a good man, he told himself. But something dark was in the room fluttering about, wings spread wide. Eyes like glass.

It knocked over the lamp, the bell shattering.

Herman was terrified, then furious.

He froze there for a second, then breathing it in, lunged into the dark.

He had the gun out and was trying to open the box of shells. His hands shook so violently he spilled them, hard metal rattling on wood. He crawled on his hands and knees, scrabbling in the dark across the wet floor. He filled his mouth with the shells, bitter, metallic-tasting. He dug into his mouth, loading the revolver, crying, dropping the slippery cold shells, chasing them, holding them in his mouth again.

ᘏᘏᘏ

The men were at the agent's cabin.

Herman stood in back of the cabin in the rain, watching through the lakeside windows. There were five of them sitting around a table, joshing each other. Herman had figured the agent and one other, perhaps, but not so many. They were playing cards and drinking. The agent, Kluney, a big, red-faced man, was telling them something: he was making a real production of it, just as he had earlier, at the weighing. The bottle went around, and the men raised their glasses. A man with a thick mustache forced his black hat onto another's head. There was a howl of laughter and the man nearest the door stood and hung his arms out and opened his mouth.

Herman went up through a stand of timber, behind the agent's cabin, and, near the place where they kept a one-lung engine for a saw, found a fifty-gallon drum of gasoline. He walked it down the hillside, cutting himself on the sharp rim. Outside the cabin there was a man in a green mackintosh. Herman recognized him from trips into Farnsworth, a big talker and strutter. A policeman.

But he didn't look big there in the rain. Herman wedged the drum between two large pines and went around the cabin. He knew the policeman had been drinking with the others. He was smoking a cigar now. Herman waited. One of the others came out. They exchanged pleasantries, the policeman and this man. Herman waited for the door to close.

"Raining like a son of a bitch," the policeman said.

"There's drink in here if you want it," said the other.

Then the door closed and Herman went down. He threw a stone into the brush, out past the cabin, to catch the officer's attention. When the policeman left the stoop, peering into the dark, Herman got up behind him, his knife out, and cupping his hand over the man's mouth, cut him. Minutes passed.

"Hey, Charlie!" It was Kluney, the agent. The door opened slightly.

"Tell him to come on in," someone shouted.

Herman waved them off. He'd put the policeman's mackintosh on.

"Come on," the agent said. "Nobody's out there."

Herman spread his arms wide and danced across the yard. He knew this policeman to be a joker.

He'd been the one in the cabin playing Del as Jesus.

"Look at that son of a bitch!" Someone laughed. "It's that timber nigger's ghost!"

They all laughed.

"All right, you stupid Polack," Kluney said. "I'll leave your glass here."

The agent set the glass on the stoop.

Herman went around the cabin with the gasoline. He worked fast, but it seemed the rain washed the gasoline away as quickly as it came out of the drum. He got under the cabin—there was a good-sized crawl space there—and, nearly fainting from the fumes, doused the dry leaves and dust. Through the floor he heard the men laughing, and the rain started up harder, a gust of wind shaking the trees to shrieking.

Herman got out from under the cabin. The lights in the windows seemed brighter. He was shaking so badly now he couldn't control his hands. He went to the lee side of the cabin and took out his matches. He always carried some in a brass container with a dry-strike lid. His hands shook so badly he couldn't work the top off.

He thought to stop. But why? He'd already done the thing not to be done.

With his boot heel he broke the container open on the foundation. It was a mess. He got the matches in his fist and, under the cabin, struck them. Not a great whooshing, but a sickly flame went up.

He tried to fan it, whimpering. The flame steadied.

He was being tested. The spirits were around him on all sides, arguing. He balled his trembling hands into fists and ran back out in front of the cabin.

The ruckus went on inside. Flames licked up around to the back, ragged yellow, and Herman's heart fell. The rain cut across it all, jagged heavy rain, and the pitiful flame licked around the chimney.

He dragged the policeman out in front of the cabin, propped the body up, and put a stick in its arms.

A window opened. "Goddamn cabin's on fire," someone shouted. Another window opened. There was a whoosh, the fumes under the cabin igniting.

"There he is!" Kluney shouted.

Shots were fired, and the policeman's body jerked one way and then the other.

"See who it is," Kluney shouted.

The man who came out came out slowly, peering into the rain and dark. He wiped the rain from his eyes. He gingerly felt his way down the steps, holding his hat on his head.

"Get out there!" Kluney shouted, slamming the door behind him.

He did not move toward the body or to the rear of the cabin, which was now—very clearly, even in the heavy rain—burning.

Cowering like a dog, the man dodged toward the lake.

Herman took his place again, behind the body of the policeman. The men were crouched inside, had all the windows open. They were arguing, deciding something.

"What do you want?" Kluney shouted.

The fire had ignited the brush on all sides, and the roof was on fire, the rain pouring down, the cabin lit in colored steam.

Kluney came out the door. "Look here, there's gotta be—"

Two men climbed out the windows, firing at the policeman and at the body of the second, up the path, where Herman had hanged him.

Herman closed the distance between them, shot the bigger of the two. The other slid to a stop, spun around and, looking at Herman, whose face was smoke-streaked and glistening with rain, pleaded, "You just can't—"

But Herman could, and did.

When Kluney appeared in the doorway, Herman came up the path, the gun spent.

He did not reload it.

"I know you," Kluney said; he was on the porch, wild-eyed and desperate.

"No, you don't," Herman said.

Hugging him, Herman drove his knife deep into Kluney's belly.

He went around the shore and got his canoe and, in the deepest part of the lake, let the other men's guns go. They were good guns, better than he would ever own in his lifetime, some of them made in Belgium and Germany. They were worth a small fortune. He thought of the walleye and pike, and of the water panthers, and of the guns tumbling down black and heavy. He thought of the manidog, in the lower four levels.

From the middle of the lake, he watched the last of the cabin burn, the clouds over it yellow-red, then went back to the service, stepping big and blank-eyed and smelling of gasoline into the midst of things.

By then they'd moved Del. They did not tell Herman where, nor did they ever, even days later, after the body had been buried.

Herman just stared, blank-eyed, his hair burned to a frizz.

Louisa rocked their boy in her lap.

She reached for Herman's hand; he could barely feel her, he was so cold.

∿∿∿

The investigators did not come until the following spring, so early and heavily did it snow. They'd expected them sooner; those investigators poked and prodded the ruins of the agent's cabin, finding nothing but charred logs and bits of melted glass and tin. Then suddenly the investigators were everywhere, in Farnsworth, at the Tip Top Diner, and dragging the shore of the lake from rowboats powered by noisy motors. They employed many, many men and used all kinds of boats on the lake, even divers with new and strange equipment.

The investigation went on for weeks. No one was talking. Why was that? they asked.

They're Indians, and there's nothing you can do with them, they were told.

One morning Herman was having his breakfast at the Tip Top.

"Have you ever seen this?" one of the investigators said, setting the note Herman had written, and Del had signed, on the table in front of him: "Quit cheating us and we'll quit cheating you. Yours, Willy."

Herman had taken to eating alone mornings. He did everything alone. He'd even left his wife and boy and was living in a cabin out in the middle of nowhere, on an island that was nothing but stone. Still, he'd taken to coming to the Tip Top, just to sit, which he did for hours, never saying anything.

Now they all watched. What would Herman do? They could see, from the side, Herman gripping the cushions of his seat. He'd taken to shaking, long before, but here he was much worse. The silverware rattled with it.

"Have you ever seen this?" the policeman said.

He gripped Herman's shoulder.

"Ah, hell," someone said. "He can't even read, much less write. Leave him alone."

"Is that so?" the officer said. "How'd you know what was on the menu here, chief?"

The waitress, hair in braids, one hand on her hip, banged Herman's plate down.

"Always gets the number seven," she said.

"This your brother's signature?"

"Leave him alone," the cook said.

"What's your name?"

"Terry," the cook told him, which wasn't his name.

"What's it to you that I ask him a few questions?"

"He's family," the cook said. "He did anything wrong, it isn't something any one of us knows of. Word gets around."

"Well?"

Herman was in a world of pain. He was causing his friends to sin. He'd taken responsibility for the killings on himself, but the others—that was too much. They could tell he wouldn't last much longer.

"Del, your brother," the officer said, "he's been missing since this all took place. Since right around the burning. You know where he's gone?"

Herman looked up from his plate.

"I have no idea," he said, and I imagine that, for just a second there, Herman smiled.

∿∿∿

"But the bodies," I ask Isabel one hot summer evening.

"Gossip," Isabel says. "That's what that story is. Those men all just ran off."

"Delbert, too?"

"Shush," Isabel says. Still, here are all the telltale signs: the furrow in her brow, how she grips the mixing spoon tightly. And although she is making something chocolate, the look on her face is anything but sweet.

"And don't ask *him*," she adds, pointing to Peke at the kitchen table.

I know that Peke and his half brothers, Herman and Delbert, were at the service that night. I've heard it from Clarence Fisher. And Isabel. I know, too, that teeth don't burn and that the police found a fifty-gallon gasoline drum hidden off in the woods.

So I do.

"What about it? Did he?"

There is a hush in that room that makes your ears ring. Peke makes a smacking noise, then goes to the front door and, after looking in all directions, shuts it.

"Don't," Isabel warns.

Which is as good as license for him to go ahead anyway, but all he says is "That boy Delbert, he always liked to swim, you know?"

4

(1936) IT WAS LATE NOW, TOWARD NOON
on an otherwise perfect autumn day, and the
thing Peke had wanted to happen, but had hoped would not happen, was upon him.

Nine o'clock had become noon, his deer hunter had not shown,
and he was free.

In the back of the boat, he tied flies, his feet propped on the gear
he'd lugged down from the car. The boat bobbed, tied at the bow to
the government dock. Peke glanced up from his fly tying, hoping the
girl had gone. But no, there she sat, resting her shoulders against the
wall of the bait shop, crying again.

Peke shook his head, redoubling his efforts to make the fly look right. It was a mess. Feathers out at all angles, the hook crooked as sin.

"Tcim-djayu, ikwe," he muttered. Go away, girl.

He knew she was trouble. He didn't need Wenebojo running at him with fire on his back to tell him that. Molasses-dark hair, a figure that made his heart tighten and—the girl was lovely and hurt and in some kind of difficulty.

And now here she came up the dock, hips gliding in that sinewy, elastic way.

Peke tried to ignore her. Her shadow got in the way of his fly tying. She stood over him on the dock, shielding her eyes from the glare.

"Can I rent a boat?" she said.

"You want a boat, ask Elisha. Inside."

Peke pointed around her, at the bait shop. Elisha waved through the open door. Peke waved back, frowning. *Cingus,* he thought, weasel. Elisha was a gossip, talked with everyone passing through.

"I didn't mean that exactly," the girl said. "I mean, you aren't busy, are you?"

"What's it look like?" Peke said.

She looked out over the lake as if trying to locate something. Peke sized her up. Gold barrettes in her hair, fine cobalt cotton dress, high-heeled black pumps. That lovely figure.

Just like that, the girl spun away, striding toward the blue Hudson parked behind the bait shop. Illinois plates. She threw the front door open and scrabbled in the glove compartment. There was something desperate and furious about it, and Peke couldn't help but go to her. Already he'd endured her crying off and on for the last hour.

He stood, waiting, just back of the door.

So what that Elisha would blabber? And something in him just then said, *All the better for it.*

The girl got out a map and flattened it on the hood. It was an old Shell Oil map and not very detailed. She pointed to an island.

"Would it really be so awful for someone to take me up here?" she said. "Is that so much to ask?"

"That the only map you got?" Peke said.

"Why?" the girl said. "Is there something wrong with it?"

Peke rapped his fingers on the map. The hood under it made a hollow bell-like sound. He took papers from his pocket, rolled a cigarette.

He could feel Trickster lurking nearby in his cap of turds with those gaily colored feathers.

"Where do you want to go . . ."

"I'm Delia," the girl said. She pointed to the map. "Right here."

Peke blinked. He breathed deep, exhaling smoke. Now he was in for it.

"Jesus, girl," he said, "that's Windigo country. You can't just go up there. That's a day and a half, two days, maybe, up there, and two or three portages. What do you want with that place?"

Delia turned away. She was a spoiled, angry girl, and she was crying again.

"That map," Peke said, touching it lightly, "that's a road map you got. There's . . ." He shook his head. "There's a good ten thousand lakes to Lake of the Woods. It isn't like that Lake Superior, you know?"

The girl held her arms tight at her sides, pacing in circles around the gravel drive. This was her fourth circuit. Peke sat on the front fender of his Chevrolet. He would wait until she quieted.

"So," he said, "how much time do you have?"

"No time," she spat back.

The girl made another circuit, back and forth, the heels of her not-too-sensible pumps turning awkwardly under her.

"Gonna ruin those heels," he said. "Gravel's gonna tear that leather right off."

The girl lifted her arms, her hands balled into fists. She made an unintelligible guttural noise. Peke could see she was near crying. He was a little afraid for what he had in his mind to do. He wanted to help her.

Isabel, his wife, was insanely jealous, and there would be hell to pay, but if he could do it with integrity and honesty, it would be all right. In a way, he could not turn from her now, he reasoned. Gitchi' manido had sent her to him, and as he'd been saved once, by a girl just like this—by his wife, though she was blond and a Swede and years younger—in his thinking, he was beholden to this stranger. And he had a daughter of his own, Nina, now fifteen, and that carried over.

It all seemed pretty straightforward.

Still, he could feel Trickster lurking about. He was messing with this girl, who didn't even know it. After all, she was an Indian; he'd seen that right from the moment she'd stepped out of her business-blue Hudson. She was an Indian girl who'd been adopted, raised in the Cities, probably Chicago, and like so many, she'd come back, and it had to be any number of things, but most likely, from the willow in her hair (what city girl would know about that?), it had to do with making an impression on her real (as she was probably thinking about it) parents, whom she'd never seen but who loomed large in her imagination.

Peke, perched on the fender smoking, sighed. Well, he'd given her enough time.

"It's about your folks, isn't it?" he said.

"No," Delia said. Then thinking better of it, she added, "I mean yes." She looked up at him, with those big eyes.

"Which is it gonna be?"

"What makes you say that?" Delia asked. There was something odd in it all. "About my parents, I mean?"

Peke eyed her askance.

44

"Oh, it isn't every city girl that washes up on a reserve in her father's car with red willow in her hair. You did a good job of it, too."
He took the papers and tobacco from his pocket. He smiled, his eyes wrinkling. Lit another cigarette.

"So who is it?" he asked.

"I'm supposed to be in Michigan."

"Can't help you if I don't know who it is."

The girl put her hands on her hips. She tossed her hair over her shoulder in a show of defiance. Peke held back a moment. He pitied her a little and felt protective, too.

"Just spit it out."

The girl considered this. "Herman Oshogay," she said, just like that.

Peke ran his hand through his hair. Now it was his turn to try not to look upset. He felt himself frowning, his lips pursed. His heart kicked in his chest.

"Do you know him?" the girl said.

Peke tugged on his cigarette, eyes narrowed. He made a smoke ring and studied it. Made another.

"Herman?" he said.

~~~~

In the time since the burning, as people had come to call it, Peke's half brother Herman had cut something of a figure for himself. Herman had sold himself to timber interests, had ferreted out some genealogies in favor of Northern States Development. Allotments could be sold only by *sagwade,* or mixed-bloods, and it had been joked for a time that if Herman couldn't trace your bloodline back to some immigrant farmer, then he could follow it back to some Hudson Bay fur trader, and if that wouldn't do, he would just go back to Adam, which it was supposed he did through the local priest, Father Edward Feeney, whose job it was to keep track of those things. Roughly a quarter of a million acres had been sold and clear-cut, Herman taking a fair slice of the pie as kickback.

Peke liked none of it, his half brother's business.

Every July, shortly after the Fourth, Herman drove into town in a brand-new Cadillac, this year a canary-yellow convertible with fancy running lights and horn, to attend Mass and chat with Father Feeney. Herman was fat and said little or nothing to people. He wore diamond, turquoise, and lapis rings. And the way he smiled at you when he smiled.

He's got crocodile teeth, people said.

Peke hadn't talked with Herman in years, not since the grain agent's cabin had burned and Herman's son had caught the coughing sickness and died. It was then that he had moved away to the island and afterward had been seen in town only on business. Usually that with Father Feeney.

But Peke was not thinking about Father Feeney and Herman now, with the girl waiting lovely beside him. He was thinking about Isabel and how she'd run off with Herman for just a day or two, not long after Herman had picked up steam. Back then Herman had been one sleek, honey-tongued talker. A city Indian, an in-between, an apple.

They'd had a terrible argument, Peke and Isabel—to sharpen knives in a circular motion (Peke's method) or by drawing the blade down and across the stone in an arc (Isabel's method). Peke had brandished the knife. This is the way it is done, he'd said, threatening. What had made him do it? How could he have been so stupid? Or had it been just self-indulgence?

Isabel had said, Fine, then.

She'd gone right out the door. Three days. He'd never asked her what she did during those days she was gone, but others had told him the places they'd seen Isabel and Herman together, one of them the Saint James Hotel.

When he thought of it, as he did now, he felt sick and forlorn, and his heart—or was it his head?—felt disconnected and strange.

"So?" Delia said, setting her hands on her hips. "Do you know him?"

"I guess," Peke said. He crushed the cigarette under his boot. "You got business?"

"I'll pay for *everything*. Really," the girl said, making doe eyes at him.

"All right," Peke said.

∿∿∿

With the girl's money he rented a boat, motor, and gasoline from Barney's, and bought bread, canned chili, milk, and apricots from Oshogay's grocery. He was discreet, businesslike. When asked who the girl was, he told them she wanted to get to the north end of the lake, and needed a guide. Since he did not wink slyly, hitch up his pants, or otherwise behave strangely, most took it for work as usual.

"We're a little late," Peke explained.

Still, they made quite a sight, Peke and the girl in the big business-blue Hudson Hornet.

More than a few people shook their heads.

∿∿∿

When he got tired of steering, the steady drone of the motor making him sleepy, he slowed, then stopped. The lake was quiet and the boat bobbed. The sun warmed his back. There was the smell of woodsmoke.

"Want to steer for a bit?" Peke asked.

The girl pointed to herself. Her hair was tangled in bright curls. "Me?"

"Yes, you," he said.

They argued there, about what her "hiring him on" meant. He explained to her what would happen if he, say, decided to jump out of the boat and swim over to that island there. He'd leave her the map, though.

"Is it a deal?"

The girl clambered back, taking the motor.

∿∿∿

Slumped in the bow, Peke was dreaming.

In his dream he put his penis in a box on his back. It talked to him. There were some girls swimming in a lake, and the penis wanted to get out there. Where woods met the lake, he took the penis from the box and sent it out, floating on the surface. But the girls said, "What is that?" and he called the penis back to shore. He tied some rocks to it. It sank. He took a few off; he wanted it to get out to those girls. He sent it out again. Now it was just perfect. One of the girls splashed up in the water. She had him in her hand and rushed to shore. The three girls had sticks and set upon him.

Peke woke, sweating, the boat giving a terrific hollow *boom!* It bounced, swerving. Peke's heart hammered, and blinded with sleep, he got the motor handle from the girl and got things stopped.

He went up in the bow. There was a huge crack in the hull, but no leak.

"I'm *sorry*," the girl said, tears in her eyes.

Peke was trying to wake himself. The dream lingered, like a strange aftertaste. It colored everything. He saw himself for the fool he was. But the damage was already done.

"Can you fix it?" the girl said.

Peke told her no.

∿∿∿

Hot, relentless sun. A persistent northeast wind that buffeted the water and created rough chop. That night they slept, Delia in the tent, Peke in the boat, wrapped in his jacket. Then, up early, Delia was cursing. Then there was another long, bright day, and it was night again, and they sat together in back of the fire.

"I'd like to ask you something," Peke said.

Delia replied, "Don't."

"Why Herman?"

"It's family," she said.

ᗰᗰ

The following morning Peke was studying her in the bow of the boat.

He was not sick of her, which surprised him. She was still beautiful, her hair, auburn, sunlight in it, tossing. But he was reaching the end of something elastic in himself. He felt a need to know *why*. Why did she need to see, of all people, Herman?

"How far is it?" Delia said, glancing back over her shoulder.

"A ways," he replied.

ᗰᗰ

On the south end of Snowbank Lake, Herman's cabin high and mighty just ahead, Peke reached for Delia's arm. Something like voltage passed between them. He had to say something.

"Listen," he said. "I want to warn you about your old man."

"My old man?" Delia said. She tossed her hair back, as if irritated.

"Your father," he said.

"What are you talking about?"

Peke felt his face heat. "Herman," he managed to say.

Delia laughed, sharp, bitter laughter.

"He *is* your father, isn't he?"

She looked at Peke, her eyes big, and dark and sad.

All the way out to the cabin Peke was silent. His hand went numb from the motor's vibration. The hull had begun to leak, and his feet were wet and cold. In front of him the girl's hair pointed behind her like a needle on a compass.

She crouched on the seat, facing the lake.

What was it, then? Peke wondered. But he could guess the remainder now. There was something full in Delia's face. When, earlier, he'd asked her about her family in Chicago, she'd said, "Oh, they're all right. But they won't speak to me anymore."

It was common knowledge that Herman made trips down to Chicago, where he stayed with friends. They couldn't refuse him, really; it was that old law of hospitality, and here, in Delia, was the result.

Alone and in trouble.

Peke was looking at her hard, wondering if Delia had had a part in it or if Herman had forced himself on her. Delia looked back just as hard.

"Yes," she said, blinking, and added, "Don't say anything more. All right? I told you not to ask," she said.

Crossing the bay to Herman's island, Peke cut the motor and put in the oars.

"What are you doing?" Delia asked.

"Giving you a little advantage," Peke replied.

They were downwind of the island, and he was sure the sound of the outboard hadn't carried. There was a dock sticking out into the lake, a weathered gray tongue. Beyond it an elaborate wrought-iron stairway snaked up the face of the island to Herman's formidable cabin.

There was a big bay window facing northeast. Two chimneys,

both stone. There was an antenna for his radios. A generator was puttering.

Now it stopped. Peke brought the boat in alongside the dock and tied the bow.

"I don't want you coming up," Delia told him.

Her eyes, he saw now, had flecks of yellow in them, so sad.

"*Promise,*" she said, and Peke agreed.

Here and there grasshoppers swung heavily over dry yellow grass, fragile wings clacking. He watched Delia climb the wrought-iron stairway. Those heels caught something awful. Her hands were balled into tight little fists.

It was a steep climb. Peke sat in the boat as long as he could bear. Just long enough for Delia to climb out of sight.

∿∿∿

I imagine him taking those steps, the sun on his back, wondering what he was getting himself into. After all, he'd promised. But the girl—but Gitchi' manido, really—had come for him. It was a tangled mess. His feelings ran from pity to cold, sweaty fear to a protective love.

Herman, he knew, was dangerous. And there was this, too, to think about: why should he mess with what he'd come to terms with years before, that pain he still sometimes felt over Isabel's having run off with Herman? What was now the smallest of irritants had grown smaller, more compact, in him with the passing of years. It wasn't a pearl, exactly, but it had healed over with the sediment of new experience.

Herman brought all that up again, afresh.

I wonder, as Peke ascended those stairs, if he whistled, under his breath, as he often did.

Just then Delia screamed.

Here was one frozen moment: Peke, his hand on that iron railing, catching his breath. Tamarack, pine, October sun, the lake, broken by islands. Shards of reflected sunlight, the chirr of cicadas.

His legs were filled with a terrible energy. He was thinking about Trickster and how, in a fit of enthusiasm, he'd killed his own family; he was thinking about Jesus and how he must have been relieved, finally getting to the cross. He was thinking about the score he had to settle with Herman. And he was thinking about the girl.

He had let her go up alone. It was unthinkable. All because he'd been afraid for himself. What was so petty in him that he'd done it?

He put his hands on his knees and propelled himself up the hillside. Over the top then, bald granite, the cabin there. He broke into a run.

When he started, it was to help Delia. Fists like stones.

∿∿∿

The boat, careening through the buoys in the channel, did not slow for the government dock out in front of Barney's Outfitters. Peke and the girl were slumped down. A steady wind was blowing; whitecaps traversed the lake in ragged blue-green lines. The bow of the boat popped up, then banged down, throwing a shower of diamond-bright water over the two in back.

Isabel, on the dock, was beyond being angry. She was white-faced with fury. She stalked along the dock, her hands bunched into fists at her sides. She had failed him only once, and now to be repaid with *this,* as if she hadn't suffered his silence long enough already.

It was almost noon, and the sun was bright and sharp.

She would tell him, That's it! That's it! I won't take it! I've had it!

The boat coming in, she could feel her rage building. Her chest heaved in preparation. All those years, those all-too-frequent silent dinners. Those looks! He was even sitting in the back with her. That hussy! Her head down, his arm around her. Something burned to the pit of Isabel's stomach. She felt so enraged that air hissed out of her. She had been reduced to this. But now, after years of accommodation and restraint, she was going to indulge herself. Her lungs were working like a bellows. The apparatus of her voice prepared itself.

The boat made a broad arc to the dock. The motor hummed. There was the hollow thud of waves on the wooden hull and the smell of oily exhaust.

Peke saw her. He did not wave or stand. He did not look the least bit shocked.

Isabel's heart sank when she saw him. She felt a momentary grief—how she ached for him!—and then an even more powerful impulse to hurt gripped her. He, in showing no shame, rent the fabric of their love.

He—

Peke jumped up in the back of the boat, tall and rough-looking, his eyes hooded and filled with warning. He gave the motor one last spurt and brought the boat in alongside the dock, which was bobbing crazily.

"You," Isabel said.

The girl, just like that, ran past her. Pretty, beautiful, even, but obviously pregnant—no one had mentioned that—her face swollen and spotted, bruised. Had he hit her? Had Peke hit her?

Peke leaped out of the boat. There was a body there. Blood. Peke was covered with it, was trying to lift the body. An arm flopped into the water, heavy hand, and big sapphire pinky ring. Isabel stared, a burning in her head. She knew that ring.

The hand got caught between the boards of the dock. Peke grunted, trying to get Herman out of the boat, onto the dock. His face swelled with the effort.

He turned to Isabel, his face contorted.

"For chrissake," he nearly cried, "could you please just *help* me?"

Delia, when it was time, came up to White Earth. That was not long after Christmas. She stayed two years with Peke's sister, Esther. When I was a girl, every now and then a card came, usually around Easter. "God bless always," the message invariably read, "Delia."

When I was younger and didn't understand silence, I asked, on a number of occasions, "Who is Delia?" When I got no answer from Isabel or my mother, I asked around White Earth. There were a number of versions of the story, but all of them included this: Your grandfather, protecting that girl Delia, just about killed old Herman Oshogay. Gabriel was that girl's son.

Some people wanted me to believe Peke was Gabriel's father. But that was just loose talk and gossip. I knew some people resented the figure Peke cut around Pine Point and down at the government docks.

Still, some said there were papers to prove it.

So I checked. There *were* papers, a birth certificate over at Our Lady of the Lakes, only Herman was named as the father. Isabel told me all that, finally, and how Peke had worked things out to ensure the boy of some future, of his inheritance, and how he'd had Father Feeney sign that certificate.

But then, I asked, why did Gabriel disappear?

Isabel gave me one of her things-should-not-be-this-way looks.

A few sons were born to women that same year, all fat, happy babies. Herman, like Herod, tried to find out which was Gabriel, she told me. He thought he could just bribe those women and that way get to the bottom of it. But how much different does a nine-month-old look from, say, a ten- or eleven-month-old?

A number of those women took Herman's money. At least five, Isabel said. Enough to let Herman know he might as well have tried to get a stone to talk as to get any of them to give away Delia's baby.

Josiah, John, Joseph, Gerry. Isabel smiled, telling me those boys' names.

She mentioned only four, and always the same four, so I wondered about the fifth.

That was my idea, she said, all those names sounding nearly alike. Just fake names. Isabel shrugged. "If he'd touched so much as a hair on one of those boys' heads . . . Well," she said, "we don't need to be talking like that, do we?"

All I could do was nod.

And there was this last thing: I had to ask who'd done that damage to Herman that afternoon. Maybe it was Delia who'd messed up Herman after all, had hit him so hard that his head hemorrhaged inside.

Isabel said, "Maybe. But you've got to know this about your grandfather. He would never hurt anyone intentionally. He's not that kind of man. It would make him sick to do that, really." And then her mouth would do this awful thing, and she would cry.

"You know, *I* really started it," she'd say, by way of leading into the whole tangled mess.

5

(1938-1943) IN LATE SEPTEM-
ber of 1938 my father, Roy
Sharrett, electrocuted the priest at Our Lady of the Lakes. I've been
told he did it with the consent and to the amusement of the other
parishioners, and he did it with some savvy.

"He did it with style," Isabel told me, grinning.

"Style?" Peke grunted. "Huh."

It was a story the older generation liked to tell, so I heard a few
versions of it growing up, but all agreed on the basics and how it
had been just like my father to take on the local priest. Roy, back
then, was cocky, a little too full of himself. But, as he saw it, he had

his reasons. He came from one of the proudest and oldest of clans, the Muskego Pillagers, known for their fierceness, and Roy was no exception. He chewed tobacco, could kick any machine made by man back to life, could break the meanest horse, and got into fights with the kids on neighboring farms, much bigger kids, and always won. All this from a boy barely into his teens. So Father Feeney was just his kind of target. The delicious fruit far out on a limb, tempting.

It was like Roy to go out and get it.

Peke put it this way: "Your old man had *kitche* Waboos." Peke always smiled saying it, as though he were apologizing for the man's behavior, as much as complimenting it. *Kitche* can mean "great" as well as "big"—as in "inflated."

Still, even as a child, I was all too well aware of the import of Waboos, or Hare. According to Peke, Wenebojo, the Trickster, in the form of Hare, stole fire for man. Blinded himself when he didn't like what he saw. Ate his own intestines. Played mean tricks. And my father, Roy, if anything, was a trickster, ran against the grain. He made a regular occupation of it, showing us our backsides, what we might have been hiding from ourselves.

Tricks, though, after a time, they'll boomerang on you, as they did to Roy.

In failure can be the seeds of success and vice versa, and that is what I think happened the day Roy electrocuted Father Feeney. The seeds of my father's demise in the Big War were planted that day.

That year, in June, Father Feeney had gotten a new Cadillac, an immense black hulk of a car, and everyone was joking about it. Must've dipped his hand into the offering basket a few times for that, they said. Maybe we could haul hay in the back, looks big enough. Sure is awful, *awful* shiny.

But this was just the way of the people. Chippewa approach things obliquely. But my father, true to character, spoke right out. "If he's so goddamn holy and all," he said, "why's he riding around with his nose in the air like that, in that big turd of a car?" Everyone gave my father a knowing look. Roy was still a boy then, just seventeen.

You'll understand, the look said.

My father, Roy, did not want that kind of understanding. That beat-down, abused, and helpless understanding. No, right then he decided what he wanted was to get inside Father Feeney's game and beat him at it.

So he thought long and hard. Right there in that hot summer sun, inspiration struck like lightning:

Feeney's car, he realized. He could get at Father Feeney, the emperor, through his car.

Roy, as I've already said, was a first-rate mechanic. So he bent himself to it, considering that Cadillac from all angles every day as it sat outside the rectory.

In those days almost everyone walked, though some still rode horses. I imagine my father as I've been told he looked back then. Wave of blue-black hair rising off his forehead, shiny with tonic. There was Pillager blood in him all right, and more than a little Waboos, the wild energy of Hare. Cheekbones like hatchet blades, a little of the prophetic Chief Joseph squint in his eyes.

And here was Father Feeney, an asthmatic owl, peering from behind Coke-bottle-bottom glasses, steering that monster of a car around the sand roads of White Earth, his nose turned up so high he could have sucked birds down his nostrils.

Roy, schooled in the rubric of democracy, saw a contradiction there, in our walking, while Father Feeney rode high in his big new car. Especially since our land had bought that Cadillac. All of them knew Father Feeney and Peke's half brother Herman had wangled allotments from half-breeds and sold them to the timber companies.

And there was this, too: toward the end of that summer, Father Feeney had taken to honking for no reason at all, and now you might be shuffling along somewhere, not hear the car, and suddenly have horns as loud as a locomotive's send you leaping.

Father Feeney thought it all pretty funny. After he made you jump, he'd go by and say out the window, wheezing: "Just puttin' the spirit of God in you!"

Roy put a lot of thought into these things. The jolt you got hearing that horn behind you. Electricity. The spirit of God. And he waited.

There came a time toward the end of September that year when Father Feeney's car needed servicing. Roy ran his own car-repair business in a rented garage about a block from the rectory, and Father Feeney brought the car over. When he was done "servicing it," as Father put it, Roy was to leave the car in the rectory drive. Which he did, the following Sunday morning, bright, sunny, the maples in full color, dew glistening on the lawn of Our Lady of the Lakes. Inside the church Father Feeney, feeling particularly inspired, gave a sermon on the difference between an open heart and a closed heart. Up behind that pulpit he lifted his hand and made a fist to illustrate his point. Closed heart. Opened his first—open heart.

"May we all see God," he said, and brought that service to an end.

At the door he shook hands with his parishioners, quivering and shaking, puppylike. Outside everyone waited. They all knew Roy had done something to Father Feeney's car, and as Father Feeney went for a drive after Mass every morning, they waited there on the lawn, which was green and sparkling with dew. They chatted about the weather and whatnot, all the while waiting for Father Feeney to make his usual perambulation, nose in the air, tripping lightly out to that behemoth of a car. Father Feeney got into that Cadillac, and with a whir and a rumble it started.

The Chippewa are not a malicious people, quite the contrary, but when that car rolled down the rectory drive, smooth as if it were floating, they were all disappointed and, of course, confused at themselves. They'd been prepared for, at the worst, an explosion. Or flames leaping out from under the hood or a rough-running motor or at the least one of those whistles you put in the exhaust pipe that sounded like a siren.

But no, none of that.

The car bumped down onto the street, fenders big as wheelbarrows, and they all turned to go home, round-shouldered, disappointed, but a little relieved, too. And then they saw Roy smile. He had the whitest, loveliest teeth you could imagine.

His smile just then was mischievous. He made out that he'd forgotten something, had to talk to Father Feeney. About what, no one could guess. He went out into the middle of the street and waved that Cadillac down. Everyone was milling across the road, all sleepy after Mass, conversation, and rumbling stomachs.

"Father!" Roy called.

For a second acute discomfort registered on Father Feeney's face.

"Yes?" Father Feeney said.

Roy set his hand on the sideview mirror. Put his foot up on the running board, cool as you please.

"How's the Caddy running?"

"Just fine," Father Feeney said, patting the wheel.

His forehead had gotten shiny all of a sudden. Roy smiled, a friendly smile.

"You know what God thinks of pride," Roy said.

"We'll talk about that later," Father Feeney said, nodding. His little beardlet twitched. He was sucking on a mint as he often did.

"You better watch out or He'll strike you down," Roy said. "Be just like lightning. He can see right into your heart."

"Yes. Now I'm late, and—"

Roy winked. "I bet He's looking in there right now. What do you think He sees?"

Father Feeney pursed his prim little mouth. "You could never know," he said. "Really."

"Oh, I could guess."

"I wish you wouldn't."

Roy reached right into the car, patted Father Feeney's shoulder. "Got a mint?"

"Don't be an ass," Father Feeney said through clenched teeth. "And get off my car."

Roy shrugged. Stepping down off that Cadillac's running board he gave a tug on the sideview mirror. Father Feeney's eyes very nearly popped out. He jumped up in his seat so hard, like a jack-in-the-box, he hit his head on the roof in there. It made a loud metallic *bronnnng!*

"You okay?" Roy said.

Everyone there turned to watch, confounded at what they'd seen. They were blocking the car, front and back. Some were concerned. What had made Father Feeney jump like that?

"Your car's looking awful shiny," Roy said. "I heard there's timber money in that polish. That true?"

"Is not," Father Feeney spat.

Roy ran his hand down the big black fender, patted the spare tire there.

"You're sure, now."

"Absolutely."

Roy gave another tug on that sideview mirror, as if to balance himself. Father Feeney's eyes bugged out again; he jerked in his seat, flopping this way and that.

And just as suddenly stopped.

"I . . . I," Father Feeney stammered. He looked from Roy to those standing around the car and back again. His mouth—a little pink O under that dapper mustache—puckered not unlike a cat's anus.

"What?" Roy said.

He gave another tug on that mirror. Father Feeney bolted in his seat again, eyes agog. He looked all around him, terrified now.

"I think I hear thunder," Roy said.

Roy gave one last tug on that mirror and stepped off the running board. Father Feeney was gunning that engine. He tore away from the curb and, racing up the block, turned right and had to slow down for old Edna Frobisher. He lay on the horn, and, my God, did that make him jump! He was tossing around there like a rag doll, hollering and carrying on, banging into things right and left.

Some said later, when it was clear how it had been done with those ignition coils, that Father's hair was smoking.

In seconds he had thrown the door open and was scrabbling away in the dirt on his hands and knees, Edna chasing after him, trying to help.

"I think you put the fear of God in Father," someone said.

Everyone laughed, great bellyfuls.

My mother, Nina, just a girl, looked over at Roy. "There was something frightening on his face," she told me years later. "Or should I call it his countenance? It was as if he'd seen something rushing at him, all fire and fury and retribution.

"It swelled there in his face.

"And then he laughed."

∿∿∿

In 1942 the war was going badly. Everyone on the reserve followed it on the radio and in the *Star and Tribune,* which was sent up from the Twin Cities twice weekly. At this time, of the 875,000 acres that constituted White Earth, all but 52,000 had been ceded to, stolen by, or condemned for other use by timber, mining, or farming interests. White Earth proper, a community of five thousand, was surrounded by farms. So it was with a certain ambivalence that the denizens of White Earth regarded this war. There were a number of ways to approach it, the first of which was to disregard it. It wasn't ours, some said.

The second was more complicated. This war, this conflagration, called into question our identity. Our loyalty. People were asking, Are you Midewiwin (medicine society) or Christian? Indian or white? A blanket-ass old-styler, as traditionals were sometimes called, or a modern?

And people were asking, What if I could fly a plane? What if I had a car? What if I had a radio? What if I lived in the Twin Cities? What if I lived like those people on the radio? But of course, there was the flip side of that dream, too. What if the Cities devour me? Are the whites as loveless as I have been told they are? Are they as tight and stingy? And if they have all these things, why are they like that? What if I don't throw tobacco on the water? What if I don't offer up prayers? What if . . . ?

Up at White Earth we were asking these questions.

Roy, in 1942, was not.

Just twenty-one, he was already a take-control sort of person. He was smart and ornery, and like any boy, didn't know himself, though he thought he did. He was thinking that, to get on in the world, he'd have to throw off this Native nonsense and his family with it, and the quickest way to do that was to enlist and join the ranks.

Which he did.

They sent him down to Fort Worth, Texas, for basic training. What my father did not know, and could not have known, was this: every last thing he held dear, every affectation, his very pride—his Indianness—the air force would try to stamp out of him, and then some.

On the back of a postcard he sent from Fort Hood—a card bearing a photograph of a truck loaded with watermelons—he wrote, "I'm getting a hell of a lot more sympathy for colored folks down here, being one myself."

A short while later, there came a class photograph. Not only had Roy made it into the air corps, but he had done so at the top of his squadron. In that picture, wearing a leather jacket and those aviator's sunglasses they all wore, he grinned crazily.

As Peke put it, showing me that picture, "You can see he's still got his Waboos here."

Sure enough, he did.

So my father got more training. The plane he started out in was an AT-6. This, for Roy, who'd driven only the most rickety of cars on the reserve, was sublime.

He wrote that "the AT-6 bumps coming off the wheels, and just like that, you pull back on the stick, give her a little throttle, and when you're at three thousand feet or so, you stall out, kick the rudder over, and there, under you, is the whole of Texas."

The whole of Texas? We knew what he meant. But if he didn't like Texas, he loved flying.

All that summer of 1942 he flew the AT-6, the trainer, but dreamed of the day they'd let him at the new P-47 Thunderbolt. For all practical purposes, the P-47 was a 2,300-horsepower Pratt and Whitney Double Wasp engine with a fuselage and wings bolted to it.

Finally he got the chance: "Your Eskimo flew a Jug today!" he wrote. "Know that roller coaster at the fair they call the Tornado? In Farnsworth? Multiply that times about five hundred, and put it way, way up over some clouds."

There followed, at times, descriptions of aerial maneuvers: Immelmanns, which I don't understand to this day, inside and outside loops, incipient stalls, barrel rolls, low-altitude flying. His training was to prepare him for combat in the ETO, the European Theater of Operations, to fly under radar to bomb German supply trains. The P-47 was ideal for it.

But he did not fly in the ETO, not even close to it, and that was cause to wonder.

As a girl I asked Peke, "If he was training to fly over in Germany, why'd he end up in the Pacific?"

Peke touched my nose. He puffed up his cheeks. "You get like that, Aja, your head all swollen with pride," he said, "it's only a matter of time before Trickster comes to give you a visit."

"You mean with the sumac leaves?" I asked.

"No," Isabel said from behind, kicking Peke's chair. "Sometimes he comes as a stump." She kicked his chair again, shaking it. "Sometimes there's a phony man that comes, looking like a friend, but he's really just ice. Trickster sends him." Isabel grinned, a not altogether friendly grin. "Did I get it right?"

Peke eyed her evilly.

~~~

In September of 1943 my father and a boy named Fred Birketts took two P-47s out around dusk. They were flying against the sun, part of a sight-flying exercise. They were to hit a target—a train, actually—and return to base at Fort Hood. Fred, who was the number two man in the squadron, had insinuated himself upon my father. He was a kid from a wealthy family out east, one who'd decided to forgo the comfort that wealth offered to become a hotshot pilot. Running second to a cocky no-good redskin like my father was not his idea of the way things should be.

Roy was unaware of his first lieutenant's resentment toward him, had his head in the clouds.

That night the 47s were running beautifully. It was cool and windless. Beneath them all of Texas stretched in tan and green checkerboard patterns. I can only imagine they did a number of wingovers after takeoff. Setting sun in the canopy, the target up ahead. Roy was on Fred's tail, a few hundred yards back.

They were to hit a stationary target, which they did, then return to base. Cruising at speed they covered the distance in a matter of minutes. Fred banked off to the north. Roy followed. Something strange was happening, some spring wound tight. My father radioed to Fred.

Roy: "Princeton? Why'd you break the flight plan?"

Fred: "What do you say we have us some fun, Redman?"

Roy: "What kind of fun do you have in mind?"

Here exhilaration surpassed irritation. They were out in the open again. Roy was squadron leader. Fred was using friendship and the promise of pleasure against duty.

Below them a rail line out of Houston shone fiery in the last of the sun.

Fred: "You got a sense of humor, Redman?"

Roy: "Depends, Princeton."

Now the decision was made. Fred climbed steeply and did a wingover, then a barrel roll.

Fred: "Catch me, Redman!"

Roy flew right up his tail. Immelmanns, outside loops—my father stayed with him, surpassed him. He fired his dummy cannons.

Roy: "Gotcha there, Fred!"

A train was just visible now on the horizon, a smudge of exhaust over it like a tail. The sky gone to lavender, the train long and rust-red and shiny out there on the horizon. A freight train.

Fred: "What do you say we scare the shit out of some Texas longhorns?"

And here the boy spoke in the man. Why not? my father must have said to himself. He was invincible. What could be the harm in a little fun? Too, he remembered how much he'd enjoyed putting the fear of God in Father Feeney, how sweet, for weeks, the laughter was.

Fred, circling: "You with me, Redman?"

Roy: "You're on, Princeton."

The train came up the tracks, glowed red in all that brown countryside. Roy and Fred swooped down from under the clouds. Two hotshot pilots.

But which was the hotter?

At the last second, nearer the ground, the planes were buffeted by a side wind. Just as Roy had thought he would, Fred pulled out, banking to the east, unable to ride with the wind shear. My father, flying on pure inspiration, got down on those tracks.

Flew headlong at the train.

A split second before colliding with the train, Roy snapped on his landing lights, hurtled over the tracks a nanosecond longer. The brakeman and engineer, thinking it was another locomotive, braked then jumped from the engine. The train skidded down the tracks as Roy banked away, laughing so hard his sides hurt.

Beautiful!

Even from the air, the train made a terrible, metal screeching.

ᴧᴧᴧᴧ

The air force line of reasoning made sense: if you're such a hotshot, Mr. Sharrett, and like flying dangerously at low altitudes, we've got just the job for you, they told him.

Somehow the engineer, before jumping from the train, had managed to read my father's rudder: A706. That was the official version; I can only guess at how Fred tipped off the railroad.

So my father was reassigned—to the navy.

And, too, that is how my father, Roy, came to fly over ninety reconnaissance missions in the Pacific in a plane the navy fliers not altogether affectionately dubbed Dumbo. A PBY, or flying boat. Light, with two small machine guns and no cannon. It was a plane used to pick up crews of disabled submarines and fighter planes, or survivors of destroyers and such. It was a slow, vulnerable bird, and the only way to survive in it was to fly at almost inconceivably low altitudes over rough seas, the alternative being to climb over the clouds and be torn apart by enemy fire.

To assuage PBY crew members' fears, each airman was given a fine silk parachute.

~~~

Roy came home on leave in 1943, his eyes glazed over and dull. His mouth was one flat line, and there was no Waboos there at all. He was cool, people said. He'd been tested. Nothing made him jump. It got to be a kind of challenge: Honking at him or slamming a door, greeting him a little too loudly, to see if they could get a response.

Just kidding, Roy, they said.

A few people went down to see him in Saint Paul over the Fourth of July. He was staying with family on the Mississippi flats before he shipped out. Some kids tossed a string of cherry bombs behind him and ran. The others sitting with Roy, even drunk old Ishtakubig, jumped up. Roy reached behind there and, sweeping those firecrackers into his hands, bore down on them, didn't so much as flinch.

Sparks and blood and smoke shot from between his fingers.

Just then, Roy grinned.

It was a start, my mother said.

6

(1943-1956) FROM THE FIRST IT was like a collision. Roy Sharrett, on leave from action in the Pacific and wanting to get home, and Nina Dibikamig, just come from home and looking to get out, glared at each other over the jukebox at the Town Tap Bar in Saint Paul. The year was 1943. It was late June, a Friday evening, and the bar was crowded, smoky, and noisy.

"Hey there, sailor," Nina said, addressing Roy.

She was with four other girls from White Earth. My mother's friends laughed nervously. The men at the bar turned and with hungry looks eyed my mother, but she was oblivious to them. She wanted the officer's attention, Roy's. He did not point to himself comically and smile, did not saunter over and do a Bob Hope impersonation, as others had done.

He glared.

"Isn't he sweet?" my mother said, loud enough for him to hear.

Roy took a sip of his drink, and then, as cool as you please, he turned his back on them, but especially on my mother.

It was a snub of unthinkable proportions. Not only were Nina and her friends and Roy the only Indians in the bar, but they all knew each other, if only vaguely. At Land O' Lakes High, Roy had been the fix-it-all man, the mover and shaker, the boy to beat, the heartthrob just so many years older. Five to be exact. Roy was twenty-three now, my mother and her friends eighteen.

"Hey, lover boy," my mother said.

She wanted him to say, You talking to me? or What did you say? And when he didn't, she spoke in a clear, sharp voice, right over "Moonlight Serenade."

"*Bastard,*" she said.

Roy, in the mirror behind the bar, grinned. It was then that my mother knew she had to have him.

∿∿∿

Nina Dibikamig—champion of lost causes, of confused identities, of the never was but was always almost—right there she latched on to something she could sink her teeth into. Roy didn't like her, not in the way the others did, and that made her want him. Badly.

Nina was not one to be thwarted.

At the plant, every day now, someone called her Ingrid, after Ingrid Bergman, or Rita, after Rita Hayworth, or some such thing. These catcalls—or gestures of attraction and appreciation, however my mother wanted to think of them—were not entirely without cause: my mother's mother's side was Swedish, high cheekbones and fine features; the other, her father's pure, unadulterated Chippewa, thick dark hair and deep-set bittersweet chocolate eyes. Nina came up with hazel eyes, green and brown, and her skin was somewhere between brick and tawny, which always made her look fashionably suntanned, which she claimed she was. She liked to play tennis, ride a bicycle around the Cities with her friends, and swim on weekends at Lake Nokomis.

And even though my mother modeled for Sears, or J. C. Penney, always looking the part of the chipper girl, the unidentifiable and exotic mix, the one who made you look twice—What is she?—her energy, in person, was something else. My mother wanted to be pert, happy, positive, all those American things.

But she was torn, at war between her old life and the new.

She wanted the kitchens she'd seen in *Better Homes and Gardens,* the fine living rooms and bathrooms from *Good Housekeeping.* She wanted the twenty-piece bone china sets, fancy silver, and a big chromium coffee urn. She wanted a Cadillac Runabout, not a Chevrolet or Ford; she wanted cashmere sweaters, a husband smoking a briar pipe and looking dapper in gray wool and shiny black wing tips (Wrights, of course), and a house to match.

All of it would have been possible, in her thinking, but for a flaw: she'd gotten polio as a young girl, and she thought it had crippled her. She limped slightly, something she strenuously tried to hide. Her attempt to mask it made her mysterious, though she didn't mean it to. Yet few noticed the limp, really. (It wasn't until I was in my teens, and we were swimming in Ten Chiefs Lake, that she pointed out how her left leg was thinner than the right. Even then I couldn't see the difference.) If anything, people sensed it. She was the kind of girl a boy might want to catch if she fell. There was something like that in her step.

As she thought of it, that leg stood between her and those kitchens and double garages and shiny Cadillacs. That leg and her awareness of being Indian, which she was also trying to hide. She'd read in a newspaper that the Ford plant in Saint Paul was hiring pieceworkers, and since she wanted to make this new life happen, and *now*, she bought a ticket to the Twin Cities at the bus depot in Farnsworth.

Peke resisted. "You're not going down there. Not alone," he told her.

It seemed a simple thing to do, find someone else to travel with her. Only it turned out that Gladys Pelly, Nina's sole friend and confidante, wouldn't go without three other girls, none of whom Nina was any too fond of: Rosie and Liza Fobister, identical twins, and Camilla Fontaine.

Nina had to convince them all.

Surely no one could have believed the things my mother told them. My mother is a consummate liar, though at times I wonder if perhaps she really believes the lies she is telling because she means well. I know that sounds like twisted logic, but that was my mother's logic all around. Still is. Rasputin and even Richard Nixon would have been no match for her. Saint Paul, my mother told her friends, was glamorous. Needed workers badly. In Saint Paul there was a glut of vacant apartments just waiting to be filled by Chippewa girls.

By the time they boarded the big forty-seat GMC Highway Master, from Farnsworth, headed for Saint Paul, I think my mother actually believed her fabrications. And besides, she must have rationalized, how were her stories different from her father's, wherein sorcerers brought back the dead, magic canoes calmed stormy waters, and thwarted lovers sprouted wings and became partridges?

I wonder.

∿∿

The girls found a basement room on the River Flats: brown cement, water pipes coiling overhead, a tiny window that opened onto a view of a drainspout, and a drunken and red-nosed landlord who looked at them as if he were doing them some big favor. He'd advertised the apartment through the War Price and Rationing Board as a single at five dollars a week, yet somehow managed to twist that into five dollars a week for each girl.

They had a hot plate and one large kettle.

They worked different shifts and so were never there at the same time, though when family passed through, the room was crowded. Then they were reminded, first of all, that they were Chippewa and, secondly, that in the spirit of generosity, they could not refuse hospitality. And so they didn't.

But if the so-called apartment on the Flats—there was not even indoor plumbing, just an outdoor privy—was an abomination, the life out of it was, fortunately enough, still an adventure.

Rosie and Liza and Camilla for the first time in their lives were sought after. The Flats were crawling with Indian men—Cree, Oneida, Menominee, Dakota, Gros Ventre—who worked at the defense plant. In a way, it was the reserve all over again, only slightly more cramped, the ratio of men to women a special bonus. Gladys was delighted; her eyes shone with the prospect of marriage, playing matchmaker, interfering.

Nina wanted nothing of the sort. She was not about to marry into what she'd just left. No, she wanted a dapper businessman in a charcoal-gray suit, a doctor, or a lawyer, just like the ones she'd seen in the glossy pages of those magazines.

So Nina was silently desperate. Nights now, when the others paraded through the apartment helping themselves to bowls of beef stew, laughing and joshing each other, she chain-smoked on the stoop, drank Grain Belt, and bit her fingernails. Frank or Bobby or Emil or whoever it was almost without exception hit on Nina and, finding her one cold fish, left her to pursue the twins or Gladys or even Camilla.

"I didn't come down here for this," Nina told Gladys.

Gladys, her hair bobbed and curled, was yanked off the stoop by a well-muscled welder from Tegan, Montana, a Blackfoot.

"Well, it's your loss," Gladys said, giggling.

One evening, to my mother's utter disgust, everyone played a Flats-wide game of lacrosse with sticks they got from the swamp bordering the Mississippi.

"It was twilight," my mother told me. "You could hear people calling to each other. The field was lumpy, and there was that damp river smell coming up from the Mississippi. For a couple years we had red sunsets, and there was one that night. I sat on the stoop and cried. I just wasn't going to give in. I wasn't going to get hitched up and end right back at White Earth or Rosebud or Red Lake. I just wasn't."

∿∿∿

This was how things stood with Nina when Roy turned his back on her at the Town Tap. Noting the stripes on his shoulders, she gathered her resources. She had time: Gladys was off dancing with some pimply-faced PFC in army green; Liza and Rosie and Camilla were at a table of Seabees, drinking beer, which they hated—horse piss, Liza called it—and laughing hysterically when they were squeezed or pinched, which they were quite often.

My mother studied Roy's face in the mirror. He was handsome but almost sinister-looking. Thick jet-black hair, a proud hooked nose, a sensuous but almost cruel mouth. Mess with me, it said.

Nina sauntered up to the bar and, giving the soldier to Roy's left a not at all subtle nudge with her elbow, took his seat.

"Are you playing hard to get, soldier, or is your face paralyzed?" she said.

Roy took a sip of his drink.

Nina'd hit him about as hard as any woman could. I imagine him trying to compose himself. Owl had visited, he must have thought.

Grandfather had bitten his heart. He had to respond. To ward off Grandfather one had to look directly into his glassy eyes and make an offering of tobacco.

He was all hot flashes. One moment anger: who the hell was she, anyway? The next, memories of a brown-skinned girl in the Philippines, flying blind over the Pacific, and Zeros. Always Zeros, that characteristic high revving whine their engines made.

He shrugged.

"Cigarette?" he said, offering Nina one out of his pack of Luckies.

～～～

There were things my mother hated about Roy. He was better than good in the Flats-wide lacrosse games, and he liked to gamble, especially at poker. He talked very little, and when he did, he often spoke Ojibwaymowin, which Nina understood but did not speak well. It put her at a disadvantage. She learned that he was a pilot, flying PBYs, or Dumbos, which explained his wearing aviator sunglasses, which made him look like an insect or a machine. And when there was business to be done, that was exactly what he was like: a machine.

"Three choices," he'd say. "A, B, or C."

Nina fought with him incessantly. "What about D?" she'd ask. "And H, I, J, and K?"

And just like that, he was gone again.

～～～

As is sometimes the case, the worst of times are the best of times. For Nina, life on the Flats changed after Roy, because she was spoken for. She hadn't gotten the doctor she wanted, but she had gotten a pilot, and I'm sure, even back then, she had visions of him flying for the newly burgeoning airline industry, in the company of movie stars, to exotic destinations. So she could date, and confidently, which caused some confusion.

Suddenly the driven one, the possessed one, was open to joking and affection, even courtship, of a kind, but only that. Word got around. My mother didn't *do it*—that would have made things serious—but she did everything else, I am told, and with real enthusiasm. (My mother never could put aside pleasure.)

All of it was temporary. Now, with the war in full swing, the tarpaper shacks and Depression-era apartments were nothing more than containers, and their station in life just a momentary inconvenience while they got a toehold in the Cities. Quilting societies were formed. Lacrosse teams played visiting competitors from Milwaukee and Chicago.

Gladys got pregnant and married.

The twins, Rosie and Liza, courted two brothers from Seattle, following them to the Boeing plant there. Camilla went off to Chicago. My mother moved out of the basement, into a two-bedroom with four other women, all Navajo. She subscribed to *Silver Screen, Better Homes and Gardens,* and *House Beautiful.* And at the factory every day, where she wrapped armatures for generators, she dreamed.

She told me, "What I saw was a big house. Oh, not like you'd see on Summit Street or anything, not a mansion. A small house. White siding. Asphalt shingles on the roof. A broad driveway. A shiny blue car. A few men down on the Flats had bought cars, though they weren't much to look at. We'd take the top down and drive through the neighborhoods, five or six of us.

"I liked the area around the lakes.

"Once," my mother said, "someone even gave us a friendly wave.

"We'd go dancing. 'Pennsylvania Six Five Oh-oh-oh.'" My mother laughed. "It was really quite a time."

Then, in August of 1945, the Bomb was dropped, the Japanese surrendered, and in a whirlwind, the Cities celebrated. And that, my mother told me, was the end of the Good War. Overnight, my mother told me, *we* were the Japanese, we Indians.

The Ford plant, switching to peacetime production, in one sweep laid off all of its female line workers. That included my mother and nearly every other woman living on the Flats. For a time she was unemployed. They all were. The People huddled together. The men, in their Hudson Terraplanes and Franklin Air-cooleds, rattled into town each morning, returning late in the evening. Mostly they did highway work: laid tar, built cement culverts, spread gravel. There was railroad work, for the Sioux Line, the Burlington Northern, and the Union Pacific. They came home filthy, exhausted, blank-eyed. The women, themselves put out, tossed away, disinherited, worked to bring the men back to life. There was the Mississippi, which helped, broad and glassy and clean and good swimming, and the bright sunsets, and games.

Harkening back to that old life was a kind of revival. A necessary resurrection. Amid all the turmoil, they played onin'djiwat'adiwin, the hand game, gambled with totems, mostly carved out of basswood: Buicks, Cadillacs, Chryslers no bigger than your thumb; tiny homes. There was a terrible irony in this, especially for my mother: gambling, you could hold everything you'd ever wanted, or what you thought you wanted, in the palm of your hand.

And lose it, just as they, in truth, had.

∿∿∿

In the end, my mother got those chromium fixtures she'd dreamed of, and the big blue Buick, the spacious kitchen. The spirit works miracles. But she got them in a way she had not anticipated. Something in her worked reverse magic, as we Chippewa call it. Wenebojo, the Trickster, had singled her out: my mother became a cleaning woman in the mansions just up the bluffs from the Flats, polishing, dusting, washing.

Suddenly she had more silverware than she'd ever wanted. She waxed Studebakers and Lincolns to a shine she could see her face in. Washed linoleum floors on her hands and knees. Listened to expensive radios and cooked in the newest and finest of ovens. Conversed with the wealthiest of Minneapolis *and* Saint Paul—the former on the west bank, the latter on the east.

She got the refinement she'd always wanted. Wore the newest of clothes (though only while working).

My mother told me, "It was like I was hung upside down and shaken. Hard. I got my fill of fancy things up on Pillsbury and on River Road. I was blinded by silver and gold, by polishing. Nights I came back down to the Flats, and the people there, for the first time in my life, looked beautiful. Craggy noses, jet-black hair, brown eyes.

"*Boju*, somebody'd say—hello—and I'd nearly cry.

"For the first time in my life I was home. I can't explain it any other way.

"Where had I been all my life?

Scrubbing, polishing, waxing, she waited for Roy's return. And she dreamed new dreams, but of old places, places that felt like home. Now she dreamed of a cabin on Ten Chiefs, not far from Farnsworth, but far enough. She dreamed of attending Mass and burning tobacco and making charms, as her father, Peke, had done. Now she wanted hardwood floors. She wanted her time back. She wanted to sit in a wooden boat on a June evening and hear the crickets singing. She wanted to harvest rice in the fall, remembered the heavy, rich smell of parched grain. Felt it underfoot, hulling.

And she dreamed of Roy.

She would cut out the nonsense. They would not fight so much.

She would make his meals. She imagined carrying him a plate: mound of mashed potatoes, a venison chop, green beans from the garden.

Garden.

She could dream of flowers all day long, string beans, snappeas, Hubbard squash, rutabagas, pumpkins, and Silver Queen sweet corn. It made her mouth water.

A life up there was possible, could still be had. It wasn't just dreaming. There were things to do, and on their own time. Sure, she could have a radio. A Zenith, even, or a Motorola. And a boat. Roy would have a car, so what that it would be a jalopy? There were dances in town and new stores. She could feel rough cotton in her hands, warmed at the thought of sewing and appliquéing in fine robin's-egg blue, coral red, spring green.

There were things to do up at White Earth. *That* was her revelation. All she needed was Roy's return.

~~~~~

On the darkest day of that year, December 21, 1945, shortly after three in the afternoon, a car pulled up to the River Flats apartment, number 108. My mother, darning socks, looked out the window. It had been nearly two months since the navy had found the wreckage of Roy's PBY somewhere in the Admiralty Islands. Nina stood, her heart clenching something awful. She knew that army green. How often they'd come before, to tell them someone had died. Only now there were two men in the car, the one in the passenger seat queerly hunchbacked. The driver bent over the wheel, checking something on a tablet fixed to the dashboard.

The passenger nodded. Gray exhaust curled lazily out the tailpipe.

They talked for some time, the one at the wheel shaking the passenger by the shoulder—affectionately, it seemed. My mother held her breath. Her legs threatened to give way under her.

Then the door opened, and the hunchback got out.

∿∿∿

My father, Roy, wouldn't take off his parachute, but other than that, he was normal. That's how my mother still puts it. "He just got vertigo once in a while, but that parachute made it all right." If he fell, he could always pull the rip cord, and that parachute would catch him.

As a girl, I said to my mother, But that's silly!

My mother always smiled knowingly.

Yes, it is, she'd say. And, no, it isn't.

There followed a time of attempted understanding.

Why did he have to wear the parachute? He was standing on level ground? Roy, kicking his boots in the dirt, would reply, You only *think* it's solid.

Ah ha, my mother said. I see.

After a time, push came to shove. Wearing the parachute didn't improve Roy's chances of getting a job in the Cities. This didn't bother Roy a bit. Plenty of work to do around here, he said, making a sweep of his arm to indicate the flats.

I said, earlier, that their meeting was a collision, and no less was true of their second joining. Now he was hot, she cold; he was swept up in politics, she as apolitical as she could be; he inflamed with progress and flushing toilets and new cars, and she wanted mystery, the forest, a wooden rowboat on a calm lake.

Yet, when they made love, something strange happened. There was some powerful alchemy between them. They were like opposite poles of a magnet. Poles that switched now and then, but were never the same, though always powerfully attracted. When Roy's political fervor ebbed, my mother's burst into full fury. When the apartment on the Flats went to hell, my mother depressed and apathetic, Roy cleaned like a tornado.

Throw it out, throw it all out, he'd say.

Yet he would not take off the parachute. Only at times of intimacy, my mother beckoning, would he carefully set it beside the bed and, with his left hand clutching it, make love to my mother. This I know because Isabel told me so. "I thought you should be aware of who your father really was," she said one evening. "He had some disadvantages there, after the war, you know."

Peke grunted. "That boy was always touched," he said, which to the Chippewa means he was gifted or he was crazy—or a little of both.

That winter Roy and five others reroofed the Flats apartments. Built a veterans' hall. Got a bus and took the kids over to Minnehaha Academy on Cedar, got a court injunction to get the city to let those kids into classes. They put up a machine shed, and Roy went back to working on cars.

Nina continued to keep house for the wealthy.

ᴨᴧᴧᴧ

Then the winter passed, and the willow buds were out, the snow melted, and the Flats acres down to the Mississippi greened. My father, now known simply as Chute, threw himself headlong into his business. All day, wrenches, grease, timing and advance, starters, carburetor rebuilds, motors roaring, clouds of too rich bluish exhaust. He worked spells on those motors.

Nina worked, too. To get pregnant and to get him out of the Flats and "back home," as she thought of it. She got him to eat oysters, brewer's yeast, chicken livers. His color came back, at least most of it. And if those hands could make motors purr, he did that with Nina, too.

Time passed.

"When are you going to take that off," my mother would ask Roy, meaning the parachute.

"When it's safe," he'd reply.

"Safe?"

"Yes, safe."

Twelve new apartments he put up. A seamless cement drive. A basketball court—my father loved to play basketball. He repaired Packards, Lincolns, Pierce Arrows, once even a Rolls-Royce.

The Flats community grew from some two hundred to nearly eight hundred. "It wasn't a bad life," my mother told me, "not really.

"Except that I couldn't get your father to sit still for so much as a second." And there she would smile, a smile I didn't understand until I was much older.

"Never?" I asked.

"Just now and then," she'd say, and smile that smile.

It's funny how, oftentimes, couples trying to make a baby, if they're unsuccessful, decide to adopt one, and right about there, when they stop trying, the miracle happens. So it was with my mother.

Peke told me this: *You know, maybe we shouldn't have named your mother Sweetheart. Did you know that was her real name? Ninamuch?* My mother did have one of those heart-shaped faces. And yes, of course I knew, I'd been reminded of it a hundred times.

Isabel, fixing coffee, would shake her head. *What kind of nonsense are you telling her now?*

What Peke told me was this: *A given name makes a face. Only you have to believe it.*

He told me, *To get supernatural powers, you have to wrestle snakes.*

He said, pointing with his index finger: *The trouble isn't with the spell; it's how to distinguish between reality and illusion.*

You know, when Wenebojo killed the underwater kings, it was

Toad Woman who doctored them. Brought them back. Takes a special person to play Toad Woman.

Yuck! I said.

Toad Woman was always pictured as ugly, grotesque, with warts and bulging eyes and a rust-brown dress in tatters.

I thought about that a lot.

Who was Toad Woman? Was my mother? She was beautiful, after all. Was Roy? Or was I Toad Woman? Or was Toad Woman just something that came over you?

Early one evening in November of 1947 my mother returned from her day on Pillsbury Avenue to the gloomy and dark Flats apartment. She was tired, unusually so, and standing at the counter, rolling out a crust for a potpie, she collapsed.

Roy rushed to her.

She was trying to stand, but couldn't. She was terrified, thinking her polio had returned. Now visions of an iron lung and a slow, withering death possessed her. All she could do was cry.

She reached up and caressed Roy's face. "Didn't you want something else?" she said. "I mean, for us?"

Roy nodded.

"Just name something, *anything*. Can't you think of something?"

"I want you," he said.

Six months later Nina gave birth to a six-pound five-ounce baby girl. I was so small I could fit into a shoe box. Time went by in a flash.

〰〰〰

There is an old story about how Jidjiwe, the Sandpiper, fishing, saw himself in the moon reflected on a dark lake. Stunned at the glowing apparition of himself, he dived into the lake to follow.

Some Chippewa say you can still see him trapped in the moon's reflection. Some say he drowned.

That is how I like to think my father was recalled to service, with the prospect of righting his self-image. This time he'd beat it, he must have been thinking. This time he would fly fighters, not flying boats. This time his crew wouldn't die in a crash landing. This time he'd fly better, smarter, wouldn't hit the air pocket that had sent the plane careening into the Pacific Ocean.

This time he would save everybody. He would do that right thing he hadn't done, whatever it was. He would trim the elevator or see the moon through the clouds on the water. He would knock down that Zero with the one remaining fifty-caliber cannon.

∿∿

A group of people from the Flats gathered at the Washington Avenue depot in Minneapolis to see him off. My mother was inconsolable. (Is this my first memory? Of being held tightly, a sharp piercing sound from my mother terrifying me?) I imagine they were quite a sight: Roy, that parachute on his back; my mother sobbing; Big Bob, who had once been featured on postcards of the Mesabi Iron Range with the caption "World's Biggest Indian," towering over them, sad-faced.

There, at track 23, my father was Jack Armstrong, the All-American Boy, all over again. He was going to get another shot at it. He would rise to the occasion. Chest out, chin up, back straight!

Heave-ho, soldier!

He had his aviator sunglasses on, which he hadn't worn in some time. His uniform was pressed and his shoes spit-shined and polished to a mirror luster. There was that can-do gleam in his eye, albeit a now very artificial gleam.

There, on the platform, they waited:

A movie-star-beautiful woman amid a crush of friends all dressed for the occasion; a goggle-eyed girl, barely three, looking for something to hold on to; a serviceman wearing a parachute and grinning crazily; and the World's Biggest Indian.

The station smelled of diesel exhaust and oil, electricity, dirt, and perfume. Loudspeakers called out tracks and departure times.

They shifted awkwardly, too visible.

The train came in, immense, black, stopped with a clatter and an airy hissing. Roy blinked at that train. What was he waiting for? He shook hands with Big Bob ("Don't take any wooden nickels!"), kissed my mother's friends Marcy and Helen and Louise, stooped down and gave me what seemed a crushing squeeze. Then he turned to my mother and did the same.

"Where is it?" Nina said, recoiling.

Somehow, in the crush, Roy had taken off the parachute. Had he thrown it away? Or had he just hidden it, for now, as part of his new image?

She looked around them: peculiar orange lights, businessmen in smart suits, a jet of steam escaping from under the train, a blue poodle on a red leash. " 'Scuse me, miss," a porter said. He steered a cart around my mother.

"Roy!"

She followed the porter, trying to restrain herself from digging into the luggage. Then didn't. She heaved that luggage everywhere. Suddenly she was desperate.

"Nina," my father called. *"Hey!"*

He winked, standing back a ways.

My mother tossed yet another suitcase onto the platform, passengers dodging. He needed that parachute. What would he do without it? *She* needed him to have it. *Where was it?*

Roy threw her a kiss. "It's okay," he said, and swung up and onto the train.

~~~

On the evening of my eighth birthday I was at my grandparents' house, waiting for my mother. She'd gotten a slip from the post office in Farnsworth. There was a package for us, addressed to the Dibikamigs, and she'd driven into town to get it. I remember feeling somewhat under the weather. I was in bed, feverish, and Isabel was pampering me. My brother, Jerry, was over at the Strongholds', so he would not catch whatever I had.

Now Peke puttered around the cabin, smoking when Isabel wasn't paying attention.

"Stop that!" she'd say, turning and eyeing the doorway into the kitchen.

There followed a period of relative quiet, in which Isabel read to me. I don't remember what. She usually read *Grimm's Fairy Tales,* or H. R. Schoolcraft. Between Peke and Isabel, I'd already gotten quite an education about shape-shifters, windigos (cannibals made of ice), giants and ogres, and elves (pukwanjinini), princesses, maidens, magic incantations, spells, and coats or hats that gave special powers. Most likely she read "The Enchanted Moccasins" that night. I never tired of it.

But that evening I was suffering. Always, on my birthday, I was most aware of my father's absence, and this birthday was no exception. He had mysteriously disappeared after his term of service in Korea.

In all those years we had not received so much as a postcard. Nor did I have so much as a picture of him. In my imagination he was sometimes tall, sometimes short. He sometimes had a big hooked nose and the near-Asian eyes that Chippewa often have. I knew his name was Roy and that he'd been a pilot, that we'd lived along the Mississippi in the Twin Cities, in a place called the Flats, and that Jerry had been born after my father left.

If I asked my friends' parents about my father, they looked at me askance. "Well, your father, Roy, now . . ."

It is a belief among the Chippewa that to speak of the deceased is to bring them back. To speak badly of Roy, then—since it was assumed he was dead—was more than a little risky.

Your father was, they said, brilliant, his own person, different, dashing, one determined Indian, a real ladies' man, one hell of a big asshole.

John Fisher, whom I had a crush on and whom I saw at the off-reserve school, put it differently. "Your old man was crazy," he said. "He went windigo out there in the Pacific."

I didn't even know where the Pacific was.

Now on my birthday, my hopes were dashed again. In that way children do, I'd imagined a tearful, happy family reunion—as I had on my fifth, sixth, and seventh. Every year I denied my longing for this father, and it quietly grew larger in my mind, more mythical, our eventual reunion.

If I thought about it enough, it would happen, I thought.

"Knock twice on Wenebojo's canoe," Peke had told me, "and it will take you anywhere."

I wanted to be taken into my father's arms.

∿∿

"Well, what's taking Nina so long?" Isabel said.

My mother had gone to get the package at the post office, and more than an hour had passed.

Peke, in the kitchen, grunted. *"Kiwitag'icig,"* he said. She's flying around all over the place. Isabel waved his smoke away from her face; it had snaked into the bedroom where it curled now at the foot of the bed.

"You shut up," Isabel said.

I pulled the quilt up around my chin. The smell of burning cedar comforted me. Peke was out there praying. But suddenly I was angry. What good did any of it do?

"Is he coming?" I asked.

Isabel smiled sadly.

"I don't think so, sweetie," she said.

~~~

A short while later my mother returned.

"Goddammit!" she spat, slamming the front door behind her. "I order some cloth and those yahoos send me this!" I got out of bed and sat at the table. There the package loomed like some giant brown carbuncle. My mother kissed me on the forehead and went around to the cupboard for a knife. Isabel patted my hand and winked, then mouthed the words, "Just be patient."

Sure enough, there were packages in red and yellow and blue paper and a coconut cake—my favorite and what Isabel baked for me every year—on the sideboard. I opened, we ate, I cried.

Peke nudged my foot under the table. "Are you twelve this year?"

My mother set her fist on her hip. "Come on, Pop, you know how old she is. Don't tease her."

"She's eight and she's one thousand," he replied.

"Right," my mother said.

She set to opening that package she'd gotten at the post office. It was big—as big as the crate of grapefruit that had mysteriously arrived from Florida one Christmas—wrapped in twine and heavy brown paper.

The return address was Harney's Carburetor Service, Topeka, Kansas.

Isabel pointed to it. "Wasn't that some other place you sent off to?"

"Oh, hell, who knows?" my mother said.

By then she'd gotten the paper and cardboard off. There was some dirty green material underneath. We all looked into that crumpled box.

My mother's face went through some strange contortion. I got that awful feeling that everything was about to change, that my birthday had gone sour.

There was a card on top: "For Aja on her eighth birthday. Love, Roy."

My mother lifted what looked like a pack out of the box and, barely able to control her shaking, handed it to me. "Here," she said in a voice I didn't recognize.

I was afraid.

The pack was canvas on the outside and smelled musty. I could barely get my arms around it, it was so thick. I popped something on the end and began to pull out yard after yard of creamy white material from inside it. The fabric was silky smooth when I ran it over my cheek. I swooned, it was so smooth, so warm. I ducked under it, the room lit up like a cloud, billowing and white and pure and going on forever and ever.

I imagined I was an angel up high.

I must have giggled.

"What is it?" I asked. I did not really want to know, floating in all that whiteness, peaceful, and quiet, and feverish.

"It's a parachute, *ninamuch*," Isabel said.

I peeked out. "But why?" I said.

Peke glanced up from his carving. "Don't take it all out," he ordered. "It won't work."

"Don't joke with her now. It isn't funny," Isabel said.

"I wasn't being funny," Peke replied.

My mother kissed my forehead and went into the bedroom and shut the door. The lock made a decisive metallic click. Then, seconds later, something was banging off the walls and I could hear her crying in there. I'd never heard anything like it, a high, ululating shrieking.

I draped the chute over my shoulders, thinking to make it look like wings, waiting for the noise to stop. I looked to Peke, those sad brown eyes, then back to Isabel, who shook her head. She took my hand in hers, stroked the back of it, the way she did when she told me stories.

"Your mother and father," she said, "from the first it was like . . . a collision."

(1957) FROM THE TIME MY MOTHER took the job at the VA hospital in Farnsworth and moved us back up to White Earth from Saint Paul—hoping, I suppose, to hear some word about my father's whereabouts—my brother, Jici'goko, tried the patience of us all, but especially me.

I was my brother's guardian, my brother's caretaker, my brother's saving angel; his nemesis, his obstacle, his pain-in-the-ass older sister (by five years). And every morning, after my mother left, I was his keeper.

I sometimes think there are two kinds of mothers. Our mother was the first: after we were no longer babies, my brother and I, she didn't take much interest in us. The second category, I fit into: after my brother got out of babyhood, he became interesting to me.

He intrigued me (he managed to make an explosive out of an old mayonnaise jar and a little gasoline and some BBs); he surprised me (rodents would jump out of the most unexpected places—the bread box, for example); and he often exasperated me (no, he could not put peanut butter on his hamburger, but he did anyway).

His very name, Jici'goko, meant "contrary." Everyone just called him Jerry.

Those first few years, when my mother was off at the Veterans, I watched Jerry all day every day, except when I was at school. Then my grandparents, Peke and Isabel, had him, and he was always worse in the evening, because he came home full of things to be afraid of: Pauguk, the Skeleton Man; underwater panthers; shape-shifters, especially Grandfather, as he was fearfully called.

The only thing those nights that kept me from being terrified myself was Jerry.

"All of that is bunkum," I'd tell him.

The wind would be howling, the cabin creaking, and the brighter the cabin got inside, the darker were the windows. My imagination would begin to work powerfully. All kinds of evil things were out there. And then something would happen in me. I was not afraid at all. There was an ax by the door, for chopping wood, and I knew how to use it. The clock kept turning, and at one, Nina, our mother, would be home and that would be that.

"Want some herring and peanut butter casserole?" I'd ask Jerry, and that usually stopped his whining.

Finally Jerry started first grade.

For six hours I was blissfully free while my contrary brother, down in room 105, was twisted into shape by Old Lady Richert, a woman of vast, indefatigable energies. Every year Mrs. Richert took it upon herself to set straight those minds contaminated by the confusion of Native thinking. While I was reading about the Erie Canal and George Washington, and learning penmanship, my cantankerous brother was taking a beating.

I tried not to smirk when he looked defeated as we walked home those first few weeks. Jerry had met his match.

"I asked her why glue sticks, and she told me that was the stupidest question she'd ever heard," he told me.

"She's a bitch," I told him, surprising myself. "Don't listen to her."

That year, Mrs. Poehling, my fifth-grade teacher, placed me in a special group, the Cardinals, and I was more than a little proud of myself. I was also a member of Junior Great Books, and though I couldn't entirely understand Aristotle and the other classics we were reading, I made a pretense of it. When we discussed Plato's Allegory of the Cave, for example, I drew connections between those in the cave and my grandparents. I felt disgusted with myself, attacking their stories, their beliefs, but I was given tremendous encouragement.

And I *was* smart.

But there were rumblings coming out of room 105. This new kid, Jerry, had made Mrs. Richert throw her ruler. He asked insane questions, and when he was sent to the principal, instead of being given the usual punishment of standing in the corner by the big yellow cooler at lunch, he got double dessert.

"What's going on with your brother?" Louise Skinaway asked me, pointing to him.

I could only shrug my shoulders.

Egghead, they called him. Professor. And the word I hated most to hear: Genius.

I was tormented. Here was the fall of the House of Usher. An explosion. A collapse. All my reading, studying, pushing myself.

What had I come to?

A girl, eleven, wearing peculiar clothes sewn by her half-breed mother, her father gone off to who knew where; a girl raised, really, by her grandparents, both of whom were known for being odd. A girl, big-eyed, gangly, and lonely, and at this crucial moment, surpassed by the brother she was forced to watch over in her mother's absence.

I wanted to kill him.

One sunny afternoon, for no reason, I knocked him down, just like that, right in front of his friends. Cuffed him behind his ear and he fell. The whole raggedy bunch of us laughed.

"Stupids," he said, dusting himself off.

Score one for Jerry.

That night he called from his room, terrified. He said Grandfather was after him, with black wings and red eyes. I lay on my back in my bed, staring into the dark rafters, biting my cheek.

"Go to sleep, Jerry," I said, filled with bitter laughter.

"Can I come over there?"

"No."

I was the one who'd given Grandfather wings, had made his eyes glow. "Hot, like coals," I'd said.

Lying there, I imagined taking Jerry fishing, and after filling him full of stories about Mishepishu, all coppery scales and horns like on a bull, and *hungry,* I'd force him out of the boat.

He'll bite off your legs first, I'd tell him.

But now I'd done it.

Lying there in bed each crackle of wood in our stove made me jump. Each creak and snap of the house pricked *my* ears. Batwinged Grandfather hooted outside, trying to get in. It seemed I could even smell him in that musty, smoky attic, and what he smelled like was death.

Jerry whimpered. "Aja?"

"Shut up," I said.

And listening to my mother comforting him when she came in, I felt humiliated and ashamed, and hugged myself. I was not about to cry or ask for my mother's attention, as Jerry had.

Never.

So that winter was interminable. When I worked my mother up for sympathy, all she said was "You knew Jerry was clever."

And with that, she snapped her compact shut and made a face in the mirror. High cheekbones and big dark eyes, full lips and a certain *something*. She was dating again and was jittery and excitable.

"Do I look all right?"

"Like Ingrid Bergman," I told her, which was true.

Weeknights I was pestered by Jerry.

Huddled over my copy of *Little Women* or an autobiography of Abraham Lincoln or Florence Nightingale, I could not read. Jerry sat across from me, tearing through *my* Junior Great Books. I flipped pages, too, always faster, but took in nothing. It was pure, self-inflicted torture. I'd loved reading, but now that pleasure was gone. Jerry would look at me over one of those books, his big, bland brown eyes staring, and I would think: drowning, poison, electrocution.

What I settled on was kits ordered through ads in comic books and magazines. Ads that made outrageous claims. "Build hovercraft," the ad would say in large print and, under that, in much smaller letters, "Uses one and one-half horsepower electric motor, as in standard canister vacuum cleaner." We did not have a vacuum cleaner, had never had one. Which set Jerry to improvising, usually unsuccessfully.

He threw things, cursed to himself, jabbed at parts with a big yellow-handled screwdriver.

I could barely conceal my laughter.

And there were other kits: for gyrocopters; for go-carts, which were a craze then; for a one-man submarine. That kid, my brother, spent tens of hours poring over blueprints, plans, secret decoder rings, diagrams of motors and gears and whatnot.

And I could read again.

Every Saturday my mother got up late, and the two of us went into town to buy groceries and maybe catch a matinee, usually some Technicolor musical like *Oklahoma!* or *South Pacific,* which made me feel drugged. While we were in town, Jerry would be at the dump with Peke, scrounging parts for whatever kit I'd ordered to bedevil him. When we returned, there would be Peke, snoring in the easy chair, Isabel at the stove, and Jerry tangled in a mess of wire.

The last kit I got Jerry was a See the Canals of Mars Telescope. All that was in it was a cheap plastic lens, a length of cardboard tubing, a plastic handle, and some directions that smelled of chemicals.

I sniggered, thinking it would drive him mad.

~~~

"Send him out during deer season with a pair of antlers on his head," Louise Skinaway said, leaning over her tray at lunch. I glanced around the low-ceilinged room. Plaid shirts, overalls, farmers' kids. But no Jerry.

I chuckled grimly. Jerry had been pestering me to help him find things for his telescope. Lenses were expensive, out of reach, and I felt a little sorry for him.

I'd really gotten to him, but good, so much so it was coming back at me.

"No, your dad's always bringing us over venison. Never know what'd happen. And anyway I'd hate to get Jerry in a stew," I said, chuckling.

Louise didn't get it.

Here was one more stultifying day. Up in room 501 we did long division and multiplication, something I'd learned years before while grocery shopping with my mother.

It was late April. Spring was upon us.

Birds called through the open windows, and there was the scent of lilacs. I doodled on my desk. Bored. Then on a sheet of paper, I drew a picture of my father, then Mishepishu, the horned water serpent, sketched pukwanjinini, or little people, and Akik, or Turtle.

"Shoot me," I whispered to Louise, who sat in front of me.

Just then Mrs. Poehling glanced at the clock on the wall over her desk.

"Class," she said, smiling, and looking askance at us, added, "I have a surprise for you."

Into our little blue room stepped a jaunty-looking man in a charcoal-gray suit. He wore a red bow tie and thick black-plastic-rimmed glasses. He was shortish, and his hair was slicked back. I was all prepared to dislike him when he introduced himself, I thought, as Professor *Buhawuth*.

He was a Brit, a real one, and from that first second, his hands spinning apples that became planets that became solar systems that became galaxies, I was transfixed. He had a breezy way of joking, and we Chippewa kids recognized it right away. He was a bit of a trickster, this Professor Butterworth.

"Rahtha like a *cir*cus, keeping all these *bahlls* in motion. No surprise that the big G drops one now and then, eh?" he said, and winked theatrically.

He put up a chart, vaguely gestured at it with a pointer, a rubber bullet on the end. The chart sprang back into itself with a snap. It made us all jump.

"There's the Big Bang in a nutshell," he snickered. "We don't like *chahts*, anyway, do we?"

Mrs. Poehling smiled munificently from the back of the room.

"So . . . anybody know what day this is?" Professor Butterworth asked.

It was April 29, 1957. A Monday. Otherwise the day meant nothing to us. Professor Butterworth made a circuit of the room, whistling.

"No?"

We were all eyes and ears.

"Today there's going to be an *eclipse!*" Professor Butterworth said, clapping his hands together. "And we're all going to *watch it!*"

I remember thinking that we would stand outside on the cracked and broken pavement of the school parking lot, squinting into the sun, burning our eyes out.

"Won't the light hurt our eyes?" I asked.

The others in the class laughed, but Professor Butterworth nodded.

"Looking right into the sun, you'd go blind, yes. You *cahn't* look at the sun like that without a *filtah*"—he bent down and smiled at me—"or, even *bettah*, a *pinhole camera!*"

A short while later we stood in back of the school holding up grocery boxes. Mine had the Wheaties logo emblazoned across it. I felt ridiculous. The pinhole, made in a sheet of aluminum foil set at the front, projected a tiny sun at the far end. I was thinking I would be bored when I saw that sun start to shift, saw a portion of it disappear.

The light got odd out there. It was a kind of daylight twilight.

Something big was happening.

I looked for Jerry in the lower grades huddled on the grass just back of the south wing, then over by the teachers' cars and up by the poplars in back.

I looked all around me.

I was feeling sick, something in the pit of my stomach telling me all was not right. I dropped my box and ran over to Mrs. Richert's class.

"Yes?" she said.

"Have you seen my brother?" I asked.

"He's sick," she said, imperiously. "He went home *hours* ago."

I screamed.

～～～

Professor Butterworth, in his dapper tie and thick, professorial glasses, bent over the wheel, driving seventy-five on that narrow rutted road into the reserve. He had a bit of Sterling Moss in him, threw the car from side to side. We were flying. Where side roads intersected, he barely hit the brakes—a touch of Russian roulette, as we never could have stopped anyway. There was a handle on the dashboard, and I clung to it. At one point, the car lifted, airborne, and then came the long rush down Peterson's Hill. I was saying prayers. Please, please, please, I prayed. I won't make Jesus jokes anymore. I won't steal things. I won't hit my brother. I won't lie. I won't . . .

There, now, was the cabin, high pines all around, and to my horror, my brother, Jerry, in the yard, his eyes pressed to some kind of gadget, at the end of which he'd fixed a pair of binoculars. We slid to a stop, crunching gravel, hot exhaust, and dust. Jerry stepped back from his makeshift telescope. His eyebrows screwed up, and he spun this way and that, his hands out.

A thin, terrified wail rose up out of him.

That my brother was blind for three weeks did something to him. And to me. I sat up night after night, reading to him from his favorites, all space adventures. He lay on his back, his eyes bandaged. It was awful, but I couldn't help but get the feeling he was smirking.

"What?" I'd say.

And like that, he'd settle into the bed.

"Read me that chapter over," he'd say, or "Get me a glass of water, can you?"

For some time, Jerry bumped into things. He had books and toys to amuse himself with during his weeks in bed: a crystal radio, with a copper antenna; a whole set of *Tom Corbett, Space Cadet* adventures; a balsa-wood glider; and a cheap plastic microscope with interchangeable lenses. (The microscope had been Peke's idea: something safe that might motivate Jerry to his usual absorption in things.)

Now he took an interest in none of it.

"Read to me," he'd say.

But if his rheumy eyes frightened me, what bothered me even more was unspeakable: This blind boy didn't have to take the bucket down to the lake for water (we didn't have running water then). The bus stopped by our place just for Jerry. He wasn't allowed to cook, but then, when had he ever cooked? And all talk of sending him to a special school ended. I walked him to and from Mrs. Richert's classroom, tortured by that last humbling thing—leading him by the hand.

But I had my suspicions.

Around twilight on July Fourth I took Jerry to the YMCA in Farnsworth. I'd told him we were going there to swim, since he couldn't see the fireworks, but I knew the pool wasn't finished. We met Louise in the gymnasium, high and full of echoes, and waited for a Ping-Pong table to open. It was a balmy, warm night. The older kids were shooting baskets and listening to records.

I beat Louise easily, working on a backhand-over and a topspin slam. Jerry watched, his back to the wall. He was biting his fingernails. Louise, as I had asked her to, stepped out.

"Here, Jerry," she said, and tossed him the paddle, which, of course, he dropped.

"I can't," he said.

Jerry, before the accident, had been able to beat me five out of ten games, occasionally even left-handed, which had made me furious.

"Let's just volley, okay?" I said.

Jerry liked that. He stood like a dummy at the table, hitting one in three, chasing the others. In the middle of it I said, "Listen, let's play a short one, just to ten. I'll give you a handicap." Jerry frowned. "Look, I'll even play with my left hand. Okay?"

Jerry's eyes narrowed.

"Well?"

"All right," he said.

There was a wall of sound in that gym: Patsy Cline singing "and I'm crazy for loooo-vin' you," the squeak and snort of tennis shoes on waxed wood, the thump of a basketball, Louise snapping her gum. Jerry clenched his teeth, held the paddle in that upside-down grip he had. I sent a slow one over the net.

Jerry smacked it back.

The ball clipped the corner of the table. Right where I couldn't get at it.

"I quit," he said, and slumped away.

Walking home I was so angry with him I hung back with Louise until a block or so separated us. Head down, he trudged up the ridge the grader had left, as if using it for a guide in the near dark.

Behind him I was deciding what to do.

There's a lot of power in being a victim, Peke had told me, but only for so long, and then it eats you up, always from the inside.

A number of Jerry's classmates came out of the pines on either side of the road. They looked like wolves, slinking and cowering, all in a group. One of them took a not altogether friendly swipe at Jerry, knocking him down. Jerry turned to see if I was watching.

I felt ill. He was getting to be quite an actor, my brother. And the person he was acting was, no apologies, all over that reserve—it was one way to survive the pressures of life. Right there, in his stumbling, his throwing his hands up, that pitiful, helpless look on his face, he saved my life.

I tore down the hill, Louise after me.

They were really roughing Jerry up. The biggest of them was

Tom Aagard. I knocked Tom away, and Jerry did that pathetic slouching thing. He pretended he couldn't see me, thinking I'd buy it, this latest ploy.

"Is that you, Aja?" he said.

I pulled a wide roundhouse punch and smacked Jerry right between those bland, startled eyes. He squatted, held his hand to his nose.

"Get up!" I shouted.

I could hear the excited breathing of the other kids. Jerry shook his head. I lifted him by his jacket and shook him.

"Say something!"

I boxed him across the face.

"Hey! *Hey! Are you in there?*" I shouted, my voice rising, shrill.

Jerry did not so much as blink.

8

(1962) NO ONE SHOULD HAVE TO TELL a story like this. So up until now I never have. I'm in it. So are my father, my mother, Peke and Isabel, and on the periphery, my brother, Jerry, brilliant, yet as innocent as a cabbage. For reasons that will become clear in the telling, though, I'm going to back away a bit.

I need breathing room from all this, even thirty-some years later. So, that said, here it is.

⌇⌇⌇

On a clear June day in 1962, toward noon, a car shinier than shiny pulled up to the Oshogay pumps at White Earth Village. School had let out, and Aja, who was courting Oshogay's black-jacketed pump jock, stared through the door from where she sat on a high stool drinking a Pepsi. "Pepsi-Cola hits the spot! Eight full ounces, that's a lot!" she sang sarcastically. Her sweetheart, Henry Junior, winked and went out.

The driver, his back to Aja, looked for something in the car. DA, T-shirt, a pack of Marlboros rolled up in his sleeve, well-muscled arms. An old guy, but attractive. A little dangerous-looking, even. And the car! Red-and-white upholstery, big fins in back with tail-lights that looked like rockets, aquamarine paint so shiny she could see the front of the station reflected in the door, herself there, waving, a cigarette in her hand. "Oh, dahling," she said, puckering her mouth. The driver adjusted his glasses and rummaged through the glove compartment while Henry Junior pumped gas now. Aja turned to the mirror in back of the station desk. Her body was playing some strange tricks on her, and in response she was playing some on the men around her.

But this stranger, maybe he was a movie star. With a car like that. Or one of those developers who'd been coming around here since the sale of the north end, big pinky rings and flashy cars. Aja touched a wetted finger to her hair, pasting a strand back. She eyed herself in the mirror. She made what she thought was a face of melting desire, as she had seen on the cover of a movie magazine at the barber's. Then she tried to look insane, like Joan Crawford.

"I'm insane," she said to herself, exhaling a plume of smoke and twisting her mouth and staring.

There was the hiss of an air hose, the smell of gasoline and a hot engine. Outside, they were talking about the whatchamacallit and the tires and how fast the car would go and all that. There was something friendly yet sneaky in the man's voice.

Where was so-and-so? he asked.

Just up the road, Henry Junior told him.

Aja lifted herself so she could catch sight of her chest in the mirror. Her mother had sewn her a pleated shirt "to de-emphasize things," but the shirt subtly did just the opposite. Aja was a little in awe, was embarrassed, surprised, at the effect she had on men now, was secretly pleased, yet felt almost dirty.

And she had all kinds of romantic notions.

"I'd do anything for you," she breathed into the mirror, smoke curling from her nostrils. "Anything, sweatheart, koochie coo, honey bear!"

Aja laughed to herself.

She knew these yearnings were phantoms, and that was what she'd said to her aunt Betty, who'd told her she better wipe that silly Mona Lisa smile off her face and wise up. "You're going to school," she said. "Period."

"Right," her mother, Nina, had added. Aja thought her mother pathetic. Just pathetic!

But even now, Aja was waiting.

She could practice on this stranger. She held her head just right, so when he came in, he would see her face in three-quarter profile. She was just practicing; it couldn't hurt anyone, and besides, it was fun. A kind of dark and scary fun, and it was the most exciting game around this goddamn dump.

"I love you," Aja breathed into the mirror. "Always. Forever. And forever and ever and ever!"

The service-door bell rang twice, and Aja's heart jumped. Then here were Henry Junior's heavy boots and the sharp rap of an unmuffled V8 engine. She knew these things from hanging around the shop. The exhaust note dwindled to nothing in the distance.

"Guy gave me a five-dollar tip!" Henry said, ringing up the sale.

Henry Junior came around the station desk. He sidled up beside Aja. Seventeen, he had pretensions of a mustache and that hungry look she was so sick of—but not altogether; she couldn't seem to pull herself away, however much she wanted to. And his cologne stank. She liked to call it Ode to Toilet.

Henry looked furtively from side to side. He reached behind him, switching the light off. It just served to put the station office in shadow.

"Henry," Aja said in a bored, flat voice.

She reached around him and found the switch. The light was glaring.

"Not now," she said and, with just a hint of a smile, had him in her pocket again.

∿∿

Parked around to the north end of Ten Chiefs Lake, just behind Doris Second's allotment, in Henry's old jalopy, a rusted and badly dented 1951 Hornet, Aja persisted in fielding Henry Junior's advances. The car smelled of mildewed mohair and faintly of Lysol and Henry's cheap cologne.

"Stop it, you," Aja said.

Henry intensified his efforts.

Doris was throwing a party, and they were late already, or so Aja said. She hoped to meet her friend Josie there—and, too, just maybe, *him*.

Mr. Right. Ha!

Now Aja bit Henry on the neck. Hard. Henry, who'd given up on the belt buckle and was trying to go up her pant leg. A novel approach, Aja thought.

"Ouch!" Henry said.

Aja studied her mouth in the rearview mirror. She touched it up with a little Passion Pink, then made a tortured kissing and for seconds afterward—just seconds—let Henry Junior get to second base.

"All right," she said, and pushed him away.

Beside the car, in the moonlight, Henry stood with his hands hanging at his sides.

"Do we have to go in?" he said.

∿∿∿

Hours later, pricked, poked, prodded, and filled with gossip, true and untrue, Aja, on unsteady legs (beer), negotiated the steep, rutted road to her mother's house. It was a little after one, the moon out, and summer in the wind.

Now Aja had a little time to herself.

A gentle breeze rustled in her ears, bringing back memories of seashells, a trip to Florida, the only trip she'd ever taken off the reserve. She stopped to put her palms on her knees, thinking she might be sick. She was sick, all right, sick of Henry and his mooning around: But *why* can't we? I love you, girl. She was sick of all of it, of her friends Josie and Alice, and of the beaten-down, used-up feeling she had about things. She hated the goddamn off-reserve school she attended. Hated her mother's nosing around, threatening to send her to that parochial school, Our Lady of the Lakes. Pathetic! Even her grandfather's world of spirits and demons and shape-shifters seemed like pure bunkum now. Only Betty, her aunt, and Isabel, her grandmother, seemed to have anything to offer. Which these days amounted to "Be careful."

Right, Aja thought.

She dejectedly scaled the hill in the dark, rehearsing her excuse. What would it be tonight?

We got lost? No. We forgot what time it was? Impossible, Isabel had given her a watch, and a nice one, to avoid that. Something came up? What something? Well, there was this guy come over from Rocky Boy, Montana, one of those Finedays you're always talking about. The legendary whatever the fuck his name is.

Right, *him,* so-and-so.

She had to stop again and was very nearly in tears. Despite the Grain Belt and the inertia that threatened to pull her down, she struggled up the slope. The moon was at her back, full, or very nearly full. Here was the roof of her mother's cabin, rust-red in the dark, the big pine to the right of it.

It seemed to loom up before her.

She had that spooky feeling again that she was not moving but the world was moving around her. The roof seemed to grow right out of the hilltop. And just as she was thinking, Stop it, *stop it!* she saw the car, fins high and like wings in back.

Aja went around to the kitchen door. She thought to climb the pine and traverse the roof to her bedroom window, as she often did, but she couldn't get herself up for it. So what? she thought. So what that *he* was in there, that guy she'd seen at the station? She just wasn't up to making small talk. She eyed the roof again. She just couldn't hack it. No. Saw herself on hands and knees. End. Finis. I refuse, she thought. She eyed the door. Peeling white paint, green underneath. Warm yellow light came through the curtains. The hinges made an awful squeaking, which, during the day, no one noticed, but at night sounded like something right out of Poe.

Aja loved Poe. " 'For the love of God, Montressor,' " she said, humoring herself, and reached for the knob.

The door groaned as she'd known it would.

In the kitchen there was the smell of potatoes and beef and . . . nutmeg? The kitchen was spotless. The living room light was on, too. Aja felt as though she were nailed to the floor. Cologne. She just couldn't stand another gentleman friend. No way.

Aja bolted for the stairs.

Halfway up came her mother's voice. A tone in it that stopped her dead.

"Aja," she said. Was it joy? Or agony? What was it? "Aja!

"Come and see who's here!"

They had not expected her to come through the kitchen door; there they sat, on the sofa, their heads turned in expectation.

Aja recognized him before he did her.

He had a smile that could kill you. Really. Teeth as white as porcelain in a disarmingly cockeyed smile. Jack Armstrong, the All-American Boy. Only he was an Indian, jet-black hair and features as fine as any movie star's. He was full of something, she could just feel it! And right when he turned, saw her, his eyes registered—shock! And something else.

Aja's heart jumped.

"Your *father* is home!" Nina very nearly sang.

Roy took a step toward her.

"Hi," he said and put out his hand.

~~~

The following morning, after a night of worse than disturbed sleep, Aja washed dishes in the kitchen of her aunt's restaurant, the Alibi.

"A handshake?" her aunt Betty said. She was counting the eggs the egg man had brought in. "Is that what he did? Shook your hand?"

Aja shrugged. "He—"

Josie put her head through the space between the counter and the kitchen. She did not smile or say, Hey, I heard your pop's back in town, or give Aja one of those warm looks of almost perverse condescension, as she sometimes did now that she was engaged. She actually grimaced a little, tossing back her hair. "I need a number seven," she said, "and an oatmeal."

"Comin' up," Aja said.

During their break, Aja and Josie stood behind the Alibi smoking. Aja was trying to rouse herself to say something to redeem the situation. She'd let the cat out of the bag by telling Betty and Josie how hurt she'd been by that handshake, and now she wondered what she'd wanted from them. When Betty expressed anger, Aja had felt protective of her father. When, now, Josie remarked how handsome her father was, she felt the opposite—possessive, to a fault. She imagined tearing Josie's hair out.

"Asshole," Aja said.

Josie smiled.

"What's wrong with you?" Aja asked.

Josie did that grimacing thing again. She sighed a little. "Time to go back in," she said, which was a first, as Josie was always stretching her break.

Roy, Aja's father, was at table number six.

Josie's table.

Now, when she was done at the Alibi, Aja dreaded going home. What to do? She wanted to hit the man, and, like a child, she wanted to fall into his arms and cry, and what scared her was that the latter impulse was the stronger. Roy, to her surprise, turned her into jelly. The word "Dad" rolled off her tongue, sweetly real, for he had been her father all those years before he'd been called up a second time, for Korea. During dinner she tried not to look at him. Tried not to ask him questions. When she did, they came out haltingly, awkward. The questions that needed to be asked—Where were you? Why didn't you at least write? What took you so long? Do you love me still?—were not asked, nor did Aja's mother, Nina, encourage such asking. In the evenings, over dinner, they were just one big happy family.

Roy often teased Aja's brother. Although wary, he was young enough to go along with it all.

"I'll show you how to build a go-cart," Roy said.

"Really?"

Roy gave Aja a furtive glance, then smiled for them all. Roy's mechanical talents were legendary around White Earth. Stories about how he'd kicked so-and-so's baler or thresher back to life circulated like myth, Roy always somewhere in the middle with his wrench.

"Don't promise him things like that," Nina said.

They all bent over their plates.

$\sim\!\sim\!\sim$

A month later, mid-July, a hot, muggy evening, Aja stood behind the Alibi with Josie. There was the clatter of dishes inside. A lull of voices. Aja was tired and dirty and upset. She'd specifically taken the night shift to be away from home, but Roy was inside having coffee. It seemed he was always having coffee at the Alibi.

"So that's all he does?" Josie said. "Glance at you once in a while?"

Aja nodded.

"And he doesn't say anything?"

"Of course he says *things*."

"Like what?"

"Like 'good morning,' or 'hi!' Or 'Sure is hot out, isn't it? Watch out for those mosquitoes.' "

Josie shook her head.

"And all the while he's taking Jerry out fishing." Aja flicked her cigarette across the alley. She clenched her hands into fists, angry, and just as quickly felt her eyes glassing up. "Or working on that fucking go-cart."

All through her shift she was aware of Roy in the dining room. There was laughter, and in the center of it was Roy. Roy, who hadn't yet really spoken to her. Roy, who in one month had started a number of projects. Roy, who this time, others told her, had come back in one piece. Aja watched him through the divider between the kitchen and the dining area.

There was something almost parrotlike about the man, something that truly bothered her. Every now and then, when it seemed their eyes might meet, Aja at the grill and Roy there at his table demonstrating some aspect of flying to his friends—he made airplanes with his hands, the deadly Nakajima Ki-43 Oscar, the Mitsubishi A5M, and, always, Zeros—they looked away.

Weird.

I hate him, Aja thought, flipping a burger. I really do.

~~~

One evening, when she couldn't get the hours she wanted—Betty had told her, "You go out and have some fun; you're too young to work like this"—Aja went into White Earth Village to pester Henry Junior at the station. She sat on that stool again, chewing gum and smoking, making faces in the mirror.

"Oh, *baby*, I love you so much. I just can't *live* without you." She made a big open-mouthed kiss, like Eva Marie Saint in *North by Northwest*.

"Aja!" Henry shouted. "Is there any ATF on the shelf there?"

Aja reached for the can over the mirror. She tossed it out the door to Henry.

"Thanks," he said.

Through the gold letters in the window, Oshogay's Gas, she could see this customer, all belly and shuffle. Black wing tips. Yellow sweater. Jaunty hat. Aja adjusted the angle of her cigarette. The customer was watching her now in the reflection.

Aja put on her best face. "You're my everything, Heathcliff," she said. "My honey bun, my koochie coo, my baby doll.

"Kiss me, lamb chop!" she said, looking right at him.

About an hour later, right around dusk, she glanced up from *Silver Screen*, and there, behind her, was the car. Fins up to here, her father at the wheel. Rakish. She tried to make herself small at the counter while Roy was busy with the car. Henry, mystified by it all, worked the pump, not knowing what to say or do. There was more of that "How much lift and duration and what jets do you got in the carburetor" talk. Aja put her face in the magazine. "Some Enchanted Evening" ran through her head like a demented dirge.

Or was it something else? "Happy Talk." God, how she hated that goddamn song. Now Roy messed with the engine; she could see his belt buckle below the open hood.

He was avoiding her. He didn't like her.

He hated her.

He wished she'd never been born.

Frankly, Scarlett, I don't give a damn! Aja thought, trying to make light of it. But it was painful, all that posing, with her father behind her. She felt an ache in her so deep and so engulfing that she could only do her best not to cry. To so much as lift her head was impossible. She felt sick, and worried where to put her head if she was.

Henry darted in, back of the register, ringing up the sale. "What's going on?" he said. "Huh?"

Aja, on the stool, hugged herself. She waited to hear the sound of the exhaust dwindle in the distance so she could cry. It was stuck right there in her throat and coming up.

"Aja?" Henry said.

She was waiting for it.

The car started. Suddenly she was angry. Furious, in fact. Something came right up out of her middle, heated her face, twisted her mouth. Her tongue felt oddly muscular and hard.

"If I *ever*—" she said.

But she didn't finish. She felt him standing behind her. Her back felt itchy. She had to pull herself together. She crushed her cigarette in the ashtray, GOODYEAR on the side in red.

"Aja," Roy said.

She couldn't look at him.

So she looked at Henry. Baseball cap, funky mustache, that sad, self-effacing grin. Suddenly she was able to right herself. Henry did that for her. Made her feel in control, at least in part.

"What?" she said, turning to look at Roy. She smelled him, that same cologne he'd worn when she was just a little girl—lime, that was it—and she went weak again.

What? she thought. *What?*

"Come on out, huh?" he said. "What do you say, hon?"

~~~

It was an enormous car, but it felt tiny, even with the top down. Roy drove with a kind of loose verve, hand hung over the wheel at the wrist, his fingers dangling down. The radio played, some twangy western thing.

"Okay there?" Roy said.

Aja nodded. She tried not to slide over near the door. Now that she had her father's attention, she wasn't sure she wanted it. Or was it that she couldn't stand it? She didn't know what to do with her hands. She set them on her lap, then on the seat on either side of her. She stared through the windshield, her face hot. When Roy turned his head away, to the left, she studied him. Here beside her now was the man she had loathed, detested, longed for, cried over, been hurt by, all wrapped up in a package that was . . . *real.*

There was stubble on his chin, a little gray in his hair. He had wrinkles at the corners of his eyes and a fine white scar on his chin. He seemed *too* real to be real. Except for his eyes: he was wearing those Ray-Bans.

Aja straightened her legs. And, getting sudden goose pimples, pulled them back up. She was wearing shorts and a loose blouse. Tennis shoes. She felt naked. She crossed her legs one way and then the other.

"So," Roy said.

Aja grinned awkwardly, set her hands on her knees and left them there. Was she cold? Why did she feel almost chilled?

The car eased through a set of sweeping turns, up Highway 26 North.

"Where we going?" Aja said.

"Construction site."

"Which construction site?"

"BPOE."

"Right," Aja said, as if she would know what that was.

The site, it turned out, was magnificent. The two of them stood on a bluff, high and over a lake, where a foundation had already been laid.

"See over there?" Roy pointed. Khakis, shiny machine-turned watch, muscular hands. Well-cared-for nails. Hair shiny with oil. He looked like an advertisement in a magazine. "Eighty acres down to the lot line. Four hundred forty feet up to the road. Some real old pines down there"—he pointed to the north, a blue-green ridge—"sandy beach on the south. Call it Horseshoe Lake Lodge. What do you think?"

Aja shrugged. "It's nice," she said.

∿∿∿

And so started a series of awkward drives that stretched from mid-summer into the fall.

While Roy was funning (but in that calculated way he had) with Aja's mother, and building things with Jerry, he took Aja for drives. North, west, east, but never south. They might stop on some dirt track, and Roy, in his peculiar way, would describe what would be built there. "Road. Two-lane, drainage, corrugated metal pipe," he might say. "Curve widening. Six percent grade. Number ten gravel with six over." At another site, a stone chimney in a cement foundation: "It's gonna be a hotel here. Dining room seats seventy. Vaulted ceiling. Dormers. Want to see the blueprints?" And he would conveniently have them in the trunk.

Aja was struck dumb.

At first, in the car, anyway, there had been attempts at conversation. But at sites, outside the car, in the open, things became more awkward.

So, later, toward September, they simply drove. Father and daughter, top down, the leaves changing early.

But it was never that simple, really. If Roy shifted against his door, Aja shifted against hers. Every time he looked over at her, she would smile the most awful smile and look away. She couldn't help it. Her mouth just twisted up and she couldn't tell why. One evening, to see if she could change things, she took her cigarettes from her purse, and lit up. She felt a bit of her old self. Here's lookin' at you, shweet-haaht.

"So you've taken up smoking," Roy said.

Aja nodded. She wanted an argument. A launching pad for it all.

"I used to do that," Roy said, and that was the end of it.

Sometimes, Roy would take her to a roadside restaurant and buy her dinner and not eat anything himself. As often as not he'd forget to take his Ray-Bans off in the restaurant.

He looked like a bug, Aja thought then.

∿∿∿

Now she leaned against Henry Junior in his Hudson, confused at his having parked the car so near the BPOE, which was busy this time of night.

"So where did Bug Man take you tonight?" he asked.

Aja took a deep drag on her cigarette. Exhaled. The smoke curled in the car. A drunk lurched by and into the woods.

"Another BPOE."

"Biggest Pricks on Earth."

Aja studied Henry Junior there in the dark. He was not so insistent recently, didn't seem to want her so badly. She felt empty for that, and it scared her. And he was always talking about Roy.

Roy this, Roy that. He was doing it now.

"Your old man is in cahoots with some developers down in the Cities. They want to clear-cut the north shore and put some kind of paper mill in. Did you know that?"

She didn't know, she said, and she didn't care. But that was a lie. She felt a rush of blood to her head. It was all too much.

Now that Henry wasn't breathing down her neck, Aja felt she just might float away.

"Henry," she said.

Henry banged his hand on the dashboard. "I mean, who does he think he is, anyway? Jesus Christ himself or something? The way people're talkin', he's gonna raise the dead here, know what I mean?"

Aja worried she might scream if he didn't stop.

"It's like he's—"

Aja reached for his pants and undid his zipper.

"Hey!" Henry said.

He was actually trying to pull away.

"Hey! What—"

She took him in her mouth, soft top and muscular shank, musky-smelling, her hand around his balls. Ten quick strokes and he was hunched over the wheel, and she had something like bleach at the back of her throat.

There.

That had shut him up, she thought, and got out of the car.

But Roy, with a capital *R-O-Y,* Roy at large, was not to be so easily escaped.

He was everywhere now, in what he was building. A new VFW. A lodge. Drainage. Power lines. Even roads, marked with lath, on top of which strips of bright orange plastic fluttered. In town, his car was like a beacon amid all the reserve wrecks. Shiny new chrome and glass. It was a magnet, a center for talk. For speculation. The old lodge was torn down while the newer, larger lodge was being built, so the council took to meeting at the Alibi. Roy had a distinctive laugh, and even in the kitchen, Aja couldn't mistake it.

Nor could Josie.

"If he weren't your father," she said.

Aja was shocked. "What?"

Josie glanced up from tying her apron. "Oh, nothing," she said.

Cow, Aja thought.

And always, at home, over dinner, Aja sat opposite Roy. There, with Jerry talking about his latest radio triumph—he'd gotten an Australian station, or some other unintelligible thing—and her mother telling River Flats stories, Roy seemed almost comfortable.

Just . . . *warm.*

He'd get that amiable grin, and his whole face would light up. With his sunglasses off, his eyes shone. Just then they seemed to settle in.

They very nearly sighed, the four of them: life could go on after all.

Then, early one evening, Roy pulled up to the pumps at the gas station and let out a whoop.

The bell rang. Henry Junior climbed out from under a customer's Packard. Blue monkey suit, greasy hands, a length of green wire, a dwell meter hanging from it.

"Hey there, Henry!" Roy said.

Aja studied the *Silver Screen* in front of her. Sophia Loren, in all her voluptuous glory, smiled up off the page in Technicolor-blue satin.

"It's in the bag," Roy said, smiling at Aja.

His voice was extra jaunty, extra full of itself. It had to be, he'd just sold off the north end of the reserve through a clever and barely legal allotment deal, had skimmed a bit off the top for himself, and had created scores of jobs at the soon-to-be Calmenson Paper Company.

"Hey, Aja," he said, waltzing right into the station. "You want to come out and take a look?"

∿∿∿

Driving up to Ten Chiefs, she worked on a number of different smiles, none of which seemed right. Roy had his Ray-Bans on again, his eyes swimming in all that green glass as if in an aquarium. He slumped against the door, smiled awkwardly, steering the car up the winding road. One stand of trees after another flashed by.

"Ah, shit," he said.

He reached into the glove compartment and got out a flask. He took a couple tugs on it and handed it to Aja. She knocked back a mouthful, a burst of warmth in her stomach, then got out her cigarettes.

"Gimme one of those, will ya?" Roy said.

It was one of those golden, early October days. The poplars had gone to yellow, and the maples were turning. Roy took another toot. So did Aja. Everything was warm and yellow and woozy. The big car very nearly seemed to steer itself. The ground rose under them, and the car rolled up and on and on and over the flatlands.

"Nice up here," Roy said.

Aja nodded. He pointed out landmarks: where Old Man Muskeg had first built after they'd come over from Lac du Flambeau; where he, Roy, had played on a high granite bluff; the remains of the first chapel.

There were still remains of the graveyard, too, the headstones all but sunk into the ground. As Roy pointed them out, his voice slowed, like an old-time record player, the spring run down.

And like that, Roy smiled. "Ah, what the hell," he said.

Aja was not so worried about her hands now. The whiskey

helped that. She lit another cigarette, watching Roy drive. They'd drunk a good portion of the flask and seemed more relaxed. Something like gravity was pulling them together, and something equally strong kept them apart.

She didn't know what to call it.

Is it love, dahling? The voice of Bette Davis echoed in her head. And "Happy Talk" was coming at her. She tried to shut it out by listening to Roy. He was talking about flying now, high and proud and mighty. Those P-47s he'd flown before he'd done his stint in the navy. Still, no matter how much he talked or how friendly his voice, he would not look at her.

Aja was devastated.

Her throat ached, and she clenched her cold hands between her knees, trying not to cry. At one point it seemed he would put his hand on her shoulder, but what he was doing was reaching for something in the backseat. The car swerved, and Aja had to grab the wheel. Roy brought the car to a stop, grinning strangely. Something had been decided.

They stepped out of the car to take a look at the future site of Calmenson Paper. Up high, over Ten Chiefs Lake, far away from anyone, the thing with the distance got worse. Roy stood with his hands in his pockets, the sun reflected in his glasses.

"What do you think?"

There was a dull, unthinking quality to things, and the whiskey hadn't helped. Aja's eyes felt heavy, her body tired. She was really not here at all; she was in Henry Junior's arms.

She shrugged. "Nice," she said.

There was no "Happy Talk" in her head now, no Roy Orbison singing, "Cry-ey-ey-ey-ing, cry-ing!" No Bette Davis, no Ingrid Bergman, no Mae West.

In the trees, the silence threatened to swallow her.

Roy led her down a path to a shelf of rock.

Here were white pine trees hundreds of years old, a blanket of red needles, soft underfoot. Roy, tossing his shoulders, as if to throw something off, launched into the details of the deal he had just cinched.

Aja was getting that disconnected thing again, as if her father, Roy, without moving, were going away from her, down a tunnel that had no walls. While Roy talked on, eyes hidden behind those green lenses, he pointed—at what, she couldn't tell. A blue jay settled in a tree and called raucously. Aja, leaning closer to see what Roy was pointing at, stumbled into him.

Shock. Warmth. Flesh. His cologne.

He brusquely lifted her away, but now Aja had seen something in him. He was more than a little afraid of her. Afraid of *her*. Whyn't ya come up and see me some time? Mae West drawled. All those afternoons of practice in the mirror came to her.

"Take your glasses off," she said.

"No," he said.

She put her hands on her hips. She was getting tangled in that thing that repelled them, but in the dappled light, the quiet, she was tearing through. It came right out, thickened her hands, made her face hot.

She swung around, flat-handed, smacked her father's face, gritting her teeth, as hard as she could, sending the glasses flying.

She punched at him, tight-fisted, her knuckles connecting, first cheek, then forehead.

"Stop. Stop, goddammit," Roy said. "Stop it, son of a bitch!"

He got his arms around her and she continued to hammer at his head. She punched into it. Brick-colored skin. Hammered at his ears. Finally, Aja crushed in Roy's arms, they stood face-to-face, breathing hard.

He was terrified, she could see that, terrified of what this was leading up to.

~~~

On the three-day road to death, my grandfather, Peke, told me, stands a tree beside a river. The heartberry tree is heavy with immense glistening fruit not unlike strawberries: red, full-bodied, succulent. They are the loveliest berries you have ever seen.

But in reality they are the product of wrongdoing, and you may choose, here, this time, not to indulge yourself in eating them, however full or barren the tree might be.

Still, alongside the river one is hungry and, worse yet, thirsty. The river is deep in a chasm, a tantalizing blue. Across the river beckons paradise. An oddly crooked log crosses to the other side, a bridge. The dead man hesitates. Is the log safe? If one fell into the river, one would surely drown.

Here are the berries, swaying in the warm breeze.

The berries are beautiful. They glisten. They are ripe to bursting. Red. Succulent. Your mouth is parched. You can even smell them. Sweeter than anything you've ever smelled. The river below roars. To eat from the heartberry tree, you reason, will fortify you for the difficult task of crossing the river on such a bridge as a crooked log.

~~~

I once said to Peke, when he teased me that I was sweet on a boy I'd met at school, "That Parker boy, he's ugly as sin." This idea I'd gotten from Father Feeney at Our Lady of the Lakes. He'd said sin looked like a leper. A cancerous ulcer. A festering sore.

Peke chuckled.

I felt chills run up and down my spine. Here would be another of those strange things he said.

"Ah, Aja," he said, "sin is *rarely* ugly."

The Midewiwin teaches that if one eats from the heartberry tree, the crooked log, the bridge, once one is on it, becomes a serpent.

The dead man is thrown into the chasm.

That fruit, Peke said, *is hell itself.*

Just a girl, I had one last question: "What do they taste like? The heartberries?"

Peke's eyes wrinkled up, the faintest suggestion of a smile there.

"Just *terrible*," he said.

Nearly two tons of steel rolled back into White Earth Village around dusk. Fins like bats' wings, taillights like bombsights. The red-and-white interior a whore's boudoir. In Aja's mind that evening it was all or nothing, and the needle on the gauge now pointed to nothing. She smoked, leaning against the door. She was disgusted with herself, and with the strange notion that, even feeling as awful as she was feeling, given the chance, the only thing to make her feel better was to feel even more awful by doing again, with even more abandon, what she'd just done that made her feel awful right now.

It was obviously a trap, a rat wheel. Even she, barely fifteen, could see that.

It was *crazy.*

Roy was doing even worse. He was clutching the wheel, trying not to fall into himself. Gone was Jack Armstrong, the All-American Boy. Here was the father who'd been called Chute, who'd crushed a pack of cherry bombs in his bare hands. He, Roy, was not tempted to repeat what he'd done wrong. No, he wanted to kill himself, and in no short order. His service .45 was in the lower drawer of the desk back at the cabin, and when he got home he was going to write a note, leave the car for the three of them, and in the woods, shoot himself.

He stopped the car at the Alibi.

Now the big red sign loomed out of the dark, hideous.

"I gotta go," Aja said, and skipped around back and inside.

⁓⁓⁓

While Aja and Josie were on their break behind the Alibi, Henry Junior stopped by to chat them up.

"What is that, a six-gun in your pocket, or are you just happy to see me?" Aja said, trying to sound like herself.

But she didn't. Not at all. Was it in her voice? She was trying to be brave. She was horrified it might show. Both Josie and Henry turned to look at her.

"What's gotten into you?" Josie said.

Henry made a spinning motion with his index finger.

"This girl's loco," he said.

⁓⁓⁓

One sleepless cold-sweating eternal night later Aja spun herself out of bed. The birds were calling, first light rising to the east. Roy had not come home in the night. Jerry was in his bed, that benign baby face of his as blank and soft as vellum. Aja passed her mother's room. The door was open a crack, and she couldn't help looking in. There her mother sat at the window, waiting.

There was something on her face, which Aja read as stricken.

She crept down the stairs; it was all taking too long. She thought she might vomit. Too, too long, and then she was in her father's room, the bottom drawer open she would do it she would just do it now and there would be nothing more to think about she would—

The gun was gone and, in its place, a note: "I love you all terribly. Roy."

Under the note were the keys to the car and the papers for the property deals he'd wangled. Figures scrawled in an uneven hand.

∿∿∿

Running.

Running, her legs pumping under her.

Running to the rectory, pushing the bell there. No one. Running to the Alibi. Betty, shaking her, "What is it? What?" trying to slow her down. Where was her father? What was the problem? She couldn't tell them. Trees, the ground rough under her feet, just one big rush of needing, wanting, a clutching after . . .

what couldn't be
hadn't happened
was a dream
a nightmare.

∿∿∿

In her grandfather's arms she cried. Isabel sat beside them.

"There's nothing in the world you could've done, Aja, that somebody else hasn't done before," Peke said, cradling her in his arms.

Isabel lifted the hair from her face.

"Can you tell us?"

Aja shook her head.

"We understand," Peke said. "It's all right," he said, holding her.

∿∿∿

At noon that day, Roy was seen walking backwards up Main Street in White Earth Village. With him was Henry Senior, guiding him. Henry Senior slowly beat a drum. People came out to watch. They hadn't seen it in some time, but no one needed to be told what it was: Roy had joined the Crazy Dog Society.

The music was a dirge of sorts.

Dum-dum, da-da-dum-dum. Dum-dum, da-da-dum-dum.

Butter-yellow sunlight. Poplar leaves rattling in a light breeze. The drum beating slowly. Roy, the penitent, felt his way up the street, poking a willow switch behind him. What could he have done that was so awful to have to join the Crazy Dogs?

They looked upon him with a certain wariness, a loathing, but in each heart that watched, there was fear.

Things happened.

A week went by, and he was still at it. Blue plaid shirt, torn overalls, that willow stick. A Crazy Dog will walk backwards, each step leading to the thing that led him astray. Roy just didn't stop.

Roy, people began to joke, was going back to a time before Jesus.

He was walking for all of them, they joked.

∿∿∿

And me? At Our Lady of the Lakes parochial school I took an interest in my studies, an unhealthy interest. Up all night, head in the books, I chewed my fingernails until they bled, saw and heard nothing and, when I rose out of the depths of study, was into this new Catholic phase. Now I could recite the wonders and mysteries backwards and forwards, memorized all kinds of things, and in the end, won a scholarship and moved east, to a new life.

Josie married and stayed on at the Alibi.

Jerry built another radio.

Nina sat by the window at night, waiting for Roy.

Roy continued to live on the reserve, but never came back to the house. Not once.

On my grave will be written, "Blessed in everything."

It has taken me some time to come to that, and I have never before told how.

(1963) HE WOULD HAVE TO DECIDE what he wanted, Peke thought. That much was clear. He could very nearly feel her eyes on him, even this far from the cabin, a mile of water between them. Were he to squint, he could make out the cabin there on the shore, a swatch of barn-red siding and green roof surrounded by bright birches.

But he did not squint. He even took off his glasses.

Were he even to think he could see her in the window, watching him, his heart might change; he might want to turn to her, and then where would he be? Right back in it. For Isabel, if anything, was vindictive, and walking into her arms like an errant child was not

his idea of how things sho
who'd wronged her.

Now, try as he might t
with his glasses off—and
good; he was seventy or th
and looked, and hard, even
pulling at the corners of h
could see was a layer of wa
and more blue: the lake, the

He would not put his g
had binoculars in the bow o

What if she was standin
Standing there in that way with her hands on her hips? If she waved,
would he feel compelled to wave back? And what then?

It was, after all, her reaction he was fighting. Her need to punish
him.

Peke looked again. No, he couldn't see much of anything. Standing, he rocked the boat from side to side. He had two lines in the
water—one drop line and sinker with a fathead minnow on a treble
hook; one red and white Rapala about a hundred feet out behind,
trolling. Peke gave a couple of pulls on the Rapala.

He tugged at his cap. He removed it and held it under his nose.
Isabel had worn this cap years back on especially sunny days, and
her scent lingered in it.

Rose scent.

He felt a heaviness in his chest and then, putting the cap back on,
gave another tug on the Rapala. Part of him said, Go now. Take the
boat across the lake. Your brother has a trailer. He imagined driving
north to Alaska. Having his glasses off made it easier somehow to
imagine things. Made it seem as though he were just falling into
himself.

Fishing, he knew, had just been a pretense for coming over here
and bobbing out front of the cabin. He'd told himself this was about

fishing, putting the boat int
into it than Gitchi' man
make him look at w
her, he'd though
cry of need a
to stop. Th
fi

the lake, but no sooner had he stepped
...do had steered him in this direction, as if to
...at he would be losing. He would at least talk to
... But nearing the shore, apologies and a great out-
...nd desire and lust rising in him, he had forced himself

...en had come the hours of tortured fishing. Today he hated
...hing. He hated this goddamn boat. He hated himself. He hated
his boots. He hated the goddamn trees. He hated—

The boy in him hated. No, the boy in him, under his resentment,
loved. And the Trickster in him, even after all these years, still made
mistakes. Still underestimated him. Wenebojo, that old bastard,
wanted him to dance.

Well, he wouldn't. Because just when Trickster told him he was
close enough to see her in the window, he'd blinded himself. And
even as he thought this, he took his glasses from his pocket, hands
not altogether his own, was tempted to put them on, his heart beating crazily—would she be in the window?—and hurled the glasses
out into the lake.

They went in with a *plop!*

There, you old ass, Peke thought. And just as he did, visions of Isabel as a girl rose up before him, as real now as anything he could
see.

He bent over the gunwale, nearly in tears. He'd been tricked
again.

Where were those glasses?

In the reflection in the water he saw Isabel.

She held out her arms, beckoning. This was not a vision. It was a
memory now, but it came to him with the force of a vision. She had
an hourglass figure, breasts that made his eyes cloud up for the
beauty of them, strong thighs, and skin so smooth, so soft . . . His
sense of it was so painful now, he knew he had to stop. It was not

unlike pinching yourself. That was how he thought of it. He was out in this goddamn boat pinching himself black-and-blue.

Peke, counting the days, had not been with Isabel in nearly a month.

"Come back, then," she'd said. "*If* you change your mind. Or *don't,* for all I care."

Could she really be that hard? Didn't she think about him and toss and turn at night? Weren't her days one long succession of futile acts performed just to make the day go by? But no. He had seen her in town, that high step of hers, smiling, with his sister, Esther.

That had not helped matters. There had been that to contend with, too, memories of Isabel and Herman.

"Esther," he'd said on the phone, pretending friendly chat. He discussed the weather, fishing, the upcoming rice harvest. He couldn't bring himself to ask after Isabel.

"Talk to Isabel yourself," Esther said finally. "Don't get me in between. You know how I hate that."

Still, he'd pestered her.

"You got the rest of the month to think about it, as I see it," Esther said. "And as for what she's been doing? She's getting on with her life. And I suggest you do the same. But who am I to talk? You're the smart one. You figure it out."

In the boat, Peke grimaced. He'd certainly made a mess of it. Sitting, he studied his hands. Everything was a blur. Gray aluminum. Red wool pants. The fishy smell of his bait bucket.

What would happen, he thought, if I just . . .

He imagined himself kneeling. Is that what the girl in her wanted now? This girl who'd married a full-blooded Chippewa boy trying to be somebody, for somebody else? For the Muskego Pillager Clan. For his parents. Or had it been for the lot of them? Or for her? And was she, even after all these years, disappointed that he was not the

Frenchman he'd made himself out to be when he'd met her in the Twin Cities so long ago?

Isabel Rose Olsen.

Had he wronged her so, that it had come to this? Had it all been for nothing?

He remembered, when she had lain with him that first time, both of them just teenagers, she had been so afraid, and he'd wanted to calm her. The room had been filled with spirits.

Oh, you, you would kiss me with the
kisses of your mouth,
for your love is better than wine.

Ningac'kendum
Ka'mikwe'ningamgin

Love! love!

He'd heard them singing. His body sang when he worshiped at the altar of her breasts, when he drank from her. When they—

Peke lifted his head. Oh, what romantic horseshit, he thought. He was being a silly boy. He had to be practical. He looked around him, all a blur. He had drifted closer to shore, but a good deal north of the cabin.

He shook his head sadly, laughing.

He imagined Wenebojo tugging on the anchor. In the trees just up the shore was a doe. It was a sign, but he told himself, as often as not now, that he no longer believed in signs. Still, he could not help singing. Was it Isabel's spirit? Did it come unwillingly? Did it escape her, to draw him near?

He sang again, in the old language: *Ningac'kendum Ka'mikwe'ningamgin,* I am filled with longing when I think of her. . . .

With that, chuckling, Peke bent to the oars. He rowed back out into the middle of the lake. Now, behind him, from the northwest, a mass of high, turbulent clouds scudded in. He eyed them without fear. Nothing much mattered now. His whole life, it seemed, he had been followed by storms. Here was just another.

But Peke knew better. Gitchi' manido was in those clouds. And Gitchi' manido was pissed.

He could see it in the way the clouds boiled.

For a time he played mathematical games with himself, as a distraction. Strike me dead, then, he thought. The numbers came as easily as oiled gears turning. His mind worked that way. Prime numbers. Binomials. But those numbers always got tangled up in Isabel, and just when he thought he'd forgotten her, of course, there she was again. That flax blond hair that shone golden in the sun (even though he knew her to dye her hair auburn now). She had a little lump in the middle of her nose. Her eyes were gray-blue, and her mouth—her mouth was like a ripe strawberry. There was that fine curve of her neck, and strong shoulders, that lovely line of bone above her breasts.

Her breasts.

Ah, he was ruined again, he thought. He thunked down in the boat and opened his thermos. Coffee. He imagined her dancing. She spun a little circle, her hand held over her head.

She was lovely.

She was funny and insightful. It was she who'd never let him forget the old ways. And she was difficult, argumentative, thought he was a slob, and was forever picking up after him. She hadn't liked it when his face was too scratchy or when he smelled like fish. She fussed over the furniture. It was always secondhand, but it was resort furniture, some of it from Barney's Ball Lake resort, priceless, made of ironwood, with red leather cushions. Peke thought it beautiful. Isabel hated it.

She wrote beautiful letters, was brilliant, but had the tongue of a shrew when she was angry. His leaving the toilet seat up enraged her. But when he'd had too much to drink one night and had crashed the old Chevrolet driving home from the Ramblers', it hadn't bothered her one whit.

She hated his blue shirts, wanted him to wear a watch.

Why? he'd asked. So I don't wait dinner all the time for you, she'd replied.

After that, he'd taken to keeping a watch in his pocket.

That isn't what I meant, exactly, she'd said.

What do you mean?

I meant on your *wrist*.

That, he'd said, kissing her, is for white folk, *ninamuch*.

Sweetheart.

Yes, he thought, with irony.

And they'd raised two children, their own, and for a time Delia's, had been entwined in all that. The new off-reserve schools later; Isabel attending Father Feeney's church, Our Lady of the Lakes.

Still, it was Isabel who threw tobacco on the water. Who prayed to the four directions.

Peke glanced up. Was he drifting? He checked his progress by the movement of the trees on shore. If I drift beyond *that* birch, he thought, I'll take it as a sign. I'll go in. I'll . . .

Already he'd passed the tree, but he was not resolute in his decision to go in. *That* tree, then, he thought, choosing a box elder farther south. Peke shuddered. No, *that* tree. Slowly, each went by.

Now he was only a stone's throw from shore.

He felt ridiculous, blinded. The window in the cabin overlooking the lake was dark, ominous. What had he expected? For her to see him and come rushing down to say, Darling, everything is fine, I forgive you?

Peke let his head drop back. He stared up into the sky. The clouds there, to the north, were lumpy and green, the light something like the color of pea soup.

He felt that *something* again. It was like a thread, a silver thread, humming. Between them.

The breeze made it hum.

Was he imagining it? He turned to look behind him, at the cabin. Nothing. No, the thunderheads were rising now, high and mighty, light illuminating them from inside. That was what it was. See that, Isabel? he wanted to say. See that? As he had in the past.

The sky people are happy. The thunderbirds have spread their wings. *Ina'okumig.* Look at them flash!

She'd pinched him then. You old liar, she'd said. You're just making that up.

Yes, sometimes he had. But only a little.

∿∿

A wind had gathered force, cool, damp, and Peke had had to let down a second anchor to prevent his being blown in to shore. Why was he resisting this? He had counted seventy trees, it seemed. When I pass *that* tree, I'll pull up anchor and go in. It had gotten to be something of a joke, albeit a bitter one.

Now he was close enough to make out the lattice in the window overlooking the lake. But the light was such that the clouds were reflected in the glass.

Would she even want him, if he begged? Could he?

He shook his head. He was shaking. It was the coffee, he told himself. Too much coffee. His bladder protested. He thought to hold it, then remembered how Isabel, when they were fishing, had always insisted on his going ashore. He promptly stood, unzipped, and peed over the side.

You're better than that, he heard her say.

Ha! he grunted.

The clouds came over the lake like a lid on a box. When he stood again, blinded, he discovered his legs were shaking. He was a big man, and not one to shake. The clouds seemed to press down on him.

Now he could not go back. He'd never make it to the north shore before the lightning hit.

And he couldn't go in.

There was an electrical smell in the air, and the smell of wet earth. The lake lifted itself up in peaked waves, rocking the boat. Nambiza, underwater panthers, shot by, dark, snaking in the now pea-soup-green lake. There was that fresh storm smell. Electric. Wenebojo danced in whirlwinds of dust at the government dock around the point.

Om'ikeshe. I'm here, take me, he thought.

Peke was reminded of the story of how Wenebojo had made suitors for Matchikewis and Oshkikwe, the star sisters. He'd fed a tribe of wolves a great meal, and afterward, when they'd relieved themselves in the woods, Wenebojo had found each turd and stuck a feather in it. In the morning, when the sun rose, those little outfits came into camp and courted the sisters. Matchikewis, the smart and good one, saw that those men were really turds with feathers stuck in their caps.

Peke removed his hat and looked at it.

Sure enough, there was a feather in it. And a chrome number two Mepps spinner.

Peke eyed the shore there. It was not so far. A lip of white sand, scrub red willow and blue-green tamarack and, riding over it like a ship, high and mighty, the cabin.

Now for the first time he was a little afraid. The water, in this light, was bottomless and black. The shadows were moving awfully fast under the boat.

The boat rocked and kicked. The waves slapped.

What if he were to feign drowning? Would she come down? Was she there at all? But duplicity led to reprisals.

He was reminded of the time Wenebojo killed the underwater kings. Wenebojo went ashore and turned himself into a stump. The nambiza came up to sun themselves. One of them, a snake with horns, wrapped itself around the stump to test it. It isn't Wenebojo, he said. One of the underwater panthers scratched it with his claws. That really hurt old Wenebojo.

From that time on Wenebojo had three deep scars on his back.

What did all that mean? And why was he remembering it now?

He didn't have to know.

He felt her. Isabel. Watching. Right down to his toes. Isabel, his wife. His gem, his beauty, his wrath and discomfort. Hadn't she thrown a butcher knife at him? Hadn't that been enough? Hadn't he retaliated, shouting nearly thirty years' worth of stored invective at her? But in the old language, to spare her.

I know what you're saying, she'd said.

He'd been stunned. Did she really know? And would he have said it if he'd known she would understand? And had he, after all, said something true but something he couldn't say in English? That she was the most bullheaded, unforgiving, manipulative person he'd ever met? That he was sick of her teasing him, sick of her coy games, that he liked his blue shirts, and that the toilet lid would stay up from now on.

He'd called her Windigokwe, cannibal woman. He'd called her a clinging vine.

And lastly, in rage, he'd said, I would leave you if I could.

Good, Isabel said. She'd rushed to the door and thrown it open. Get out. Now.

Peke stood there, dumbfounded, the knife in the wall behind him.

What? he'd said.

You heard me. Get out.

∿∿

I love you, Peke rehearsed, in the boat, the storm bearing down on him. I love you like my soul. I love you so much I can't stand it. I love you and ache for you. I love you more than anything. I love you like the lakes, like the earth itself.

He resorted to his fine memory. Isabel had always liked the canticles.

Behold you are beautiful, my
   love,
behold, you are beautiful!
Your eyes are doves
behind your veil.

None of it seemed right.

There was precious little time. The clouds were coming in fast. The green had gone to gray-green, and the waves slapped roughly against and over the side of the boat. Peke got on his knees, drenched, searching under the seat stays for the bricks he kept there. The hull was filling with rank, dark water. The water smelled of fish and wood rot and gasoline. He dropped a third anchor.

Here was a last resort.

The clouds pressed in, and rain began to fall. There was a peninsula, all rocks, and it looked now as though the thing that would have naturally taken place would not. He would not be blown in to shore. No, he would be blown up onto the rocks. The wind had shifted. On the most distant bank of incoming clouds there was lightning. The lightning flashed blue-white. Peke counted—one, two, three—and then came thunder so violent it rattled his chest.

He studied the shoreline. The cabin, now looming over him, was as heavy as the face of God.

He could not just say he loved her. Language would not do it. He was reminded of his arrival in Saint Paul, how he had survived a fall from the High Bridge in just such a storm, how he had floated ashore with a broken arm, and how an angel—or so he'd thought at first—had found him.

Yes, she was his angel. His love was big enough for all of it.

He would tell her this. But how?

The rain came so hard now, wind-driven, it felt as though nails were being driven into his face. He stood up. Here came the lightning. Immense, jagged forks tore the lake apart. *Ka-booom! Kraaaaack-ka-booom!*

Water. Water. Water.

The boat filled with it; he did not bail. The anchor held; the lightning advanced across the lake. He was as good as blind now, the sky dark.

There was nothing, nothing left to say, nothing he could say.

He tossed his cap back, lifted his arms.

A bolt of lightning hit a tree on the peninsula off shore, and a ball of it danced across the green, violent water and set upon my grandfather's head.

He glowed like that, a man on fire, and right then Isabel burst down the bank, screaming, Idiot! Idiot! Get off that goddamn lake, you son-of-a-bitching crazy Indian!

(1965) I HAD A SECRET, AT THE WIN-
dow, the rain pouring down, a wedge at the
bottom open, so that the damp pine-laden air spilled in like melancholy itself. Behind me, Peke gave an occasional "heeerunf!" reading
in his chair. Isabel, at the stove, clattered around, making a pretense
of cooking. I couldn't stand to watch her. She was making something for me to take down to Minneapolis–Saint Paul in the morning. Now and then my brother's footsteps would cross the ceiling
overhead: Peke had bought him a chemistry set, and I half expected
the roof to be blown off the cabin at any minute, or for him to run
down the stairs, screaming, Fire! Fire!

But no. The rain continued, slanted against the trees. A June bug crawled arthritically across the screen. Thunder rumbled in the distance.

"Did you get those pens, the ones with the replacement cartridges?" Isabel asked.

I set my chin on the windowsill. Inches away, a sometimes sheet of water parted, silver, then broke up again, the rain coming down all the harder suddenly.

"Did you?"

"Yes," I drawled, irritated at the thought of it, my whole life to come in the Cities summed up in a pen. Penury, parsimony, frugality.

I could do it, too; I could. I could be good, couldn't I? I could do the right thing. I shifted there at the window. Wenebojo danced in that rain.

Run, he said.

So I gave it some more thought. I was going to live with my great-aunt's family, all of us packed into a two-room unit of her Franklin Avenue fourplex. Or that was the plan, anyway. I had always liked Peke's sister, Esther, her clever wink, her big doughy arms, her good-natured laugh. But then I thought of her son, Arthur. Arthur ran Miracle Bright, a laundry on Fourth Street. His wife was a stringy-haired white woman who always looked drowned somehow, and their two kids, disciplined into waiflike submission, were enough to break your heart.

And there was this, too: Arthur had been born again and ran a soup-kitchen ministry in which I was to take a part.

All of that, no matter how I tried to think of it, filled me with dread. Early mornings at the laundry, steam pressing, washing, battling stains.

So, at the window, like a penitent, I was hoping for a miracle, a sign.

A car, high fins and tinted windshield, pulled into the drive. Holding a newspaper over her head, my mother ran to the front door, and the spring creaking, she got the door open and came through; it shut behind her with a loud, wet slap.

"Well," she said, smiling, "it's all settled! Esther will be there. I've got the ticket."

"Great," I said.

〰〰

This is what it came down to: I'd been seeing a man in his thirties, an eighth-degree member of the medicine society and a choke setter on a logging operation. A widower who still drove the pink truck he'd given his late wife. A charming womanizer and fancy man. A *dja' sakid,* a sorcerer.

My mother and Isabel were trying to bring about a timely resurrection, though surely even they knew it would be painful. I'd won a scholarship to the University of Minnesota; the rooming plan was, to their thinking, a tremendous stroke of luck.

Industry-discipline-application was what I needed.

"We'll put that overheated mind of yours to some good," Isabel said.

Through the lot of it—the calls to Esther, the working out of a schedule with Arthur—Peke had just smiled big, contented smiles, whistling that tuneless tune he always whistled.

He knew something. But what?

〰〰

Whenever I was upset over making decisions when I was younger, Peke would say, "Think about what happened with Toad Woman."

I hated that. "I don't like that story," I'd say. "It's just about not being able to wait."

And in his inimitable way, Peke would reply, *No. Listen,* and he'd tell it to me again.

A woman lived by a lake with her dog, he'd begin, and I would see the lake, blue and shimmering, high beautiful pines around it.

Her husband had been killed, and to her great good luck, long before the year of mourning was over, another had taken an interest in her, leaving fresh meat at her door. In time, they met and had a son. One day the woman returned from gathering berries to find her husband and son gone and only bits of the cradle on the ground where the dog had tried to prevent someone from taking it.

Are you listening? Peke would say, and irritated at the interruption, I'd reply in a breezy voice, waving a hand over my head, *Mukakee Mindemoea, the Toad Woman, had whisked the boy and his dog away.*

Not exactly, Peke would say. *The mother rushed off in pursuit, through valley and forest. Occasionally she'd come to a village, and in each she would be given magic moccasins by the nocoes, the grandmothers.*

Point the moccasins in the right direction and they will take you in the direction of your son, they told her, and she did that.

Months passed, then years. The woman passed through forests and valleys, through mountains.

Finally the woman came to the village where Mukakee Mindemoea lived; by that time, her son was a man, and lived in Toad Woman's lodge with four other men. All of them, the son and the four men, served Toad Woman, under her spell, and she was powerful.

But the dog was not so charmed.

The mother called to the dog, and the dog, tugging at the son, brought him. The son was not convinced the woman was his mother, until he saw, in Toad Woman's lodge, as his mother told him he would see, portions of the cradle.

Still, Toad Woman was not to be so easily outdone.

If she could cast perpetual winter on the land, what else might she do? And the son was still under her power.

So the mother and son considered how they might defeat Toad Woman; the son killed a bear and, bringing Toad Woman the tongue, told her where she could find the rest of it, so she could eat the choicest part herself—the heart.

As soon as she had gone, and her powers had gone with her, the woman's son killed the others who had come to be with Toad Woman exactly as the son had. The son staked those men in a circle in front of the lodge, stuffing the mouth of each with fat.

The mother and son fled, the dog leading them in the dark.

Toad Woman returned to the lodge and, seeing those men skewered to the ground, gathered up her skirts and in a rush of thunder and lightning and darkness, rushed after the woman and her son. Just when she was about to devour them, however, the son tossed flint behind him, which slowed Toad Woman slightly and allowed them to get away. But Toad Woman caught up to them, and when she was about to devour them again, he tossed back slippery elm, and she fell, bleeding, her knees torn. But with a crackle of lightning and breath like carrion itself, she swooped down on them, jaws agape. This time the son made snakeberries spring up, and Toad Woman was eating, eating, swelling, until she was all flowing black skirts and teeth, approaching, yet again.

Dog, tear her to pieces, for she plagues us, the son said.

So the dog spun around, rent her limb from limb, and in that way they escaped.

As a child, I'd always shuddered at that story.

And what happened to the father? Where was the father in all of it? Where had he gone?

Toad Woman, Peke told me, was that father.

I still didn't get it.

"Has anyone at that fancy Catholic school ever said, Never look a gift horse in the mouth?"

"No," I lied. I liked horses. I didn't want Peke to ruin that, complicate something as good-sounding as a gift horse.

~~~

"Here," Peke said, pushing something at me. "You'll need this."

From the window, I watched him go out. He walked through the rain, up the rutted drive. He stood in the rain, his clothes darkening. I opened the envelope. In it were three crisp hundred-dollar bills, all the money Peke had in the world, I think.

"What are you doing there?" Nina said.

I knocked out the screen and put my head into the cold, cold rainwater, stuffed the envelope in my pocket. I couldn't have my mother see me like that, just then unable to catch my breath.

~~~

Night. Pitch dark. Rasp of tree frogs. Window open. Smell of wet pine, lake slapping on shore, dirt smell. Pine smoke. I hugged my arms over my breasts. The cabin creaked. I lay there, unable to sleep, running through my arguments for what I was going to do.

The curtains by my bed luffed in on rain-heavy air. Already I missed Clarence, his wink, his scent, a combination of woodsmoke and lime, the way he lit his cigarettes, always an adroit one-handed operation.

Thinking about his hands, I almost decided I wouldn't go.

~~~

Taking my seat on the Redbird—torn upholstery, heavy green glass—I thought, I'll do it. I could come up and visit, and they could come down. I'd show them Saint Paul, Minneapolis, the suburbs, the city girl, the first in our family to attend the university. And on a scholarship! We'd have dinner at some Chinese place, and I'd learn all the Chinese names of the dishes. (Just then, Arthur's face rose up into my little self-deception, ingratiating, bowing. Hop Sing. That's what I'd called him for years. Yes, yes, he was saying.)

From the bus I waved. Nina on the sidewalk in her well-tailored blue dress; Isabel, white hair tumbling over her forehead; Jerry, free of his sister, grinning.

And Peke, acting as if something had gotten caught in his eye.

I pressed my face to the cool glass. The bus gave an airy hiss. I took one last look: bright light, the bus depot a small red brick building, behind it Opugwun Lake, sparkling blue.

Peke turned away so I couldn't see his face, but the others kept at their good-byes.

I waved twice, and we turned the corner.

∿∿

In a small town called Wadena, we picked up a farmer in dirty overalls who told everyone within earshot he was going to visit a cousin who'd made it big in the Cities. In Aldrich, it was a mother in a red gingham dress and her very sickly looking son, no older than Jerry, who had some kind of poultice on his neck. I thought, That kid's a goner. They were going down to Rochester, to the Mayo Clinic, to see what might be done.

"What is it?" the farmer asked.

"Cancer," the mother said.

I squinched up in my seat, watching the farms go by, mostly red barns, white houses, a man on a red Farmall, a seeder in tow. A woman had a basket of chicken and passed it to the others, coming back. I took a drumstick. The woman thumped down beside me, so heavy her big thighs bulged into me under the armrest divider.

"What you all doin' in the back here, girl? There's the whole *front* to sit in!"

I had just been thinking of getting off at the next stop, Brainerd, to take the bus back up to White Earth. I'd settle for that life with Clarence. Only now I was pinned in.

"Could be my husband is hurt down in Cincinnati somewheres and not run off like everybody says," the woman said, and took another bite of chicken.

The bus lumbered along, smelling of diesel fuel and of urine from the rest room, which the mother of the sick kid used more than a time or two. When we pulled into Brainerd, the fat woman did not get up.

"Bus driver! How long we waitin' here?" she called up to the front.

Then the bus started again, lurched away from the curb in a cloud of diesel exhaust.

"Where you headed, child," the big woman said, "if you don't mind my askin'?"

"I'm going to the university," I said.

"Oh, you're a *smart* one." She winked. "My husband went, but it didn't do him any good. He did all right, I mean, but he got *ideas,* I think."

I was thinking, You fat tub, shut up. And I was thinking of Esther. She'd be getting ready to meet me. I could imagine her, smiling, driving that old Hudson down to the Greyhound station.

"Is that why you got all them bags?" (She'd seen them in the rack overhead.)

I told her yes, it was.

"What you gonna study?" She pushed another leg at me. Fried chicken.

"Things," I said.

"Ah," she said, as if with great satisfaction. "Always *things.*"

I was remembering Peke's story about Toad Woman. I was thinking about Clarence and his big, loving hands, his sad-funny face. I was thinking about Peke's money, in my pocket. Was thinking about Arthur and his laundry. I started to cry a little.

"Here, honey girl," the big woman said, throwing her arm over my shoulders and squeezing me, "I know you're not travelin' for nothin'."

Which just made me struggle against crying all the worse.

~~~

Hours later the bus rubbered up to the station on Washington Avenue. Cement everywhere, now jammed with rush-hour traffic. It was late afternoon, and there were all kinds of people waiting in the lot there, the men in natty hats and gray suits, the women in coral-pink dresses, black patent-leather shoes. In the middle of them was Esther, Pete's sister, brick-colored skin, sensible blue dress.

"All for Minneapolis–Saint Paul off here," the driver called out.

He stepped down off the bus. The kid with the cancer on his neck did too.

The fat woman stood. "Let me help you with your luggage," she said. I could see the hair in her armpits. There was an accordion of fat around her neck.

"*Please,*" I said, crouching to hide from Esther.

She gave me a certain understanding look, as if to let me change my mind again, then rummaged in the overhead tray, I'm sure now, for nothing. I scrunched farther down in the seat. There were voices outside. I was suddenly, and horribly, frozen there. I couldn't move. The voices came nearer, those of the bus driver and Esther.

"I know she's gotta be on this bus. I just talked to her family this morning. I know she got on."

The bus shifted slightly to one side, the driver and Esther coming up the aisle. The fat woman leaned over me, a big pillow of flesh. It was like a cave under there.

"You see that girl, was on earlier?" the driver said.

The big woman pressed in, all darkness and rose-scented woman flesh. I was staring into the back of the seat. Brown vinyl. Someone had carved a heart into it, inside it, "M + H."

"She must've got off earlier," the woman said, forcing me farther in with her dinner plate–sized knee.

I heard Esther give an irritated but concerned sigh.

"That *girl,*" Esther said, lumbering back up the aisle toward the door. "You try to do something for her and she just won't listen. Got a mind of her own that one, and then some.

"All right," she said, and the bus sprang back a little as she got off.

The new passengers boarded, now smelling of mint and after-shave and polished shoes, new wool clothes, all set for the long haul to Cincinnati. The bus was so heavy it gave a *whump,* dropping over the curb.

I raised my head just enough to see Esther, her hat in her hands, standing in that lot by herself, shaking her head. Arthur came striding up behind her, arms ticking at his sides with clocklike precision, no doubt fresh from parking the car.

The bus surged and thrumped over the expansion cracks in the highway. The fat woman snored. She had a bit of a mustache, but I didn't care.

I sat upright in my seat, wondering why she'd done what she'd done.

I thought of Peke, that money burning a hole in my pocket.

The world will dream your dreams, ninamuch, if you have the strength, he'd said.

I sat up, watched the last of the light fade, the countryside go dark. A short time later the fat woman woke. She looked at me. I must have been frowning.

"Don't take it so hard," she said. "My husband run away too."
She smiled, a warm, good-humored smile.

"It gets lonesome, don't it?" she said. She nodded to herself.
"Amen," she said, and began to hum, then sing, in a melancholy,
lovely voice, a voice like dark molasses:

> There is a tree in Babylon
> that stands so straight and true.
> The good Lord had me kneel there
> when I was feelin' blue.

Listening, I rested my head against the seat in front of me and
wept.

(1969 - 1971) Knowing my former husband, Myron, as I
do now, I regard our meeting, courtship, and marriage not as two
ships anchoring in a calm foreign harbor; not as "Some Enchanted
Evening," Mary Martin and Ezio whatever-his-name-was gazing
dreamily at each other; but rather as something more akin to those
demolition derbies you saw on TV on Saturday mornings years ago.
Mud flying, cars humping and sliding around that figure-eight dirt
track, exhaust, engines roaring, all speed and charging headlong.

To meet or not meet at the intersection of that figure eight.

To the Chippewa, eight is a holy number, the number of death and regeneration. The eighth degree is the highest awarded in the medicine society. Eight is my totem number. Mysterious eight, always looping into itself, ending and beginning nowhere and everywhere, a snake twisted double, biting its own tail. In it always that blink of an eye when, for whatever reason, the scene changes—again, at that point of intersection.

As it does now.

∿∿∿

Imagine an oval track, shoulder-high white fencing in front of me, leaning against it, a horse charging by, clop of hooves, others in pursuit; behind me large canopied green bleachers, hundreds of spectators, some of them Mafia dons and their wives, in dresses so loud they make your eyes ache, fingernails painted red and curved like talons. Others promenade slowly out in front of the bleachers, their bright-eyed children socking one another for paper bags of peanuts or tussling over Sno-Kones and cotton candy.

A carnival atmosphere. Upstate New York. Saratoga or Sarachtoge, the headwaters. The racetrack, circa 1969. Over a PA system, statistics on the horses run endlessly: "On the inside track is Firedragon, out of Miami, sired by . . ."

"I don't like that smell," Miriam Clark, a colleague of mine at Dartmouth, said. She stood to my left, wrinkling her pert nose. She gave a finger-wave to the others, Dwight, Harold, and Jilian, who were off to our right, comparing scorecards.

Jockeys in black-and-white striped shirts walked this last field of horses by, headed for the stables, smell of sweat, a salty musk to it, muttering rasp of breath, heavy swish of tail.

One of the horses let go a horse apple.

Just then I was reminded of old Ishtakubig's stable. Cool mornings, riding down to the lake with Peke, the tall leafy elms. Pea-green storm clouds, and always cedar smoke. The memory caught me right behind my eyes, a heaviness. My eyes got all glassy. I was homesick.

"You lose again?" Miriam said, shining me that million-dollar smile of hers.

I dropped my ticket on the ground. The windows under the bleachers had lines of people backed up and around and nearly out to the gate. A looping multicolored snake. I squinted against the bright sky.

I shrugged.

"That's the way it goes," I lied.

I'd won the last three races, bet a dollar each, but didn't think it worth the wait in line to collect. I didn't want Miriam to pester me over it. Winning. I wasn't so sure about that now. I'd been accepted into a Ph.D program along with Miriam, Jilian, Harold, and Dwight. I had expected to be elated, having won my way into the club, but I was feeling morose and crazy.

Just the thought of five more years of school made me want to do something, scream, or run wild, make love in the shade under the trees. Stuff grass in my mouth, kiss a stranger, lick the pavement.

Anything, just something . . . *real.*

Earlier, Miriam had insisted on standing off in the shade where we couldn't see anything.

"I hate to sweat, don't you?" she'd said.

I'd thought of my evenings with Clarence. Slow-moving late spring evenings. Body heat. His big, tender hands, his hot—we'd sweat plenty.

Miriam dabbed at her forehead with a monogrammed hand-kerchief. MOM. Miriam Oliver Morris. Why did that make me shudder?

"Well?" Miriam said.

I threw her another winning smile now. "Excuse me," I said, imitating her high, reedy voice. "I've got to use the ladies'."

I went down to the stables, my head a tangle of revulsion and desire, and stood there in the middle of it. Dusty-smelling feed bags. Curry combs, horse apples, the metallic ring of bit and bridle. Slap of saddle. Green smells, saddle soap, leather, pungent straw, cologne. Watery gulping in galvanized trough.

Mud. Motion. Ritual.

I tossed my hair back. I was soon to be twenty-two, had made quick and good work of one program, why ruin my track record? I thought. There's an old Chippewa belief, and it's tied up in all our thinking about windigos and prideful people. Just when you find yourself saying it's good, we say it goes like hell.

Maybe I was just afraid. Maybe that old thinking was just more horse flop.

Yet, there in the stables, all those smells were perfume to me. I loved it, all of it: Warm air. A horse—urinating—enormous, which made my stomach twinge. I felt at home. Wood, dirt, dust, men talking in low voices in a language all their own. I imagined myself a jockey. But no, that wouldn't do, I decided.

I stood in the middle of it, in the stables, taking it all in—a fish in familiar water. Sooner or later I'd have to go back to the track and then to dinner with the chair of the program.

A jockey was giving me a once-over. I liked his horse—muscular, black sides shiny with sweat, bristly mane, crazed-looking eyes. I set my hands on my hips, as if waiting for someone. Somewhere the celestial clock was ticking; here came the cars around that figure-eight track, engines running near redline, mud flying, here the gears turning in the belly of the Great Silence, preparing for those cars to meet at the apex of that figure eight.

Standing there among the jockeys, horses, horse flop, I was trying to decide something. I was waiting for that flash in the brain, that moment of certainty, for the thunderbirds to pull back the scrim of blue sky and the All One to beam down on me and make my decision easy.

One of the owners, in chinos, pastel shirt, spit-shined oxfords, stepped gingerly through the horse flop. "You may as well marry money," Miriam had joked. When he saw me there, his eyes darkened with interest. Tall, well-heeled, in his shoulders an insouciant, entitled slouch.

There would be another life, but . . . no.

There was no heat in it.

I glanced at the clock at the far end of the stable: it was 1:45. I had fifteen minutes before I'd have to go back.

Decide, I thought.

The owner bent away from his horse to talk with the jockey, a small squirrel of a man, the skin on his face pitted like orange rind. The owner didn't want to touch the horse—he gingerly pinched the bridle, dropped it to one side—and all the while, the jockey was brushing in enthusiastic, even loving, circular sweeps.

The jockey and owner led the horse out of the stable, and stood talking by a stand of trees. The owner thrust his hands in his pockets, giving the jockey an appreciative glance now and then. The horse stomped its hooves, impatient.

Suddenly I felt torn all over again. Decide, I thought. But what? I couldn't return to the reserve. That felt like death. But then I thought of Miriam and of Dwight, Jilian, and Harold. I went outside and stood just up from that jockey and owner, under those immense oaks. A horse shooed flies so close to me that its tail brushed my back.

Okay, I thought. Regroup. Rethink.

The contraries will always be with you, *ninamuch,* Peke had said. Just choose the better.

I heard a car, big engine, bad muffler.

(Right then, a car headed for the apex of that figure eight while my car was careening on loose soil, closing the distance.)

An aqua-blue late fifties Oldsmobile convertible roared into the lot and around the trees, to slide to a stop inches away from that squirrel of a jockey, who stuck his rear out in response to the car speeding at him. The horse shied a bit and the jockey tugged at the bit in his mouth.

"Myron," the owner said, and the driver jumped out of the car, literally, right over the door, braids, wound in red cloth, brick skin, pumped the owner's hand.

He let loose a yell, "Yeeeeeeee-haaaaa!" and slapped the horse on its rear. "That son of a bitch ran like he had a windigo on his tail, didn't he? Didn't I tell you this horse'd do it?"

The owner was excited, but uncomfortable, smiled a smile full of rigor mortis. I thought I recognized the driver now, but couldn't believe it. What, after all, had brought him up here, to these people?

"Well?" the driver said.

The owner pressed something into his hand.

"Fuckin' A! Frogskins! I am *happpp-peee!*" he whooped.

He looked over at that clock, hanging askew at the far end of the stable. I looked at it, too. Time's up. It was five minutes after. Some bell in the bowels of the earth struck. Our cars hit that last stretch, full tilt.

This . . . Myron leaped over the car door and back into the driver's seat.

"We're late, Jack, goddammit!" he said to the jockey.

The owner gave a curt nod and sauntered away. The jockey ran the horse into the stable, closed the door, then swung around in front of the car and got in. He said something, cocking his head in my direction. The wheels of that car kicked up dirt, engine rumbling, the car suddenly careening toward me, then skidding expertly, so the driver's door stopped at my waist.

"Hop in the back, beautiful," Myron said. "We're gonna have a night on the town!"

There was no noise, no explosion. Not then. But that's the way it is.

Ten years later you know the moment for what it was.

I stepped into that car, right over the door, as if into a chariot. Myron hit the gas. The trees flew back, spinning out of there.

♒♒♒

I speak with Myron on occasion now, and he always tells me, "I was a mess then. You gotta forgive me that much, you know?"

He runs an Apple dealership in a small town and has become something of a wizard with computers, bits and bites and Bernoulli drives and whatnot.

"You didn't play straight with me, either," he tells me.

I have to agree.

"Not even from the start."

That is true, too.

So I remember that afternoon we met, and I try, just a little, again, to be fair, I think.

But nothing in life is fair, *ninamuch,* Peke's voice tells me.

Yes, I know. But . . .

♒♒♒

Dancing at the Golden Corral in Saratoga, we did the fish, the Watusi, the chicken; we did the freestyle, the breasts jouncing, near-drunken-loving-flailing we-won-the-frogskins dance. It was a mostly black crowd in there, a small, cramped dance floor, but they were hip to the mix. It was novel, it was new, it was exciting. It was the tail end of the sixties. Myron and I danced, cold beers at our table. Jack, the jockey, took up with some serious-looking six-footer, who, as far as I could tell, might have been a man in drag. I didn't care.

Dancing, I threw my head around. Myron's face, with each beer, got more familiar. I was taking a shine to him. I had that hot spot going in my middle, I was shaking all that Miriam out of my joints, especially my hips.

Overhead was a mirror ball, light reflecting off it bright as diamonds. A reefer was passed around the dance floor. I took a puff, gave it an anxious go.

Myron and the jockey exchanged glances. I felt, just then, a potential danger: "Body of Coed Found in Ditch," the headline would read. There would be the picture, legs twisted unnaturally.

A strobe light came on in one explosion-bright flash, with it a deafening thump of bass. Myron threw his arms around me, brought us both crashing to the floor. The other dancers tumbled over each other to get some distance.

"Jasper! Hey! I got ya, Jasper!" Myron shouted.

He had his arm around my middle in a powerful grip. I was too shocked to be embarrassed. He was poking at something that wasn't there, was dialing.

The lights came on. Myron blinked, standing, looking around. Jack, the jockey, whisked us outside and to that car of Myron's. Put something in Myron's hand.

"Take it. Come on, that's a good boy. Take it," Jack said.

Myron shook himself.

"Whoa there, boy," Jack said, putting his hand on Myron's shoulder. "Hey, now, that's better, isn't it?"

I was edging away. Jack opened the door to that aquamarine car, slid Myron in. Myron leaned his head against the wheel.

"Oh, man," he wept, "I'm so so sorry. I am just so sorry."

That got to me. It just did.

~~~

Of course, I'd been pretty sure all along who he was, but I hadn't until that moment on the dance floor been totally convinced. After all, I'd known Myron and Jasper only through Henry Junior's letters. Henry, after he'd left Oshogay's Gas, went off to Vietnam. He'd written me,

There's this Myron in my barracks, and his buddy, Jasper. Myron's one of ours from around Red Lake, the Turtle Mountain Band. Jasper's just a kid. I mean a real kid, lied to get in and everything. I'll bet he isn't a day over sixteen. I feel like we oughta rat on him and get him kicked out. Myron says it'd hurt Jasper's feelings too much. I say screw his feelings. I can't see any good coming of it. After all, this is just the place for some wild-ass kid to show his stuff and get his head shot off.

Well, girl, I love you.

Pray for me. It's a lot worse over here than anybody's letting on.

So I sat there on the hood of the car, waiting, for what? Myron, at the wheel, weeping?

"Go away," he said. "It's all for shit now. I don't want you around. Go away."

Part of me, just then, did go away. But the bigger inside-part stayed. I was afraid of him, a little, so didn't move. After a time, the ragged sobs stopped coming, and it was quiet, but for the thumping of bass in the bar.

"Oh, well," he said. He turned on the radio. Bright, coppery voices, harmonizing: "There's a moon out tonight, oh, oh, oh . . ."

We listened to the music. Myron lit up, and squinting, held the spliff out and around the windshield. This time I really inhaled.

Just like that, the night seemed to take on mythic dimensions, ballooned out all of a sudden. Here was warm air, hood of car, heat, lime-scented cologne, stars overhead as if the only stars *ever* overhead, the stars I'd seen up at White Earth, my home stars, and here was Myron.

That was the feeling. As if it were preordained in the very workings of things, the night, the dark, it had to go further. I wanted it to go further.

Myron was Myron. My hand my hand. What mystery, what wonder, just being there.

I went around the car, got in the passenger seat. I was oddly in love with Myron. It was a spell. He'd touched something in me.

"Go over there," I said, pointing to a liquor store across the street, all lit up like a chapel. We got a case of beer and tossed it in the back of the car. We popped a couple.

"Heya," Myron said, grinning.

We pulled away from the store, driving into open air, mystery, a night like a Chinese puzzle box, one moment inside the other inside the other.

The engine ran lumpy, but with the top down and the stars out, that ride was magnificent. The sky was broad and dark, stretching into infinity. I had a cold beer in hand, and school and Miriam and the others were orbiting at a distance like some odd and unpleasant dream.

"Jeez, anyone tell you lately that you're pretty?" Myron said happily. He grinned a big grin. "I'm okay now. I mean, really."

We cleared a rise and, going down the opposite side, passed one immense home after another—swimming pools, manicured gardens, some of them with a little statue of a black man in the front yard with a lantern.

Here was America, too. I suddenly felt like I was in orbit. It all came down on me.

I looked over at Myron. What the hell was I doing out here? In Saratoga? With the horsey set? What was I doing taking crap from someone like Miriam, and so what that I held my fork the wrong way, dressed oddly, according to Miriam, clipped infinite verb endings, or had, anyway. I hate it when you say "goin'," Miriam had said.

Suddenly I felt very pissed off. Three and a half years of that. Why had I done it? For a worthless degree that was going to get me another just as worthless? And a double major?

And then what? Administration? Writing silly, phony papers?

I recalled what Peke had said once. Just because you can do something, he said, doesn't mean you should. A sign flashed by, bright in our headlights. Heritage Park, it read. Permit Required.

"Back up," I said.

Myron looked over at me; we were still sailing along happily at seventy.

"Back up," I said.

He did that. Right in the middle of that highway in the dark.

"Pull over here," I said.

He craned his head around, stopping the car on the shoulder just back of the sign.

"Now pull in," I said.

"But there's a chain across," Myron said.

I smiled. "So what?"

Myron smiled a smile as big as a half-moon. He understood me. The chain gave way with a snap. I handed Myron another beer. Gliding down the hill into the park, I said, "Horace, tell the children to be quiet, will you?"

"Certainly, *dah*ling," Myron said. He turned his head around, winked at me. I thought he was going to say something like "Amanda? Randolph? Please let Mummy have her moment."

"Shut up, you little shits," he said.

I laughed.

"Ahhhh, life at the club," Myron said, grinning, drinking his beer.

There was a dark arch of elms and maples overhead, then a breathtaking view of a quiet lake, a par five golf course—that's what the sign said, anyway, Braemar Par Five—and a pool. From up above, on the hill, the pool was the size of a postage stamp, moon shimmering in that unnaturally blue water.

Here was something, I thought. I'll always remember this. Sickle of dark horizon, clouds moonlit from inside, call of night birds.

Myron stopped the car near the swimming pool.

"Out," he said, the car door making a loud *ca-thunk*. I strode onto that first tee. Worked the ball cleaner up and down in its grooved slot, pumping it, just kidding, then was struck by its slick motion, felt suddenly . . . exposed.

Myron laughed. He teed up an imaginary ball in the moonlight, took a big roundhouse swing, mimicked missing the ball, tried again. He rolled down the hill and lay at the bottom laughing.

I rolled down, too. Soft, springy grass, warm soil, thump and roll of my body. A child again. The night turning around me, golf course carnival. Dizzy. The last time I'd done that I'd been five. We lay at the bottom of the fairway, laughing together.

"Christ, my back hurts," Myron said.

I propped my head up. "Why?"

Myron pulled a six-pack from under his shirt. He popped one open.

"Just the size of a box of M-60 shells."

He got that distant look. I snapped my fingers in front of his face, and he grabbed my hand. I felt something like darkness itself run through me. But then he was studying my fingers, each one.

"Man, you've bitten these down so—"

I jerked my hand away. I'd bitten my fingernails so badly they bled, were always sore, were an embarrassment to me. But I did it only when I was alone, and I was careful, usually, not to let people see my hands.

"Why?" he said. His eyes shone in all that darkness.

"Stuff."

"You don't fit."

That really hurt. "What do you mean?"

"You're too good for those people you came with," he said. "Especially that prissy-looking one you were standing with at the rail. Miss Ivory Soap."

Myron looked off, sighed. "Oh, I know who you are," he said. He was lying on his back. "You're Roy Sharrett's daughter. You're an Au-au-wak. Don't think I didn't notice you when you came down and stood by the fence there, in back of the track. But then, some don't want to be recognized, so I didn't say anything.

"Lemme see your hand," he said.

I did that, stared off into all that dark sky. He pressed my hand between his. Warm. Soft.

"That won't help," I said.

"I know."

"You do?"

"Wishing it didn't happen doesn't change things. One day here," Myron said. "The next there. But you have to do what you can, no excuses."

I stood up and pulled at my hand, and Myron rose and came with me. Something as big as a heart went loping up that hill toward the pool. I wasn't going to fight it.

I swung the pool gate open, and Myron said, behind me, "I don't think that's—"

But I was already in the water. Myron came in, too. I was reminded of the story of the Woman Who Made Love to a Bear. All those winters afterward she was alone, because she and the bear didn't understand each other, not exactly, but they loved each other tremendously, selflessly, the bear leaving meat at the woman's lodge in the winter, the woman making love with the bear in the spring and summer. And at that time the wild rice flourished, and only then, when the Woman of the Lake was making love to the bear.

Myron came floating at me. He'd lit another spliff.

Smoke, floating. The moon overhead. I undid the buttons of my shirt. My breasts floated, all of me floated. Naked now. The world, acres of smooth skin, water, nipples, soft, caressing hands, floating.

"Ah, God, you're beautiful, Aja," Myron said.

His life, what I knew of it, lay like a kind of wreckage out there. I thought I knew what he was living with—I'd seen the nightly news, Huntley and Brinkley, at Betty's. He thought he knew mine.

Just then, in that moment, gliding in that water, a truthful almost non-time, our self-murder stopped, the voices stopped, hurt became wanting, became need, became desire, became beautiful.

The bear above me, hot, slow-moving, my legs like floats to either side.

I let my head drop back, talking with my body.

What it said was this: Wild rice, wild rice, oh, *wild rice!*

〰〰〰

The following morning, like most following mornings, was not so mystical.

We ate breakfast at a restaurant, the Photo Finish—bacon, eggs, hash browns—stopped by Myron's room at the Cozy Inn, for clean things to wear, cutoff shorts and sweats, then washed what we'd had on, grass-stained and dirty, at a coin-op laundry, hot air smell of soaps, women in maternity clothes, and racetrack riffraff looking at least as rough as we did. In the bathroom, I looked into my eyes. I had a mild sense of unreality, a pot hangover. I didn't like that, and the light was too light.

I opened the door a bit and studied Myron through the crack. He was talking to himself.

All of this is a cliché now, I know that—the distant stares, the almost catatonic cringing at the backfiring of a car, the occasional emotional explosions, and at the worst, what happened to Myron at times, full-blown episodes of psychosis.

Try living with it. Let one of those clichés have you hiding under the bed with him, fearing for your life.

I was thinking to sneak out the back when he smiled a winning smile. Beautiful bittersweet chocolate eyes, high cheekbones, dark,

dark skin, and those big hands. Big, gentle hands. I was a sucker for those hands.

So what if he talked to himself now and then?

Did it start right there? Our life together? Or had it started the moment I got in the car? Or was it winning those races and not standing in line to collect my money?

I nodded to him, hooked my finger. I counted back from my last day; it was still safe.

While the machines thumped around, off balance,—or was it someone's tennis shoes thumping around and around,—or—I am almost ashamed to think it—was it Myron and me thumping against the wall in there?

Just then the darkness went away again.

Oh, wild rice! Oh . . .

∿∿∿

To this day I don't know how to think of all that. I moved out of Miriam's and into my own apartment, a beautiful ivy-covered older brick tenement. I was at home with the coloreds, as those at that school still put it back then. Black, Hispanic, Indian, I told them. What's the difference? Miriam said.

I continued in my program. Myron worked for the track weekends, did finish carpentry weekdays.

Back and forth.

He beat me only when it all started coming out, when he was over there—as I thought of it, in his imagination trapped in Vietnam, in Khe Sanh, or Gia Lam, or Pleiku.

I got to know those stories. How that kid, Jasper, had volunteered to walk point. One moment Jasper was a mouthful of laughs and sarcasm—"And I'm supposed to be scared? Little snake like that? Hey?"—the next he was just a foot in a boot, a whole lot of open space where the rest of him had been.

I got more focused on my studies, the more often it happened.

I looked outside myself. Those papers and tests were puzzles. I gave myself to them. When time permitted I worked for a corner rehab as a paraprofessional. It got so I very nearly ran the place.

When Myron hit me, I could not hit back. It made me hate myself. I couldn't add to his misery, and I couldn't take away from mine.

We were stuck.

But at that school, I was leaping over hurdle after hurdle. Maybe marriage would help?

During the second year of it, we tried to separate.

Don't let anyone tell you that pain doesn't bind. We had our own Vietnam by then. We had our snipers, our first colonial invaders (I'd been unfaithful, and so had he, it was the first year of the 1970s, but the sixties still lived on, at least as an echo). Now and then there'd be a high-altitude bombing, and Myron's lovely and loving hands would turn into burning napalm.

Me, that girl in that picture, running.

Don't let anyone tell you that you don't touch pain in love.

But don't let anyone tell you, either, that it has to be acted out, has to find an object.

Boyish man, mannish boy, joker, teller of lies, smoker of cannabis, my anchor, in all that theory my lifeline and sinker. There were elms in him, my elms, my maples, the old songs.

Nights, though, the bear still visited, the waters parted, we breathed each other alive.

That rice still grew somehow.

But when the wild rice was not growing, when the nights did not light up anymore, did not take us away, not even a little—not because they couldn't but because the wreckage, the wreckage was too much to ignore—I sent the bear away.

Something like a seed fell in that pool of so many nights before. Of Heritage Park. When the world was alive, the night, night itself;

water, the womb of the world, and Noka the bear visited spring, a woman. A shell hardened over it, that seed.

Up grew a tough stalk, wild rice, tossing in a light breeze, green stalk, under a bruise-blue sky.

Perhaps never to blossom again.

Never.

(1972) NEARLY SEVEN YEARS TO THE
day after I had left, I returned to White Earth,
not exactly with my tail between my legs and cowering, but not
kicking butt like we Indian girls back then were supposed to, either.
This was the time of "Fry Bread Power" bumper stickers, loud PA
systems and shouting radicals, and just plain-out craziness: shoot-
ings, explosions, sit-ins at the White House and whatnot. I was
tired, felt beaten down, and wanted a little quiet. My marriage had
failed, I'd dropped out of a Ph.D. program at Dartmouth, at least
for the time being, and felt somewhere between lost, ruined, and just
plain done for. During the drafting of a paper titled "Toward the

Operationalization of Empowerment Strategies for Rural Popula-
tions at Risk," I'd lost it, as surely as if I'd been riding a bicycle and
a pothole—reserve size, and named Myron—had swallowed my
front wheel and thrown me off. Empowerment for others? Who was
I kidding? I hadn't the slightest notion what to do with *myself*.

That my brother, Jerry, had just won a full scholarship to Cor-
nell did not make me feel any better, either. Or that he'd chosen to
pursue a "sensible" major—medicine.

So I went home.

Two days later—forty-eight hours of cigarette smoke, stale
breath, and frigid air conditioning—I stood in front of Oshogay's
Grocery in Farnsworth, that Greyhound burbling behind me.

The driver whistled from inside the bus. "Got your luggage,
miss?"

I held up the carry-on I'd brought with me. I intended to stay just
that week. To think things through, get myself together. I was going
to get back on that Ph.D program treadmill if it killed me.

Wasn't I?

The driver tipped his cap. I smiled a big, tough smile. The door
slid shut, the bus geared up, engine puking out a cloud of diesel exhaust. Then, like some pregnant beast, it lumbered north, took an
abrupt right onto the highway, and was gone.

Farnsworth.

I stood there, staring. In the park in the center of town, where
there had been a gazebo and lilacs, was a blue-and-green northern
pike as big as a railroad engine, under it a sign in neon: Buy
Farnsworth Baits. Up the street, Oshogay's Grocery had gone for
red letters that glowed even in daylight. There were parking meters.
And yellow curbs. At the north end of Main, where it intersected
with Highway 26, an immense billboard—a garishly painted map
of the area—dwarfed cars passing under it. Opposite, at the south
end, was an Old West facade, fake red lanterns in the windows and
mechanical broncos smack dab in the middle of the sidewalk. But

worst of all, across the street now stood a place with a story-high neon tomahawk on the roof, the sign reading Tomahawk Bowling and Grill, a red arrow to the right commanding, Eat!

"Christ Almighty," I said to myself.

~~~

In a tiny booth at the Tomahawk, over a frontier burger and fries, I considered my situation. Before leaving Dartmouth I had contacted no one, had not so much as written a letter or postcard to Isabel or my mother. I was still, I told myself, footloose and fancy free. I could decide whatever. And what did anyone here know, anyway? Nothing. No one so much as recognized me—not the girl at the counter, all of sixteen, or the pimply kid sweeping or the woman in her forties waiting on tables.

I thought to go back east. Another bus would be arriving in an hour or so.

I was free and alone.

I huddled in my booth, trying to eat. I had to force the food down, as I was queasy.

In seconds I was crying, albeit quietly.

I felt her there before I saw her. Or was it that I smelled her perfume: Tabu? (It seemed, now, just about any smell made me feel a little sick.) My aunt Betty set her hands on her hips and shook her head. My heart raced: I was caught. She saw what I was hiding in my face. But that, I told myself, was just superstition.

"So you aren't going to say hello or what?"

I looked up from my burger.

"You look a little green around the gills, sweetheart. You don't like the cooking?"

I slid from the booth and gave her a hug. It was like falling into a pillow. Big, full breasts like bumpers, all that perfume, talcum, and costume jewelry.

She held me at arm's length and looked at me.

"I've got a cold," I said.

Betty gave me a sidelong glance. "You aren't running away from Myron, are you?"

Just the thought of it got me crying again. "Betty," I said, but it was too complicated to explain.

~~~

"Yes, she's right here," Betty said, shoving the phone into my hand.

I took the phone, furious. Betty had lured me into her office, and while I'd flipped through an album of family photographs, trying to collect myself, she'd rung up my mother, on the pretense of talking business. What business?

My mother cleared her throat. She always did that.

"Hi, honey," she said. "So you're down there at the Tomahawk?"

I told her I was. I didn't say anything about school or Myron. Or the pothole I'd fallen in.

"I just happen to have dinner all put together here. What do you say to coming over around six? That'll give you some time with Betty. That all right?"

I didn't know what to say. Already things seemed to have veered out of control. Empowerment? Everything I had learned in the past few years seemed ridiculous. Here I was already caught in the intricate web of family, although, given my situation, it was not an altogether bad feeling.

"I take it you have no car."

What did she mean by that? I reluctantly told her that she was right. I'd taken the bus, remember?

Betty was grinning at me. "Ask about your father," she said.

"Betty wants me to ask you something about Dad."

"Oh, all right," my mother said. "Bring him, too, then."

I said, "I didn't ask you to ask him, Mom."

"What do you mean, ask him?"

Now it was my turn to be confused. "Mom . . ."

"You talk to Betty," she said. "Seven o'clock."

"But you said six."

"Did I? Well, make it seven."

∿∿∿

In my booth again, I was wondering what I'd do with three hours, aside from avoiding telling Betty anything—she was a terrible gossip—when she appeared at my elbow with a mop.

"We're shorthanded," she said. "How about you help out a little?"

I could smell ammonia in the bucket; I felt sick. But what could I say?

"All right," I said.

In back of the dining area of the Tomahawk, four young toughs were hunched over pinball machines festooned with big-titted girls in skimpy yellow bikinis. The machines rang and clattered and shuddered. Sublimated sexual thrills all around. I worked the mop along the walls, got at the dust bunnies. I vomited in the bucket, then felt better. I refilled the bucket. I was beginning to get angry. It takes me quite a while to get angry, really angry, but when I do it drops over me like a dark blanket.

I was working myself into a fury there.

Who the hell had done such a shitty job of mopping? Who had wiped the tables? What kind of son of a bitch wouldn't clean around furniture or fixtures? Who the hell was Betty to ask me to mop in the first place?

When I finished mopping the diner, Betty sent me out to wax the bowling lanes. They opened at seven, she told me, a strange look on her face that I could not read. I sprayed and buffed. Here and there were bad scratches. Cracks. Who owns this place? I complained. How come it's so goddamn ugly? And Tomahawk? Isn't that a little condescending? I mean, what do *you* think of that? Betty put her hands on her hips.

"It's visible is what," she said. "You got anything else nice to say?"

Yeah, I thought, I'm leaving, but didn't say it.

By seven-thirty a number of well-groomed kids up from the Cities were putting on those red-and-green bowling shoes. We were late for dinner now, still waiting for the night man, the pinsetter. I was thinking to just stride to the phone beside the register and call a cab, escape while I still could, when the front door opened and something came through. I say "something" because that was what I saw.

He was hunched over and walking backwards. Blue-and-silver plaid shirt, green pants, and heavy, thick-soled cordovan shoes. He carefully descended the stairs backwards, using a walking stick like a feeler.

"What's wrong with him?" one of the kids down on the lanes said.

I lifted my head. I felt my mouth purse with indignation.

Part of me thought, *Quiet!* Here was a follower of the old ways, the old religion, a man in dream time. He was walking backwards to reach the source of his wrongdoing, to fix it, I wanted to say. It took a lot of guts to do what this man was doing. He was making public what had shamed him.

I empathized with him, admired him.

"He's a Crazy Dog," I said.

"He's crazy, all right," the boy wearing the cap said.

The man hobbled toward the back of the lanes, that feeler going behind him. Now I could see his face: fine sharp features, eyes focused fiercely inward. Something like electricity ran up my spine and into my head.

"Best pinsetter we've ever had," Betty said matter-of-factly.

"Yes, he would be," I said.

It was my father, Roy.

∿∿∿

As Betty was driving me to my mother's, I became shockproof.

Or was I *in* shock? Betty, her big round head bobbing cheerfully, let me in on all the latest developments. The murder-suicide of Thomas Little Bear, his wife, and their two children. Who did it? I asked. His wife did it, Betty said. Hmmm. There was the new school. The teacher who had pestered certain students. What did she mean by "pestered"? I asked. You know what I mean, Betty replied. We got rid of him, all right.

She steered the car up the now badly rutted road. Sitting beside her, I was thinking about my father and the Crazy Dogs. About my life out east. My Ph.D. program. I wondered what the big mistake was that had sent me off the true path. Was it my having been attracted to Myron, my ex? Or was it that one night of attempted reconciliation? And what had I expected, calling him to come and get his things? I should have known better. No doubt I should have put those fancy snakeskin boots right into the trash.

And was it any surprise that I had chosen a man as absolutely unavailable and as badly damaged by the armed services as my father had been?

Or was it my decision, way back in third grade or so, to be myself and fuck whatever happened?

When I started thinking about it, I saw a lot of places where I'd gotten off the path. Maybe I was off more frequently than I was on the path.

It probably started when I was born, I thought.

At the dinner table, suddenly I wanted to tell them. All of them, right there. Kitsch candy-glass candleholders, little red-and-yellow saltshakers in the shape of Indian braves with corks plugging the holes in their bottoms. Roast beef on a Rose Bowl platter my mother had gotten who knew where. A picture of Chief Hole in the Day, from whom, my mother claimed, we'd descended, watching it all from the west wall.

We'd descended all right. I was trying not to cry again. It was tough. Peke kept gazing off, and when he did, he'd start to lean to one side or the other. Isabel kept having to right him. Every now and then he laughed to himself, spoke in the old language.

Peke and Isabel had aged terribly. Wattles, wrinkles, double chins, milky cataracts. I felt as if they were all passing away right there in front of me. A whole generation, with their magic.

Just so much dust.

Poof! Gone.

For the first time I saw that what I'd despised as a child had formed me, was me, and now, before I could grasp it, it would be gone. I wanted Peke to tell a story: of Wenebojo or Bebukowe, magic canoes, or pukwanjinini, the little people. I wanted to hold Isabel and whisper, as I had as a child, *noko,* grandmother. I wanted my mother to run off in her faulty Ojibwaymowin, angry, for someone, Betty, or my mother's latest boyfriend, Louis, to make a proper offering for the dinner, with tobacco and red willow, in the old spirit of things.

And I wanted to tell them. But everyone was consciously steering around subjects that would lead to the question of why I'd come home. There was no natural opening, is what I'm saying.

"We're gonna do something about Roy's old boondoggle," Louis drawled.

He meant the damage Calmenson Paper had done. Everyone knew how my father had wangled that land for them, how Calmenson Paper had returned the favor by polluting the Wabigoshish River with mercury.

That stopped conversation dead.

"Noko," Betty said, and passed Isabel the potatoes.

Now Isabel launched into a discussion of ring-necked pheasants and how the population was up since the Department of Natural Resources had left them alone. I looked around the table as they bent over their plates again, eating.

The cuckoo clock on the wall sounded.

"Shut that thing up," Peke said, and everyone laughed, a lightness coming back into the room.

ᘛᘜᘛᘜ

Later, over a game of twenty-one, Peke looked at me slyly. Memory loss or not, he could still beat just about anyone at cards. Already had.

"So you think your father is nuts?" he said.

"*What?*" I said. I must have nearly shouted. Peke was supposed to be incapable of remembering things from minute to minute.

"Shh," he said, and grinned.

"*Mishosha!*" I said. Grandfather.

But already he'd slid back to wherever he'd just come from.

ᘛᘜᘛᘜ

Washing dishes. Orange and yellow and red Fiestaware. The messy turkey tub. Sudsy lemon-scented water. Isabel, behind me, wrapping leftovers, stooped and bowlegged. Betty and my mother, Nina, stout and going to gray, drying, discussing the best way to can beans, which neither did anymore anyway. Three generations of women there in that tiny kitchen. And in my belly a fourth—my secret, or so I thought.

"So," Betty said. She poked Isabel in the rear with a meat fork. Isabel jumped. "You comin' to Wednesday's bingo?"

"Can't afford it," Isabel said.

"I'll slip you a few free cards, how's that?"

Isabel grunted.

I wondered, there at the sink, how Betty could do that: she was, humor aside, scrupulously honest.

"Your grandma's gettin' to be an old sourpuss," Betty said.

Isabel slammed the refrigerator door shut. "Speak for yourself," she said.

"Now, Mom," my mother said. She set her hand on the Formica countertop, suddenly businesslike. "You know what the doctor said."

I spun around, frightened. "What did he say?"

The three women smiled.

"It's nothing," Betty said.

～～～

That night, at my mother's, on the north end of Ten Chiefs Lake, of all places—lying beside her, in fact, unable to sleep, my mother snoring like a lion—something came to me. It came to me with the power of sunny resurrection: I had been off on an entirely erroneous tangent. My pothole wasn't a pothole at all!

Empowerment, I'd thought, came from the outside. Through government agencies, political leverage, group action. But here, up at White Earth, as it had for ten millennia, empowerment came through interrelation. Or power *in* interrelation. Right there I saw my whole premise was wrong; I had assumed a Western slant. It was that simple.

Lying there in the dark, I saw how a baby might bring us all closer. Renew things. Make us even stronger.

I thought of a new title. A new project: "The Universality of Anthropology's Western Knowledge Base in Intercultural Context: Myth or Reality?"

Hmm.

I imagined a buzzer going off, as for a wrong answer on a game show. *Buzz!*

Bor-ing! *Wrong!*

Suddenly I felt more nervous than I had before.

The thought of researching such a topic very nearly made me sick. What would be the point? But what other choice did I have?

I tossed and turned. I woke, shocked. My mother was looking at me strangely, at my stomach.

"I'm bloated," I told her. "It's that time of the month."

"Oh," she said, and promptly went back to sleep.

Lying awake, I thought of my father setting pins. I'd watched him, before we left. From the wreckage of a strike or spare, from scattered pins, he formed one perfect triangle after another. He was fast, but not too fast. With the completion of each, he smiled. It was a meditation of sorts, I could see that now. One that fit a Crazy Dog perfectly.

Ten pins.

Ten chiefs. Ten tribes. Ten . . .

It's the only thing that calms him down, Betty'd said, shrugging. You know how he always built things.

Uh-huh, I said.

Before we'd left the Tomahawk, I'd watched his hands form one perfect set after another.

I had never really known my father. He'd always been away—in the war earlier on, then off doing one thing or another. Building. For a time I'd hated him for that. And for his painful looks when we did meet, looks that said, I wish I could. This, of course, before the unspeakable happened.

As a child, I'd always thought, But why, Daddy? Why not?

In that way children do, I took his inability to make time for me as a judgment of my character. To mean there was something lacking in me. Something flawed about me. Something not deserving of his love.

At the Tomahawk, somehow, right there, my father perched like a monkey over those pins, I saw we were not as different as I had thought.

It scared me: all that repetition of perfection, how his world had shrunk to accommodate it.

In my dream that night, Betty came to me, jolly, laughing, a baby cradled to her ample bosom. See? she said, holding it up for me to see.

What's her name? I asked.

It's your call, Betty said.

∿∿∿

Morning. Sunlight. But light I did not want to greet. One of those awful, sick mornings. My mother had already gone downstairs, was in the kitchen.

Even the cheerful green curtains in the windows made me queasy.

I would not get out of bed, I thought. But then, when the smell of bacon hit me, I had no choice.

"Were you sick up there or something?" my mother asked at the table.

"Mother," I said.

She set a plate in front of me. Pancakes, eggs, bacon, and a pork sausage patty. I must have sucked my cheeks in.

"Eat," my mother said. "You're too thin."

Around ten I walked into the Tomahawk.

"You look like shit, kiddo," Betty said, grinning from behind the counter. "Think you could wait a couple tables?"

I had to think about that. "You're short again, right?"

"Five-two and three-quarters."

"Uh-huh," I said.

Betty took that as a yes. Of course, I could have said no, and she'd have thrown me the menus anyway. And I'd have caught them—pure reflex, old softballer that I was. I rolled my eyes.

Betty came out from behind the counter and wrapped a frilly apron with an orange tomahawk around me.

"You know," I said, "I should tell you that I find more than a disturbing level of cognitive dissonance in this exchange."

"You mean you're pissed off?"

"Yes, you could say that," I said.

"Good," Betty replied. "At least we're getting somewhere, then, aren't we?"

Waiting on tables, I had time to ponder what she meant. I'd waited on tables in New Hampshire, as an undergrad at Dartmouth, and now the morning crowd at the Tomahawk was cake. I smiled and chatted, set my hand on my hip, playing sassy with the men.

Guaranteed a better tip.

We were busy. I had very little morning sickness, and with the light streaming through the blue gingham curtains, Dexter busing, and Betty at the register, its bell ringing clear and loud, I felt almost at home.

So where did Betty think we were getting to?

I felt part of some strange conspiracy, although, in my family, I'd always felt that way.

What was she getting at?

I poured cup after cup of coffee. Orange vests and tables of men away from their wives, giving way a short while later to the blue-haired set and, last of all, the Indians.

"Aren't you that Sharrett girl?" a woman with eyes as dark and squinty as raisins asked.

I just smiled.

So it came to me as a shock when I slipped and fell in the kitchen and couldn't get up for crying. I didn't even know what I was crying about. Not exactly. It just all seemed so *impossible* suddenly.

Over my shrieks, I could hear Betty at the counter. I could sense people looking at me.

"Go away now," Betty said. "Shush, you. Leave her be."

∿∿∿

All those years earlier, when I tore things up irreparably, leaving White Earth, when I left my great-aunt waiting for hours at the Greyhound depot and did not call until weeks later to let anyone know where I was, I'd made a pact with myself. New life. New image. New possibilities. I thought I'd done that, succeeded in throwing it all off. I had won a scholarship, knocked off a degree, easy stuff, and gone on to do graduate work, which also seemed not all that difficult.

Yet, all that time I'd been acting. I couldn't get beyond the feeling that I was kidding myself. (So this is what I'm going to do with my time? I kept asking.) So I'd applied myself all the more. Social anthropology. History. Political science. I was going to get a perspective on things. I was something of a whiz kid, all seriousness and good intentions.

Midway into that Ph.D. program, though, I'd gotten bogged down. I'd thought it was Myron, how tangled and crazy and circular things got. I'd thought it was having to escape him.

But I'd done that now, and could see I'd been wrong. I'd come to the end of something, and Myron had just happened to intersect the sweep of my trajectory, now a shooting star, earthbound, or so it seemed.

All that work, suffering, and study, and I had been reduced to a girl crying in a heap of potato skins.

Right back where I'd started, and bringing someone with me.

"You get outta here, Dexter," Betty said. "I'm closin'."

There was some complaint about money.

"You want me to beat the shit out of you, Dexter?" Betty said.

This is what she whispered in my ear, kneeling beside me.

"Girl, you haven't fooled me for five minutes. Nor have you fooled your mother or grandmother. Not even your father, and surely not Peke.

"We may be queer-looking folks to you now—"

"I'm sorry," I blubbered.

"We're all sorry," Betty said. "Now you listen."

She said, "Every generation has got its storyteller, its in-between person. That's why you're in such pain. You aren't here, girl, and you aren't there. And this baby, this baby is like . . . well, it's like everything balances on it. Which way to go? You think you got a choice of this or that. But, Aja girl, you are right where you're supposed to be. In the middle.

"Peke's dying.

"I know he singled you out. You thought he was just telling you a load of bullshit, didn't you? All those stories and whatnot. Just teasing.

"He was testing you.

"What you gotta do, girl, is give witness. That's what you're here for."

I looked around me. Yellow-and-black tile. Stainless-steel legs of french fry vat, Hobart stove, cooler. I had an order clutched in my hand: "2 #7 hold pickles, C, Sprt, one lemonade."

"Oh, Betty!" I said, and started right in again.

I worked there at the Tomahawk right through February, when I started getting comments about how I'd put on a little weight. Every day when I opened, I counted the money, keeping an eye on Dexter. He was a thief but not an incurable one, Betty thought. Of course, it turned out that none other than Betty herself had put that neon tomahawk on the roof, had sewn those hideous aprons, and had painted Pikwak, the turtle, pukwanjinini, little people, and other mythic figures on the walls.

It was Betty who'd had that northern pike put in the center of town and had had the sign, straddling the road, erected, now with a gold star in the middle, just to make sure people got the message: You Are Here. Eat!

And it was Betty who'd hired my father. Gave out loans, sold her property to finance the Tomahawk, which every other week someone or other was telling her would go under. I would hear her on the phone in back. Always married men, ones she knew in a biblical sense, I suspected.

"Put your money where your goddamn mouth is, Ed, or shut up."

"You heard me," she'd say. "Cough it up."

The following day, there were cans of the best paint, wallpaper, and trim in the back room.

Somehow we were too busy to put the trim up. To paint. To renovate.

∿∿

With me, though, Betty was caring, involved, even hovering. I didn't catch on until her too frequent visits to my mother's in February tipped me off. She had more than a small interest in this child I was carrying. Her adopted son, Henry, my former boyfriend, had died in a boating accident years before.

"Remember, you're going back to school," Betty'd tell me.

"That's right," my mother would echo. "You listen to her."

"But how?" I asked.

"It'll work out," Betty said.

ᴧᴧᴧ

My delivery was difficult. A breech birth.

Thirty-six hours of struggle. One black hole of pain. I shocked my doctor. I shocked Isabel. None of them had any idea of the things Peke had taught me. There are some dark stories in our heritage. Dark practices. I screamed some of that out. I had, through Peke, been initiated into the medicine society before I'd left the reserve that first time. One night at the medicine lodge, I'd eaten a dog's heart. Back then, I'd spent afternoons with a Wabunowin, a sorcerer, who'd had me purify myself with an emetic, after which, I hallucinated for what seemed like days, traveling back to the navel of the world. What I'd seen then had been wondrous, and horrifying. It had so scared me, I'd tried to forget it.

All of that pressed in on me during my labor as I fell time and again into that dark, dark hole of unconsciousness. Grandfather, with eyes of glass, loomed close; Toad Woman, with her warty, bulging nose, sniffed at me; Pauguk, Death himself, a skeleton, flew circles around my bed.

Late in my delivery I imagined myself on a lake, then knew the lake for what it was, and what being on it meant.

I screamed, tried to climb out of the bed, thinking it was a canoe. I shouted and pushed people away until they gave me a spinal. That old serpent's tail got wrapped around my forearm and I bit at it.

How could I fight it?

"Hang on. You're fine," my doctor told me, his eyes fearful.

It was Betty's arm I'd bitten.

"Listen, *please*," I said, and pulled that doctor closer, desperate. But how could he understand?

~~~

When I was just a girl, Peke told me this story about Wenebojo's daughters. He told it when I'd pestered him overlong about Delia and Herman and Gabriel.

I'd wanted to know how Delia could have gone off like that, without Gabriel, her baby.

Peke said, *Listen, ninamuch.*

He said, *There were two camps at opposite sides of a lake. One of them was having a powwow, and Wenebojo's daughters, Matchikewis, the older and infertile, and Oshkikwe, impulsive and silly, decided to go.*

Oshkikwe took her son. She sat in the stern of the boat, where she could paddle and steer. Matchikewis, in the bow, held the boy. It was a big lake, and with each paddle stroke, to Oshkikwe, it got bigger.

Matchikewis sang to pass the time. But behind her, Oshkikwe was becoming impatient. The line of shore seemed to stretch into eternity, around and into the clouds that had formed on the horizon.

Wenebojo, in those clouds, danced.

Straight across, daughter, he said. The shortest way is best.

He was testing them.

A bad smell came from the island in the center of the lake. Everyone said a manito, a bad spirit, lived there. The island was not much more than a brown spot on the water. Everyone paddled around that island. But Oshkikwe headed straight across.

What are you doing? Matchikewis said, cutting her lullaby short.

Why, sister, Oshkikwe said, I'm taking us there.

Matchikewis gave her sister a long, hard look. The boy was struggling in her arms. Matchikewis tried to right their direction. She had a small cedar paddle with her. Her paddle was useless out on the lake, Oshikikwe said, and began to argue with her sister. Why had she brought such a small, useless paddle?

And anyway, Oshkikwe said, look.

Matchikewis did. Truly, the lake was as narrow as a river now, just that stretch of mud between them and the opposite shore.

I'll just go by on the outside, Oshkikwe said.

So they did that, but as they got closer, a whirlpool pulled them in, right over the island, and so they paddled faster. Out of the lake reared a great horned serpent, hissing.

Give me ssssomething! it said.

The waves came up, so that the canoe was nearly upset. Water splashed in. Matchikewis clutched Oshkikwe's son in the bow.

Give me the boy! the serpent hissed.

The great horned serpent clutched the gunwale, wrapped its tail, all coppery scales, over the stern. The canoe went up on end.

Just as they were about to go under, Matchikewis took out her tiny paddle and, saying, Thunders with me! brought it down on the beast's tail, cutting it off. The serpent roared and darted under the waves.

The tail writhed so hard in the bottom of the canoe it nearly overturned them.

Oshkikwe, terrified, paddled to shore. Behind them the whirlpool closed up.

Everyone from the powwow rushed to meet them. The men wrestled that coppery tail onto the sand. It writhed there, this way and that.

Matchikewis comforted the boy, who would not be comforted by any other.

Who decided to cross the island? one of the older women said.

I did, Oshkikwe said.

The woman bent down and cut off the tip of the horned serpent's tail. She handed it to Oshkikwe. The tail was heavy, copper-scaled, filled with a wild electricity.

For years it would have special hunting power.

Oshkikwe bought bread and, in hard winters, the hindquarters of deer, with just a sliver of it.

During the night, it grew.

But never was there another son.

And Matchikewis? From that hour the boy clung to her. Matchikewis came to be with child and, in that way, gave birth to generations.

〰〰〰

It isn't fair, I said, upset.

Peke had laughed, a deep, sad laugh. I know, *ninamuch*, he said. I know, darling.

〰〰〰

Thirty-six hours of labor and a day of recovery later, I was still exhausted. Could barely lift my head from the pillow. When I convinced the staff—all strangers, as I'd only been able to get into a hospital a hundred miles away in Bemidji—that I had to see my baby, they put me in a wheelchair and took me into the nursery.

The baby had been badly jaundiced, and the doctor had put him on an IV—antibiotics—just to be safe. Now, just out of his incubator, Betty held him, as if she always had, at her breast. I felt a sudden bitter rage. I very nearly expected to hear a boom of thunder, feel the floor awash under my feet.

Betty held the baby out, and I took him.

He cried. Smelled of skin, of lotion, of warmth, of cotton blanket. I hugged him to myself. Nearly crushed him. Ears not much bigger than cashews. Dark blue eyes, small grasping hands. But not for me.

Isabel was there, too. And my mother, Nina.

Through the open door, where Peke and two others sat, a conversation concerning the real things of the world was going on. Snow tires. Engines. Fishing lures. "Mepp number five is the one," Peke said.

Betty did not move toward me. I would have killed her. No doubt about it.

"Goddammit, I'm not going to cry," I said.

But that baby was, and when I lifted him up and away, a horrible wrenching in my chest, he reached for Betty, as if those nine months he'd been practicing to do just that at this very moment, and Betty took him.

I did not want to get hysterical. I held myself, swaying, biting my cheek.

The baby cooed and clucked in Betty's arms.

"What will you call him?" I asked.

And Betty replied, "Prosper."

(1981) ONCE, WHEN I WAS JUST A CHILD, Peke told me over checkers that a man without a story is a man without an identity. I remember the black-and-red board, the checker pieces, the smell of the room—tobacco, cedar smoke, and fish: at the stove, Isabel was frying bluegills in onions. Jerry was twisting some coat hangers into something or other, by the front windows. Nina was out at the VA. I only wanted to play checkers.

"So what?" I said sullenly.

Peke did not laugh, as he usually did. He lit a cigarette, set his hand behind him.

"Don't get her started on smoking," Isabel said from the stove.

"I'm not doing anything," Peke said. He let go a smoke ring, which dissipated slowly and evenly. There was a kind of grace in him, a refinement, which was unusual for so big a person.

"So," he said, leaning close, and nearly whispering. "What's your story, huh?"

∿∿∿

Out at Cheshire Academy in New Hampshire, where I taught high school after bitterly leaving White Earth again, Betty taking Prosper as her son, I had a story, all right. I told people I'd grown up in the Twin Cities. That I attended South High School. Had lived in a split-level ranch, white with green trim and shutters. It was that life my mother had wanted, and somehow came as an easy fabrication. I knew the particulars of it, could talk Tupperware, or the merits of a top-loader washer versus a front loader, with the best of them—better, really, because, since I'd never used those things I could be unabashedly enthusiastic. I was like that about all kinds of homey things, was good with details. My deluxe Waring blender, I might say, has seven speeds and an overall high and low setting.

To this day, I have never owned such a blender.

My clothes? My oh-so-conservative black pumps, virginal blouses, and tailored navy-blue skirts? I bought at Dayton Hudson, from the world's first indoor shopping center, Southdale, built in 1956. In Edina.

That's a suburb of Minneapolis.

Uh-huh.

I wonder now if my colleagues didn't think me a little crazy, for spitting these little koans of Minneapolis–Saint Paul trivia at them. I mean, who cared that the Foshay tower was built in 1936? Or that Saint Paul was once called Pig's Eye Landing?

A tourist, that's who. Or maybe the mayor. Or a travel agent.

This was my life out at Cheshire: up at six, oatmeal with honey and milk, two two-cup mugs of black French roast, a drive into downtown Manchester in my Volvo 240 DL wagon, marching into Civ 1, beginning with the Battle of Hastings in 1066, and moving on from there. No pagan contamination in that lot. Straight blue-blood history. Chalk dust, the rise of murky old England, the Norman influence, which I made much of, being French-Canadian. (At least that wasn't a complete lie, since I'd lived up at Red Lake, near the Canadian border, for some time and could mimic the accent: a-bowt—well, most of it, eh?)

Weekends I went to a movie now and then, graded papers, and, once, made the mistake of fixing the brakes on my Volvo.

Fixing them was a mistake because Jerry had taught me all about machines, and it got me thinking about him and how he'd killed himself months after he graduated from medical school, and that put me in a black mood. And, too, there was the garage, which just darkened my feelings all the more. Just off a busy street where some pretty dangerous types liked to do business in narcotics, I was always jumpy lying under the car, a big, rusty tire iron by my thigh where I could get to it.

Still, even with all that discomfort I reasoned, why should I spend four hundred dollars for a new caliper, when I could buy a couple tools and do the job myself?

So there I was, in the apartment garage, the car up on tripod jacks, a trouble light on, digging around underneath, cursing Jerry, cursing myself, half out, half under, when I heard someone come in. In a snap, I was standing beside the car with my tire iron raised and ready.

But it was only Marcie, Cheshire's secretary, hair sprayed into stiff curls, bringing me the papers I'd left on her desk by mistake.

"What are you doing?" she said.

"The brake pedal went soft so . . ."

And as I was explaining about the master cylinder and the spots on the garage floor, her eyes took me in.

I was wearing my old clothes. Moccasins, which Nina had embroidered. My hair in braids. Black jeans. And worst of all was my T-shirt: "Free Leonard Peltier," it said, across my breasts, in bold red letters.

All that fury I'd been working myself into, arguing with ghosts, evaporated right there and then.

I felt a rush of blood to my face. I felt like a complete fool.

"I'll take those, thanks," I said, and slid back under the car, papers and all.

∿∿∿

Did people look at me with some amusement the following Monday? Or did I just imagine it? Marcie was a compulsive gossip, a world-class chatterer in that office. I'd fed her pieces of trivia to hand on to everyone from time to time, and by God, it had worked. But now she'd seen me. And so, terribly self-conscious, and feeling I'd been found out, I poured on the stories of my childhood in 1950s Minneapolis.

In those stories my parents were always taking me to a restaurant downtown, no longer open, called the Forum. Or to Como Park. In the teachers' lounge, I got people started on old memories and added a few myself: how you could buy an ice-cream cone at Bridgeman's for a nickel; swim at the Taft Park pool on hot summer days for a quarter.

It got so I almost believed it myself, that carefree, manufactured life.

And like that, another year went by.

So it came as something of a shock to me, and a violation, when I was called down to the office to receive a phone call from a certain Betty Stronghold, long distance from . . . "I think she said White Earth," Marcie said.

I marched through the little spring-loaded gate in the office.

What could Betty be calling me about? Marcie watched eagle-eyed from her typewriter. Always, in offices, those fluorescent lights. Minty smell of floor wax.

I took the receiver. Should I act as if I didn't know who it was? "Hello?" I said.

"Aja?" Betty replied.

"Yes," I said. Why did I say yes? Why not "What is it, Betty?"

"Sweetheart," she said.

I turned my back to Marcie, facing the doorway, students going by in the hall, surprised to see me there. I smiled, a certain rigor mortis in it. I knew this was going to hurt.

"Sweetheart," Betty said, "Isabel died yesterday afternoon."

I set my hand on the counter there so as not to fall.

"I'll call you back," I said and set the receiver down, even though I didn't have Betty's number and was certain she hadn't given it to Marcie.

I took the afternoon off, went home, sat on my bed, and stared out the window. I picked at the yarn tufts in my quilt until the batting came out in tangled puffs that I couldn't shove back in. I ran my hand through my hair and, finding kinky hairs—probably white, anyway—broke them in half.

I sat and sat. Hours passed.

I beat myself up with memories. Isabel making saltwater taffy. Isabel laughing. Isabel and this kid, Rory, she'd been taking care of. Isabel and Peke arguing in that crappy little rowboat they'd gone fishing in. Isabel saying, time and again when she was angry, "God bless it all!" And always, in that cabin, the first cabin, Isabel cooking something, Nina off at the VA, Jerry busy with some new experiment he'd ordered through the mail, and Peke letting me beat him at checkers, but slowly, so he could confound me with stories that seemed to make no sense.

Isabel squeezing my hand, saying, "You always take things too hard, *ninamuch*."

I thought hard and long on that. Beat myself up with it. I wanted to feel something, but whenever my eyes glassed up and I felt an impulse to give in to it, the feeling would stop.

It had been that way with Jerry, too.

~~~~

I watched the six-o'clock news while I ate dinner. Plane crashes. Terrorists. A drop in the Dow Jones. More political claptrap. Screaming advertisements for Ford tough trucks with I-beam front suspension. Hanes underwear. Candy. I finished dinner, then watched the nightly cop dramas. *Hill Street*. Reruns of *Kojak*.

I ate a pint of ice cream. Ordered out for Chinese. Popped popcorn. Felt sick. Turned off the tube. I felt terrified. I was in some box, holding myself in.

I had to think about class preparation. I'd get up early to do it, I told myself. Fat, I thought. I'm going to get fat if I eat like this. I promised myself I'd walk for an hour before I did my lesson plans.

Finally I slept. And, sleeping, I dreamed.

Peke, in a sorcerer's black pants, shinnied down a rope into a well. I was trapped at the bottom, stone walls all around. The rope wouldn't go all the way down, so Peke made it thinner and longer. I watched that rope come down, thinner all the time.

Finally it was the thickness of straw, just golden straw.

"Come on up," Peke said.

I bolted awake.

The window overlooking the street was open, and the curtains luffed out. In a childhood story I remembered someone wove gold out of straw. There was some price attached to it. Was the straw in my dream gold, then, or just straw? And what was I doing at the bottom of a well?

And why wasn't there any water in it?

I did not return Betty's call. I left a message at the council office, said I wouldn't be able to attend the funeral.

That did it, I thought.

~~~~

Weeks went by. A month. I worked even harder. Yet I was distracted. My thinking began to get a little strange. I didn't wash every morning, didn't care. Slept badly. A worm was eating into my perfect apple.

Betty wrote, "I can't imagine what could have been so important that you couldn't make it up for the funeral. But so be it. I just wanted you to know the last thing Isabel did was buy a dog. A big dog, some wolf-mix thing, at a store in Farnsworth. What do you make of that? Take care, ninamuch."

What did I make of it? I made of her letter an attempt at manipulation. She had never used that term of endearment before—"ninamuch." Why now? And so what if Isabel had bought a dog?

But I began to wonder, about Isabel's death, my work at Cheshire Academy, my reasons for not going back for the funeral. And like that, the doors at Cheshire began to close. Things began to go wrong. I had a fling with the math teacher, Jim Kline—married, two kids; his wife called to let me know what she thought of the affair, which was . . . interesting. I stopped interjecting mind twisters in my civics classes, didn't prepare, gave them reading assignments in class, smoked at my desk.

Dog . . . "some wolf-mix thing."

Betty called me at school to ask about sending some of Isabel's things. She left her number, and her address: Stronghold, 28 Maple, White Earth Village, White Earth, MN 55743.

"Is that where you're from?" Marcie asked, bobbed nose, red-lacquered nails, in her breathy, overinterested voice, handing me the note at the office desk.

I felt oddly calm. No blenders, IDS towers, fake childhoods.

"Yes," I told her, surprising myself, "I grew up on the reserve. I'm an enrolled member of the Big Grassy Band of Chippewa. Anything else you'd like to know? Any juicy gossip? How many scalps I've got on my wall or anything like that? How about, I fucked your old friend Jim Kline. Will that do it?"

Marcie just smiled.

~~~

In November I skipped a four-day teachers' conference and went up to White Earth. Cold gray sky, hard ground, an inch or so of new snow, echo of gunshots in the distance—deer hunters. I sat on Isabel's porch. She'd been found in her rocker, her head between her knees. She'd had hypertension, so bad, she'd been told by her doctor not to so much as stoop to pick something off the floor. So how, unless she'd done it intentionally, could she have had her head down like that?

I rocked in Isabel's chair. Hugged myself, as if I were only cold.

Across the road, I could see old Herman Oshogay's son Charlie in his cabin. Big, hulking, nervous, he peered out the back window at me.

I felt the hair stand up on the back of my neck.

~~~

Walking back to my rental car, I saw all kinds of things I didn't like. Roads washed out and rutted, trash everywhere, Styrofoam cups, bottles, cans, old tires, a rotten mattress. The front window of the council office was cracked, duct tape run over it like giant dirty Band-Aids. A kid went by, dragging a plastic bag behind him.

"Aren't you supposed to be in school?" I asked him.

"Yup," he said, and just kept going.

∿∿∿

I felt a kind of fury mounting in me, but kept it held in check. I passed Betty's restaurant, and it looked like a million bucks. The name on the roof in gold lights: Tomahawk Grill. Across from it, in the park, that big fish, newly painted. That sign over the highway bright as ever: You Are Here. Eat.

I wanted to go in and ask her what the hell had happened, and so I did.

Betty was at the grill, mustard-stained apron, some kid running like a squirrel in back, her prep cook. Ten or fifteen guests talked at tables over combo plates; most of them I recognized at a glance, Highclouds, Fishers, Finedays, a few Strongholds.

It was a little after four.

"So look what the cat dragged in," Betty said in a not too friendly voice, flipping a hamburger and pressing it down with the spatula so it hissed. "Come up for a vacation?" she said.

I remember thinking, Do not hit her. "I'm back," I said, sitting with the Highclouds.

"Like hell you are," she said. Betty came around the grill with her spatula.

"I'm talking here, okay?" I said.

She saw right then I meant business. I had my notepad and pen out.

∿∿∿

In the air, forty thousand feet over Ann Arbor, on the way back to New Hampshire, two gin and tonics to calm me, I began to let a very dark seed settle in my stomach. I had poked around the whole weekend, and the story I'd come up with was truth, not conjecture.

It involved that boy Isabel had been taking care of, Rory, his sister, and their father, Charlie Oshogay.

And one dog, half wolf, half husky.

In the last afternoon of her life, late and a bit off balance, Isabel had limped down the cabin stoop and out into the road. She heaved her left leg around and, bracing herself with her cane, took yet another step with her good right leg.

She was in gear. "God bless it all!" she cursed to herself. She'd always said that.

The old road out of the reserve was narrow and hilly, and she headed uphill as she left the cabin. She tried to keep her head up. Never stoop, her doctor had told her. You'll bring on another stroke.

To hell with it, she told herself. She would make it out to the old highway and worry about her heart then. She wouldn't think any further than that.

She leaned on the cane and cursed herself for not asking one of her neighbors to drive her, but then, she couldn't let anyone know what she was doing.

Some distance from the cabin, her good leg went rubbery, and her left side numb. The sun came down hot from overhead; cicadas shrieked in the pines. She tried to rest, standing still.

The side of the road had a soft, sandy lip, and she eyed it as though it were a lover—"Temptation is always a lover," she'd told me. *Sit,* it seemed to say. Her good leg buckled a little, her thigh burning. The pain made walking all the more difficult. Her good leg refused to obey her, and she waited, short of breath. She was not going to sit down.

She braced herself on her cane and, balanced now, recalled the time she and Peke had slaughtered their pigs, rather than having the local butcher do it, and the water in the scalding trough had spilled over, splashing her. "There was real pain, Aja," she'd told me. She'd always compared pain to that.

As she rested, she remembered how her skin had come off in layers. How her mother-in-law had laid her on a cot and fanned her, had sung songs, and the end had still been far away. But now her Peke was dead, her daughter living too far away to visit much, her grandson a suicide, and his sister—her granddaughter, Aja—silent out in New Hampshire. And now healing seemed an impossibility.

Isabel had been badly hit by the stroke, her left side paralyzed, but worst of all, her ability to speak had been taken from her; no one seemed to understand her. Only the boy, Rory, did, and his sister, and thinking of them, she straightened her rubbery leg.

Isabel, still angry, worked her palm around the cane's sweat-slickened handle and pushed off again.

She tried to focus on the marsh up the road, cattails and yellow box elder. Still, she couldn't help seeing the boy with his father, Charlie, standing over him with the jack handle. When Charlie broke the boy's arm, word had gotten around that the boy had fallen, and Isabel had dragged herself down to the council lodge.

At the lodge, no one would listen to her or even try: Charlie Oshogay was well known and respected, and his wife had been revered as something of a saint. And Isabel was white, even after a lifetime on the reserve with Peke. Oh, how she had struggled. You're just overexcited, they told her. Go on home, Isabel, they said.

She looked around her. Hot sun, the cicadas buzzing menacingly, the sand warm under her feet. God was testing her. I know she was thinking that. God in the trees. In the sun overhead. In the very ground under her feet. I know she waited for something decisive to come to her. Minutes passed.

She was thinking, too, of something Peke had told her, years back, about man-eaters. The only way to kill a windigo is to become one yourself, he'd said. You gotta become ice. Of course, you gotta get real big, too. He'd always said that. The thought of it made her shudder. It was clear that she could as easily be devoured by fighting something evil as by giving in to it, but what choice did she have? She'd prayed for another solution, and none had come. Night after night she had listened to the beatings in the house on the corner. He, in all His omnipotence, had done nothing.

It disgusted her.

You, she thought, and spit into the road.

She made good time on the flats, all five miles of it, to the highway. There she found she could swing her bad leg around and even push off from the asphalt. Now she was nearly enjoying herself. She hadn't been out walking since the stroke. She felt herself smiling, but just then, caught off guard, she pitched forward, her chin striking the cane, her glasses flying off as if yanked away. Somehow she managed to stop her fall.

But the glasses. She could see them, barely, down in a pothole. No doubt He had put them there, just to thwart her. Worked out the bottom of the hole so it was especially deep. Had been waiting for her all these years. She squinted. The lenses reflected twin yellow suns. Her chin throbbed hotly. She worked her hand down the cane, stooping as little as possible. Her pulse hammered like thunder in her temples. She reached for the glasses and missed. Then again. On the third try she got hold of them and slowly worked herself back up. One of the lenses was cracked.

Isabel chuckled.

He would take her down piece by piece, but she would do what she had to do anyway.

Later, after an interminable struggle walking, on the shoulder of the old highway, she turned to face the oncoming traffic, but none came.

Isabel set her cane in a pock in the road. After a time, a dull throb, then a roar, came from far up the highway. Then a bright red spot, a chrome grille, bent hood, and cracked windshield, convertible top down, brick-red faces, and just like that, the car roared by. "Get outta the road, you old bag!"—voices tearing along after it.

Big cottony clouds lifted into the broad blue sky. Isabel turned like a compass needle around her cane. She kicked her feet deeper into the sand at the side of the road. She smelled herself: rose scent and a ripe, bitter tang. Far down the asphalt the heat haze looked like a lake, all cool and watery. She thought of the tea her mother had made, in tall, narrow glasses full of ice, with fresh mint leaves from the garden. That had been back in Saint Paul. She could feel the glass in her hand, sweaty with cold. She'd made tea like that for Peke and for their daughter, and then for Rory, after his sister was sent off to the home. Isabel had sat on the steps out front with Rory, had brushed his hair and fussed over him that afternoon. "I want to stay with you," he'd told her. "Camilla's pregnant."

Camilla, Rory's sister, was sixteen, a pretty girl, and shy. "Is the father going to fess up?" Isabel had asked.

Rory had looked away.

"Rory?"

"I gotta go," he said, and ran from the yard.

Something in the way he ran, stumbling, his arms windmilling, made things clear. It had shocked her to think it: Charlie. It was Charlie's, their father's, baby.

That evening Charlie broke the boy's arm. He did it in the front yard where Isabel would see from her rocker. The nearest neighbor was blocks away; Isabel's phone was broken and useless.

"You don't talk to him!" Charlie'd shouted at her. "You hear?"

When it was over, she went inside and smashed every cup in her cupboard. Don't get all worked up, her doctor had told her. It'll kill you. So she smashed her cups. She smashed her plate set, too. She thought of poison. An ice pick. She thought of all kinds of unlikely ways to fix Charlie.

Right about then she must have stumbled onto her plan.

It was beautiful and awful.

She had seen a man, somewhat drunk and careless, stumble into old Ishtakubig's yard, across from Our Lady. Ishtakubig's dog had leaped up at the end of his chain, teeth bared, snarling.

Only the chain had prevented worse.

I imagine Isabel, as she waited for another car to come up the road, must have smiled, remembering Ishtakubig's dog with his sharp teeth.

Yes, a companion was what the boy needed, she thought, the boy and, later, his father.

∿∿∿

That same red car shot out of the lake of heat haze.

Isabel pulled herself out into the road and leaned on her cane. The car roared, widening, closer, then swerved and slid, tires howling and smoking. The car came to a lurching stop just feet from her. Delbert Fineday, alone now, threw the door open. He was wearing a baseball cap, his braids run out the back.

"Jesus, you're a crazy old bat," he said.

Isabel, getting in, lifted her skirt and nearly fell. The floor was littered with beer cans. They clanked and clattered when she tried to settle her feet.

"Where ya goin'?" Delbert said. He said it in a tired and exasperated way. But she knew he liked her, and she him. Delbert often drove her places.

Isabel pointed through the windshield. There was a statue of Mary on the dashboard. It froze her up for a moment. Delbert lifted his can of beer, and his Adam's apple worked up and down like a pump.

"Where?" he said again.

Isabel stared down the road. She would not try to say it. The road went only one place, anyway: to town. Delbert shook his head and put the car in gear.

"You don't make any goddamn sense these days. You know that, don'tcha?" he said. "Texas it is, then!" And when she didn't smile, he glanced over at her, concerned.

"Man, Isabel, lighten up," he said.

~~~

At the Oakwood Mall tens of people elbowed past her. Some of them she knew. The Finedays, the Highclouds, the Morrisons. Some said hello, but Isabel was gruff, didn't want to be seen.

~~~

A short while later, she stood back of the register at the pet store.

Dog, she said again, to the girl there. Dog! But it didn't come out right. The girl shook her head. Her hair was done up in stiff, exaggerated curls and flips, her nails painted bright green. In her right ear she had what looked like ten earrings of all kinds, gold and copper and silver, a set of brass bangles on her wrists.

"I'll get the manager," the girl said. She reached under the counter.

Seconds later a tall potbellied man came through a door off to the right. He was breathing heavily and pulled nervously at his mustache.

"Yes?" he said.

~~~

He led her into a small, quiet room, the ceiling low and textured. Cages lined the walls, the dogs in them pacing or sleeping, or worrying the cage doors with their teeth. The room smelled of dog food and wet paper and Lysol. Isabel shook her head. No, she did not want a Pomeranian. Or a cocker spaniel or a beagle. Yes, they were wonderful, happy dogs. No, she did not want one of them. Did he understand?

"Listen," the manager said. "I've got *the* dog for you. Just about cleans up after itself, small, short haired . . ." He led the way to yet another cage. The dog in it leaped at the wire mesh. Its eyes were soft and inviting, its ears floppy. "Isn't this *just* the thing?"

"No," Isabel said.

The manager scratched at his mustache. He breathed deeply, then snapped his fingers. He tugged a notepad out of his back pocket and opened it.

"I've got it," he said. "Can you write?"

Isabel eyed him flatly.

∿∿

In a room farther back were full-sized pens. Some of the dogs were half grown, chewing bones and toys and barking. Here it was very noisy. Saint Bernards. Rottweilers. Retrievers. Isabel shook her head. Again, the manager took out his notepad.

Puppy, Isabel scrawled on it.

"Puppy?" The manager shook his head.

Isabel took the pad again, wrote: *Big dog.* She underlined the word "big," and wrote after it, "puppy." She did not want to elaborate.

"House," she wrote.

"Oh," the manager said. "*That* kind of big. You mean, like to keep burglars away or—" He made a face, his lips pulled back over his teeth, and growled. "Like that?" he said and laughed. "A guard dog, you mean?"

Isabel nodded. Yes.

~~~

Isabel stopped to adjust the knapsack. The pack was heavy, but the puppy had settled down, finally, and she had regained her sense of balance. It was late afternoon and cooler. She had taken her shoes off and was walking barefoot. The sand underfoot was damp and packed in around her toes, felt nice. She moved within sight of the fat, loamy lip on the right side of the road. Now and then she stopped to poke at it with her cane. You son of a bitch, she said to herself. She knew if she sat down, there would be no getting up. She would fall onto her back, and the puppy would squirm out and away, but she would not let that happen.

She thought of the boy—dark, chocolate eyes, copper face, and wry, bashful smile.

"I got a joke," he liked to say.

The puppy turned in the knapsack. Isabel swung from side to side. The puppy seemed to like that. He was such a happy animal that she was tempted to keep him, was tempted not to think about Rory, his sister, and their father, Charlie.

She lifted her head to see how far she had to go. A turn to the left, then around a stand of birch, and she could rest. Maybe.

~~~

The boy shuffled along, his head down. He kicked bits and pieces of things, knocked a pinecone out of the sand, then chased it. He had a pubescent gangliness about him that charmed Isabel. His legs were long, and he kicked the pinecone and darted after it, all legs and arms and big feet. When he saw Isabel, he stopped, stood blinking, then thumped down beside her.

"Whatcha doin' out here?" he said.

Isabel shrugged. She could barely move. Her good leg throbbed, and her mouth was dry, and a high-pitched whine bothered her now.

"Charlie's gonna be down in Chicago," Rory said. "Maybe I can come over?"

Isabel reached for his hand.

She shook herself. Dreams stretched into the quiet spaces. Peke, her husband, joking with her in that wry way of his. "Come on, Isabel," he said. "You're actin' like you've got a whole band of pukwanjinini fightin' in that head of yours. Just let one side win, okay?"

She motioned for Rory to close his eyes. It was something she'd done a hundred times. She liked to give him things: knickknacks, cookies, Peke's carvings. Peke had loved the boy and his sister.

Isabel slipped the pack off her shoulders. It came down on the road with a bump, and the puppy shot out, tail wagging, chewing at her hand, all excitement. She got hold of him under the rib cage, the bones there tiny, the skin loose with fat, the hair sleek.

"What is it?" Rory said.

With a decisive turn, Isabel set the puppy in Rory's lap. He opened his eyes wide and put his hands around it. He looked up at her, thrilled. One of his eyes was slightly higher than the other, fragile-looking.

"Aw, jeez!" he said.

The puppy licked the boy's face and clawed at him. Rory pressed the puppy to his chest. But just as quickly he frowned.

"Charlie won't let me keep him," he said.

Isabel poked at the puppy and it gnawed her finger. A husky mix, his teeth were already sharp and nearly cut her; his eyes were watchful and intelligent. His claws, in the store, had made a hard clattering in his cage.

The dog between them, Isabel tried to form the words in her mouth. She took a stick from behind her.

"Don't show," she scratched in the sand.

"How?" Rory said.

Isabel nodded. She turned to face him and did not smile.

"Yours," she wrote.

She pressed the puppy down in his lap, the dog whimpering and snapping playfully. She poked the stick into the sand, working herself up to it. The boy sensed something strange. It was as if a cloud had passed over the sun, casting them in shadow.

"Big dog," Isabel wrote. "Char—"

She pressed the stick down so hard it snapped in two. The boy gave a little shudder, his eyes narrowing, but then he laughed, as if he'd gotten it wrong.

Isabel looked away. There, it was done.

"Jeez," the boy said. "Can I really keep him? I'm gonna call him George," he said.

Isabel smiled.

∿∿∿

It was when they'd nearly reached the cabin that Isabel's head began to pound something awful, big red drums and black stars. Rory had his shoulder under her, and they went up the road to the cabin. He had tethered the dog out where he slept at night when Charlie was drinking, an old pump shed with a creek nearby. Rory would work out the rest, she thought, and leaned against him. The cabin loomed up ahead. Rory struggled under her.

"Isabel," Rory said, "are you okay?" She felt a little lighter. "Isabel?" Rory said.

They climbed the cabin steps, the broad red siding aglow. The porch roof stretched strangely high, then came back and over her like a lid. She'd lost her glasses and her shoes and her cane, but that didn't matter.

"Over here," Rory said. "Here. Sit down."

His voice had risen. He was trying to be calm, an adult, but his voice gave him away. She wanted to reassure him. It's all right, Rory, she wanted to say. He eased her down into her rocker. He tried to pull away from her, but she clutched his arm, squeezed hard, and he ran from the porch.

"Hey! Hey, *anybody!*" he shouted. "Hey!"

Isabel settled in her chair. The leaves in the maples were beautiful. The air coming up from the lake was cool, reedy-smelling.

The pounding in her head was deafening.

The boy would understand later, she thought. Then she slid her useless leg under the chair, let her head drop between her battered knees, and offered herself up.

∿∿∿

Back in New Hampshire, I gave notice of my resignation, sold or gave away all I couldn't take with me, packed up, and left within days.

Night, darkness outside, hour after hour, I drove west on I-80, concrete like a ribbon, dotted yellow line running under the hood of the van. Was *that* the straw I'd seen in the dream? The rope that stretched down to the bottom of that dry well?

I worked the van's big wheel this way and that.

I remembered that evening so long ago, Peke leaning close and whispering, "What's your story, huh?" Just then I saw that one chapter of my life had ended and another had begun. I belonged back with my people.

I had a school to run, for kids like Rory and his sister, a place for them to go to.

I had some stories to tell them.

Maybe they'd even listen.

14

(1983) ON AN OTHERWISE ORDINARY
Friday morning in November, John Crow Jr., a
stunted boy with coal-black eyes, burst into my office, slamming the
door so hard that I came out of my chair like a jack-in-the-box. We
stood, staring, my desktop between us—clutter of books, broken
lamp, and my $8.95 Thrifty coffeemaker, which once again had
burned my coffee.

"Sit," I said in my most imperious voice, motioning to the chair
to the right of my desk.

He did that. The clock on my desk ticked sonorously; the cof-
feemaker let go a ruined, steamy *oafff!*; far off, the bells of Saint An-

drew's rang. I was trying to collect myself. Every second or two John lurched forward in his seat, anxious to pitch this new and oh-so-exciting trouble at me.

Just to be safe, I made him wait.

∿∿∿

I have said it was an ordinary morning, but at our school near pandemonium was ordinary. As usual I'd just been trying to get through it, phone ringing, visits from teachers, complaints. It's too hot. It's too cold. Where are those atlases we ordered? And now, too, this morning, the building inspector was coming, which had me in a state of terror.

There wasn't a pipe in that old building that didn't contain lead. The wiring was standard Stone Age, the wall switches made of some kind of Bakelite Sir Isaac Newton had probably invented. Worst of all, the furnace, a big octopus of a thing in the basement, was wheezing its last gasps, which came to us, upstairs, as mysterious sighs and odd smells, so that we kept the windows open a crack.

At my desk I was trying, as best I could, to ignore all that. I had on a huge sweater that a cousin of mine had woven of dog hair; it itched. For those who had complained about their cold classrooms, I thought, *You're* cold? You should try the office! Light slanted in through the windows behind my desk, winter-crisp, that hint of blue in it. I drank cup after cup of coffee, cringed at the fiscal report I was preparing.

We had been at the once Melrov Hat Factory too long. The heating bills alone were killing us, sure as Custer.

Every morning, driving east from Minneapolis, I was greeted by the big black bowler painted on the side of the building, which, on better days, I thumbed my nose at.

The Melrov was drafty and noisy, and something in the walls

made voices echo. The hallways were too narrow, and the ceilings weren't quite level.

I tried not to hate it too much, since I'd sold my allotment up at Turtle Lake to get it. And, too, I'd breathed the place alive, brought that boy down, Rory, our first student, which had been a gamble, since that dog Isabel got him had nearly killed his father.

What kind of boy would do something like that? people said, would sic a vicious dog on his father? I let them think the worst. How much more a miracle, then, that he got into Dartmouth, and just after his sixteenth birthday? (So what that Isabel had told me he was as sharp as Peke had been once? So what that I had tutored him to the limit of my endurance?)

Almost overnight our school had grown to bursting. All Indian kids.

Directions? Come on out. It's a snap, I told them. Take Hudson Road east; when you see a place with a black bowler on the side, you've found it.

That building, like the hat on its side, was a bit of a joke.

So I had mixed feelings.

∿∿∿

John Crow slid toward me in his chair; he had a fine-boned, expressive face. He was blinking with both eyes, trying to contain his excitement.

I added up a column of figures in that fiscal report. John kicked at the floor. When he stopped, I looked up. "All right," I said, "what is it?"

John gave me a big, winning smile.

"*Fire!*" he shouted.

∿∿∿

I broke the glass in the alarm box outside my office; a hellish honking filled the building. Twelve teachers burst into those too narrow hallways, one hundred forty-three students. I ran from room to room, beginning on the third floor. Now there was thick, oily smoke. Through a window I looked out; in the parking lot teachers were counting heads, while here and there the boys, bright as colored confetti, played a crude form of touch tag.

One of our teachers, Lorraine, ran across the lot, her arms out; something like electricity ran up my back, prickling. "It's Trudy," she shouted.

I charged into the hallway and up those queer stairs; fell, picked myself up. Ran into room 302, Lorraine's classroom, circumscribing the walls—Christmas trees, elves, and thirty-one turtles, a crudely written name on each.

The floor was hot. The sprinklers cut in, producing a veritable rainstorm.

I dug through the cupboards. There was a sink in the back of the room, and I looked under it: Windex, Comet, a pipe snake. I ran around to the clothes closet. Jackets, boots—red, yellow, and black. Then I faced the classroom. Smoke as thick as cotton filled the room,

"*Gi'dub'ena!*" I shouted, in the old language. "*Are you here?*"

Broom closet. Under the teacher's desk in the front of the room. Tearing through the waste bin. I couldn't stop coughing. Had to crouch now. Fire shot up the hallway, an orange tongue. I'd looked everywhere. I went to the windows to go out, but couldn't do it. Wouldn't. That girl was somewhere.

There was a toy locker, not much bigger than a filing cabinet, in the far corner of the room. I crawled on my hands and knees to it, threw the lid open.

Huddled inside it was Trudy.

"Come out," I said. And she did.

"Climb on my back," I said, and she did that.

We went through the window backside first. A power conduit ran the height of the building. I clung to it as I climbed down past that black derby.

I felt something on my legs. A blast of hot air and smoke made my skirt billow.

I saw now, climbing down, a television crew in the parking lot, black-jacketed, in red hats, like vultures. One of them, an oafish, mustachioed cowboy journalist, shoved a camera in my face as soon as Trudy and I were on the ground.

I stooped to pick up a length of two-by-four that had been lying there in the lot for months and smacked the lens right off that journalist's camera.

~~~

At my apartment at the Fair Oaks, I would pick up the phone and, without even listening to a hello, slam it back down. The phone wouldn't stop ringing. I got requests for interviews, crank calls, even threats.

"You *deserve* to burn, timber niggers," one caller had said.

There'd been a picture in the *Star and Trib,* my name under it.

I was mortified. In that news photo, I saw a woman coming down what looked like a drainpipe, a monkey in a dress on her back. The woman's skirt billowed up, her panties showing in firelight—panties that crimped a bit, making me look fleshier than I am.

But the worst of it was that I was waiting for someone to notice what seemed all too apparent to me: I had been wearing the panties Betty'd sent me. They were always the last pair I wore, and the signal that laundry would follow the morning after. (They were one hundred percent cotton, and comfortable. How could I throw them away?) It was bad enough that they were white, that with the dark background and all, they (and I) gave new meaning to the word "moon."

But that wasn't all: in that photograph, if you looked closely, you could just make out—or was it only me, since I knew?—in black letters, the words "Hot Stuff!"

There it was, for everybody to see. Betty's joke.

∿∿∿

First thing, when I reconnected my phone, my mother called.

"Why didn't you tell me?" she said. "You have a fire at your school and you're almost—"

I put my hand on my forehead. "I wasn't almost anything, Mom," I said. My mother rambled on. I was waiting for her to say something about the picture. "I thought we'd been getting along better lately," she said, a tone of accusation in her voice.

"Give me the phone," Betty said, in the background. "Let me talk some sense to her."

"Bye, Mom," I said.

∿∿∿

I got a card from Trudy's mother. "Thank you and God bless," it read. On the front was a picture of a shooting star over a cobalt-blue background.

Or was it a falling star?

∿∿∿

That same afternoon Stuart Rice, who'd helped fund the school through the Big Grassy Tribal Council, called to tell me our insurance had gone belly up.

"Our adjuster told me our building inspector should have nixed that furnace."

I stood at the window trying to make sense of it. A woman in a stylish mink coat, her daughter skipping beside her, went past on the sidewalk.

"Listen," Stuart said, "I'll call you back. I'll talk to some people and see what I can do."

I was inconsolable. Was drowning in self-accusation. I was carried by currents here and there, all of which amounted to one thing: pain. I poked food into my mouth, or didn't. Microwaved dinners, not meant to be microwaved. Watched old Clark Gable movies I got from Psychedelic Pizza, a video place down the block. Went on a date with David, who lived in the unit opposite mine.

In front of my door, he kissed me, but I didn't respond.

"Did I say something wrong?" he asked.

How could I explain to him that just then I felt worse than nothing?

By then I'd taken to driving for whole days when I couldn't stand my apartment any longer. I circled block after block of east Minneapolis. Abandoned stores, factories with broken windows, automotive places, empty and fit for nothing.

A week passed like that, days of nearly comatose driving.

Christmas was around the corner. I slept less, drove more.

One evening I made a wrong turn just off Franklin. I was aware of a strange sensation. The night grew wide with darkness, a kind of magic in it. Everywhere were pine-green wreaths, yellow and blue and red Christmas lights, golden bells, red ribbons.

I turned up a street to my right. A dead end.

"Shit," I said, then stopped, hunching over the wheel, trying to see better.

In the distance I saw Cyclone fencing, a sign, crude red lettering on white background. I couldn't read it, so drove closer. Something hulked there. Immense. The tires scrackled in the cold snow.

For Lease, the sign said.

I put the van in Park and, pulling on my mittens, hat, and scarf, got out.

A boardwalk careened up and through a closed gate in the fence to an old school, the kind they built around the turn of the century. Red brick, pitched roof, high ceilings, and tall windows. Some kind of renovation had been under way, piles of lumber here and there, new windows, each with a cheerful yellow decal.

A hunched figure came out of one of the houses up the block. He was a big-chested man, wearing a straw hat, cocked at a friendly angle. He crushed his cigarette out under his brown corduroy slipper.

We stood there, taking in some air.

"Aren't you cold?" I said.

He shrugged, looked at me askance, then glanced at the school.

"Couple lawyers bought that place, gutted it, then backed out. Didn't like the neighborhood," he said. "Be nice if someone could set up school again. Now it's just a crack house."

The moon lifted over the roof, big as hope itself. Far off a dog barked. It was a vision I saw there, how that school came clear out of the dark.

I got all choked up. "How did you know to come out?" I said.

He chuckled. "Oh, thought you all might want to know what you're getting into here," he said. "But now I see it's just fine."

∿∿∿

I wanted that school, wanted it bad. It was one tall drink of water, and I was thirsty. I woke the following morning at four. I had the names of the construction company and the Realtor. Pacing in my apartment, I ate Pop-Tarts, jamming them into my mouth whole, then, disgusted with myself, polished off the ice cream in my freezer, two pints of Rocky Road.

The hands on the clock over my stove moved so slowly they seemed to grow into each minute.

I dialed the Realtor at seven-thirty.

"I told you *not* to call anymore, Larry," a woman said. "I love you, but you're—"

I was so surprised I set the receiver down. Then, just as quickly, picked it up, dialed again.

"We've been through this a hundred times," the woman continued. "We don't like the same clothes, the same *shopping places,* the same *movies.* I mean, why *foreign* films? Do I have to read *subtitles,* for God's sake, every time I go to a movie? And I *hate* that car of yours, and your house . . . I could *never* live in Robbinsdale . . ."

She paused.

"Is this Eckles Realtors?" I asked.

"Yes, it is," the woman said, her voice winding into itself. "We're closed," she said, and hung up.

I called again at eight.

"Are you open now?"

"No," the woman said.

∿∿∿

"What do you mean, I've got to assume construction costs to get the lease?" I said.

In a tone as snooty as you please, this Vicky gave me the figure again.

I tried not to let her hear me gasp.

"You won't need to talk with one of our agents, will you?" she said.

∿∿∿

I paced in my apartment. Spun out scheme after scheme. I'd sell the van, drive up to Mystic Lake, and make a killing at the casino. I'd win the Publishers Clearinghouse drawing, the one I'd been suckered into, had bought a year's subscription to *Popular Electronics* to enter. I'd sell . . .

But I had nothing left to sell. I went through my trade bead collection: cobalt blue, teal, and amber glass; old silver trade tokens; handmade charms. Now it all seemed like so much junk.

As a last resort I got out my credit cards, tallied my usable credit. Maybe I could play a little credit-card bingo, as Betty called it?

But no, they were all, to the last card, near the limit; I'd bought all those new jackets and boots for our students, trusting some seasonal windfall to cover the cost.

Finally I called Stuart Rice.

We talked about the unseasonably cold weather. The Polar Bear Club and what a bunch of crazy guys they were, hey? I knotted the phone cord around my neck, made faces at myself in the mirror above my dresser. I laughed like a hyena at some awful joke of his, went off on some tangent about wild rice, how the market had been ruined by California growers, trying to bring the conversation around to the subject I dreaded.

"Aja," Stuart said, cutting me off. "If I could just get people to listen, I might be able to do something. But you know how it is this time of year. How much do you need?"

"Never mind," I said.

Minutes later that old horned serpent herself called.

"Just say the word," Betty said, "and I'll go to town for you." I imagined a scaly tail wrapping itself around my neck and squeezing.

I was sure Stuart had called her.

Then my mother called. I picked at a muffin, let the answering machine take the message.

"Darling," she said, "I know you're suffering. I know you. I know you're listening. Just pick up the phone. Can you do that?"

I heard her sigh.

"All right. But, darling, just don't do anything desperate, all right?

"Please?"

In my dreams that night I wrestled with underwater demons. The darkness itself seemed to breathe. I swam across a bottomless lake.

I shuddered, woke drenched in sweat time and again.

Finally I put on my coat and went outside, the bitter cold air a reassuring slap in the face.

I think better when I'm moving, so I walked up Third, toward downtown, a light snow falling. I was thinking how ridiculous I'd been. From the first: My school, My teachers, My kids.

What had I thought I was doing? I was ridiculous. What could I have expected? After all, who did I think I was, Kwasind? That old doomed hero of legend?

I kicked at that snow, threw my arms wide, ran a loopy circle under a streetlight, climbed a snowbank.

Who could run the fastest? Kwasind, in a flash of powerful legs. Who was the greatest hunter? Kwasind, with his bow. On and on it went, Kwasind surpassing them all.

But to what end? I stopped clowning. Thinking of Kwasind was suddenly more than sobering.

I looked around me: dark trees, dry, ashy smell of new snow.

Yes, Kwasind beat them all.

And then, in that old story, it had snowed. It snowed for twelve days. All day, all night, the snow came down, heavy blue-white snow, and with it came Peboan, the west wind, haughty and threatening, looking for challengers.

The snow swirled and eddied, crested, drifted as high as the rooftops.

People stayed inside. They would wait out the storm, hungry.

But not Kwasind. He took up his bow and arrows, and ventured out into the blizzard, killed twenty deer and slung them over his shoulders, and like that, singing "Who is the greatest, who is the greatest hunter of them all?" marched toward camp.

Out in the trees were the pukwanjinini, the little people. It was their task to aid man—as well as, at other times, to play tricks.

What could they do with one like Kwasind near? What purpose did they have in life?

And who was Kwasind to challenge Peboan? Was Kwasind a god after all?

They would find out. Kwasind's power was in the crown of his head. The little people would test him. In the snow they made merry atop two crags where the path wound by. Kwasind came striding toward them. "Who is the greatest hunter?" he sang, paying no attention to the pukwanjinini. "Who is the greatest archer of all?"

As Kwasind passed, the pukwanjinini, laughing and dancing, dropped white pine seeds from atop the crag. One fell on the crown of Kwasind's head.

Just the lightest of all things, as light as a snowflake, a pine seed. Kwasind fell dead.

∿∿∿

Just short of the Eleventh Avenue bridge I stopped to watch the snow fall. It fell noiselessly, laying a blanket over the city, a hush in it, so that I was reminded of one of those winter scenes inside a glass ball.

Yellow taxis, exhaust rising like tails behind their bumpers, shuttled people home.

In some homes, lights were on, warm and inviting.

A fire rig, returning from some unpleasant errand, its engine muffled by the snow, rumbled by.

Right then I turned toward my apartment, a spring, not unlike hope, in my legs. Snowflakes schooled and spun around streetlights, lively as minnows. I felt buoyed up, as I hadn't in some time.

That fire rig had me thinking. I'd been proud not to use that moment, Trudy and I coming down from that burning school building, and the attention that followed, for my kids. I'd been selfish. So what that I'd looked foolish descending that conduit? So what that I'd shown my backside? So what that it'd been a bigger moon in all that darkness than I'd ever wanted it to be?

Hot Stuff!

I grinned to myself, kicking through that light snow.

You bet.

〰〰

The following morning, a day so cold that rainbow crystals hung in the air, I bought rolls of construction paper a yard wide, and in my apartment, singing to myself, I crudely drew, for a decorative sash, thunderbirds, their wings spread wide in a kind of ecstasy. I drew Hare, fire on his back, bringing light to man; Pikwak, lovable old turtle, who bore the earth on his shell; pukwanjinini, the laughing, teasing little people.

I called Stuart. I was throwing a party at the new school, I told him. Why not move things from the projects gymnasium, make an event of it?

"This is a joke, right?" Stuart said.

"It's no joke," I told him.

〰〰

There, at that vacant school on Twenty-fifth and Franklin, I was a traffic cop. Vans, heavy to bursting, bumped in over the fence I had knocked down just hours before.

Inside I'd put the decorated sash I'd made up on the walls as a kind of welcome.

Now everyone came, with food, with streamers, with lights, with an enormous tree. Brick-colored faces, bright eyes. It was a miracle. A wonder. A gift! We moved inside the school, laughing, joking. There was a huge fireplace and a Franklin stove. The Thunders drove down to the river bottom for wood in Stuart's souped-up and now cheerfully noisy pickup.

The Highclouds, in the front yard, piled deadwood, for a bonfire. One gaggle of children after another raced through the cafeteria and back out, threw snowballs, chased one another up the hill in back, then rolled down, laughing in voices as bright as bells.

Still more cars lumbered in. We hung green-and-red crepe paper streamers. Decorated the tree. Lit candles, hung dream catchers.

Everyone swooned over the tall windows, the broad hallways, the immense high-ceilinged gymnasium.

"How'd you do it, Aja?" they said. "It's *wonderful*." I just smiled.

It got all warm in there. Smelled of fresh pine boughs and woodsmoke. We had no working cookstove, so the Standing Rocks brought over a big propane tank and a range, right out of their kitchen.

"Hell, wasn't nothing," George said. "We'll get another."

When we were ready, there was venison stew with hot potatoes, fry bread, and wild rice, served from huge pots, and ten kinds of cakes in oblong pans. Odinigun gave a blessing.

We ate. We chowed. We feasted.

It was pandemonium, a choir, a song. Rattle of crockery. Hum of conversation. The Rassmussen Thunders, the Finedays, the Morrisons. Thirty, fifty, one hundred twenty kids I counted. Men ducked out to get more food. The older men, white-haired and stooped, had set up a table and were playing bugesewin.

As I swung by the table, their game caught me up short. They were playing with those hand-carved pieces my mother had told me about, from the River Flats. Cars of manufacturers long defunct,

Franklins, Pierce Arrows, Packards; tiny homes; rabbits, beavers, deer. All of them charms of a sort, every last one a wish.

Stuart, from across the room, gave me a hard, sharp look.

I looked back, the same.

Aja, Peke had said, be bold. I wouldn't let him down now.

In the middle of the dinner, I went outside. Jim, the man who'd come out that night I'd stumbled on the school, as he'd promised, was standing there. It was eight-thirty. The sky was dark, the stars out, twinkling.

High, bright laughter carried out to us.

I'd called a road-construction company earlier, rented those white-and-red sawhorse barricades. We'd set them up at the end of the block. I checked that all of them were still standing.

I watched everyone through the windows, warm light, candle glow.

"Looks nice," Jim said.

"Why don't you come in?" I asked.

"I'll come in later," he told me, nodding. "This is your night now."

I took a deep breath. It was such a beautiful picture, I hated to spoil it.

"You ready?" Jim said, chuckling. He would make the call from his house.

"As ready as I ever will be," I said.

"Just remember what you're after," he said and, winking, added, "keep your eyes on the prize, right?"

∿∿∿

The KSTP Crime Stoppers van arrived. Bright lights, cameras ready. I thrilled to see that fattish journalist—the one who'd poked his camera in my face—doing his best to be obnoxious when the cops pulled up, cherry lights flashing, and knocked down the barricades.

It was an ugly scene. A bullhorn. Shouting. Cops tugging at people who wouldn't move.

We'd just gotten the bonfire going, and we were all standing in a circle around it, singing, the children closest to the fire.

"What the hell is going on?" Stuart said, glaring at me.

"I'll take care of it," I told him.

I walked out into the lights, blinded. A policeman grabbed my arm and bent it around my back. It hurt so bad I felt my eyes cross.

Gene Highcloud came out from the circle, looking as big as a windigo and meaning business.

"Go back, Gene," I said.

"Break it up," another policeman was calling on a bullhorn. "Disperse. You are trespassing on private property. Disperse at once."

No one left. They gathered in tighter around the bonfire and sang. What were the police going to do? Spray us with fire hoses, use tear gas on us?

But Gene Highcloud just had to come over. One of the policemen lashed out at him with a nightstick. Gene grabbed it and just held it. "Stop it," Gene said.

The fat journalist put his camera on us; the policeman let go of my arm. Around the fire, they were singing an old song: "*Ina'kone',* the flame goes up, *awinegi'cig,* beautiful as a star.*"

"What do you think you're doing here?" the officer in charge of the operation said.

I took a deep breath. I was terrified. My legs threatened to buckle under me.

I reached out for that journalist's hand and, like that, led him and his crew into the circle, the policemen behind us.

~~~

We made the ten o'clock news. A five-minute spot. I let Stuart do all the talking while I sort of faded in with the others, until they took me away to the police station.

There were pictures in the *Star and Trib* the following morning. An attorney offered us his services, gratis.

Cards and letters came in: five dollars, one dollar, ten dollars, fifty cents.

All those little people, all those big hearts. The letters came in for weeks.

We signed an elaborate lease and got to work.

∿∿∿

My mother called just after we moved into the new school. I was in my office. The place was a mess—papers everywhere, smell of fresh pine and wet plaster, saws whining in the background, carpenters going by in the hallway, file cabinets gaping, a Mr. Coffee gurgling on my desk. Nina was rambling on about the weather, the sun dogs we'd had.

"I gotta go, Mom," I said, and hung up.

The phone rang again. "Hello, Little Red—"

There was a scuffling on the other end. I heard a kind of angry wheezing. "Oh, so you're *there* now," Betty said.

"Where did you think I'd be?" I said.

"Maybe in Stillwater Prison," Betty shot back. "That was some stunt you pulled."

"Why don't you get to the point?" I said.

"Think you're pretty hot stuff, huh?" Betty replied. "I mean, you think nobody noticed your panties, Ms. Fancy Britches? Miss Hot Stuff. You don't think people had a laugh at that? You don't think people are a little angry? And just what the hell were you going to do if it all went south on you? Huh? What then? What if it had all gone wrong?"

My mother was saying something to Betty in the background. Listening, I felt duplicitous, guilty, reckless. I knew there was something almost sick in how I'd gone about things.

"Are you listening?" Betty said.

"Yes," I said.

And as Betty was cutting me down to size—how I'd looked fat on the TV, how TV always made you look heavier, how I'd put Stuart on the spot, how we'd all looked like a bunch of ragamuffins, the kids in all those secondhand clothes—I began to hear something else in her tirade.

"I mean," Betty said, "just *what* if that lawyer pal of yours *hadn't* stepped in? What then? I mean, just what did you think you were going to do? Do you know what we felt like, watching them take you away? Do you? *We were going crazy up here.* I mean, where do you think that lawyer and bail money came from?"

Her voice had risen, shrill. I'd never in all my life heard her sound like that. So . . . *hurt.*

Something broke in me, layer after layer after layer. I bent into it, falling and falling and falling until her voice caught me up. A buoy in all that water.

"I mean, *Aja*," Betty cried, unable to hide her concern any longer, "*just what were you thinking?*"

15

(1987) I MET BENJAMIN GRUNFELD AT
the water fountain in the Hennepin County
Courthouse in downtown Minneapolis, during the hearing of *Minnesota v. White Earth*. I use the word "met" loosely, as we had been glaring at each other for the better part of a month and had said more than a few cutting things to each other. Perhaps it would be more accurate to say that we came within striking distance.

Alone together in the hallway now, after all that time, we regarded each other with a certain good-humored hostility.

"You first," Benjamin said.

"No, you go ahead," I replied.

There seemed to be an almost theatrical antipathy between us, a stiltedness, with me playing Hepburn to his Tracy, and it embarrassed us. Bowing and dipping, moving closer to the fountain, I couldn't help myself, and he couldn't seem to, either.

It had been a long and hard month. I had, with the help of a nasty, shortish lawyer in polyester plaid, argued for the return of what I knew to be fraudulently purchased allotments. The tribal council had asked me to go to bat for them, and I had; Benjamin, representing the state and Department of Natural Resources interests, had maintained that the allotment sales should be upheld.

The case had been leaning toward the state's favor until this very morning, when I'd thrown a monkey wrench into the works: Herman Oshogay, who'd held title to a majority of the acres in contention, I claimed, had an estranged son, Gabriel. An heir.

It was as if a bomb had been dropped on the proceedings. An adjournment was called. Papers fluttered out of briefcases.

"What the hell do you think you're doing?" my lawyer had whispered fiercely.

"I'm going out to get a drink," I'd said.

Now, bowing, I motioned to the fountain. Benjamin smiled.

"I insist," I said.

"I defer," Benjamin said.

The fountain, that fifties green, gurgled. A slow stream of water escaped from under the bent lever where one was to drink. I liked his cologne. Nemesis, I thought, just to get things clear. He was not about to budge, but then, neither was I.

"Charming," I said.

"Isn't it," Benjamin replied, and with that, I strode off down the hallway.

ᨓᨓ

On Sunday morning of that week, at the Rainbow Café, I had my head buried in the *Tribune*. I was perusing the classifieds, on the lookout for bargains. It was a habit of mine, almost reflex, after years of keeping Little Red afloat. I tallied debits and credits, tapped the tabletop with my pen, worked columns of intimidating figures.

The Prideaux kids needed jackets. Could I get Louise, a rich old lady I knew, to spring for them? The sinks in the faculty lounge were a wreck. The van needed . . . what? Everything, including an engine. Here was an ad: "400 Chev Holly, Muncie w/high-stall speed converter, $75."

The price was right, but the last ruined it. Only a motorhead would want a high-stall speed converter, which meant the engine was shot. I ran my finger down the column: 283, 305, 307, 327—all small block. The van needed a big block. I took in other columns. Fluorescent fixtures. Kitchen supplies. Office furniture.

A blue plate special steamed seductively in front of me: two eggs over easy, hash browns, white toast, and a slice of steak. Blackberry, strawberry, and kiwi jam.

I hummed, jotting prices and phone numbers in my notebook, relishing the moment. It was all before me: the length of Sunday morning, breakfast, the paper, and a bottomless cup of the Rainbow's finest. Work that got something accomplished, turned the gears, which would keep Monday rolling, which kept Tuesday rolling and on into—

But Monday was an eternity away now, and working, I could guiltlessly enjoy myself—except for an occasional bolt of shock at what I'd done. I had no idea if Gabriel was alive or where he might be. It was a wild card I'd thrown, a bluff.

Otherwise, bliss: alone, free, at the Rainbow.

I took a bite of my eggs. Salt, creamy rich yolk, a corner of toast with it. I shook the paper out flat. Kitchen sounds, hiss of griddle. Soothing, someone else cooking. Tire sales. I calculated size, diameter, sidewall height. Did the van take an M sidewall or an H? If a troublesome thought popped into my head, I forced it out with calculation. But now one stuck.

I was aware of being watched.

There was the heavy thump of someone sitting down across from me in the booth. Outrageous! I buried my face in the paper. I was tempted to just kick at whoever it was, and hard. I stared into that newspaper. The gall of it! Newsprint swam in a sea of gray, too close. A piece of him showed under the paper. Navy sweater, jeans. I didn't want to deal with whoever it was, but the thought of bifocals was worse—I couldn't read now; the paper was too close.

"Yes?" I said, dropping the paper suddenly.

"Hi," Benjamin said.

"Ah . . ." I grinned, thinking that my morning was ruined. What did he want now? Could he possibly think I'd talk to him? And, to my surprise, I was also thinking, suddenly and with a rush of blood to my face: Is my makeup all right? Is there egg on my mouth? Will he think I'm a pig with all this on my plate? Go away, I was thinking. And, too, I was thinking, Kiss him. He's beautiful.

Not in those words, exactly, but like that. A flash. I imagined that, kissing him. Jesus! What was that all about?

"What do you want?" I said.

He shrugged. Picked up the saltshaker. Dashed some into his palm and rubbed it off over the ashtray. Nervous. What did he have to be nervous about? He had fucking City Hall behind him. He smelled of something nice. He had a long face and those sharp features I was attracted to. Big blue eyes.

"I just want to know one thing."

I shrugged.

"Why did you wait so long?" he said. "To make your pitch, I mean, bring up the kid like that."

"Why did I wait?"

I took a bite of my eggs. My heart was hammering, but I played nonchalant.

Why had I made them wait? Bringing Gabriel into it had, after all, occurred to me earlier. Just thinking about it was beginning to make me feel more than a little angry. Or did I feel more . . . frustration? *Why?* I thought.

Because the state had made us wait since 1978 for a hearing, and then wanted us to be in court on a week's notice. Because people's lives depended on this silly courtroom drama. Eminent domain? More like eminent theft. I had not liked the dismissiveness of the other state attorneys, and I wanted to stick it to the sons of bitches. Because Calmenson Paper had been involved, that land robber and rapist, and I'd come to hate that company more than just about anything. Because I needed time now, and badly.

And because . . . I just felt like it.

Or was it, I realized, because I'd been watching Benjamin, had enjoyed looking at him, all those weeks? But no. No, I thought, that was just something that had been there. Like fine furniture or well-made lamps.

I smiled for him. A not altogether mean smile. He was handsome in an odd sort of way. Kind of eccentric-looking, but I liked that. Interesting. Benjamin studied me studying him.

"I know *you don't like lawyers*," he said. "It's like this—what do carp and lawyers have in common?"

I grimaced.

"They're both bottom feeders," he said. "Does that kind of hit the nail on the head?"

"Bingo," I said, but I found myself laughing.

Bingo. What was I saying? A waitress stopped by and filled my cup.

"You didn't answer my question," Benjamin said.

I put my face back in my paper. Benjamin hooked his finger over the top and bent it down, peering in at me with those big blue eyes. "Well?"

"Maybe I don't intend to tell you."

I set the paper down, sipped at my coffee. Things were somehow . . . delicious. I felt engaged in the moment in a way I couldn't then explain. Benjamin set his chin in his palm, studying me from across the table. His eyes had flecks of warm brown in them, were set deep in his face.

"I think what we have here is a failure to communicate," he said.

"*Cool Hand Luke.*"

"You like movies?"

"Is this a friendly chat we're having now?" I said. "Or is it business?"

"What do *you* think?" Benjamin asked.

"You tell me."

"I asked you first."

I took a deep breath and, thinking, This has gone on long enough, regarded Benjamin with all the warmth of a stone. But my eyelid twitched. Go away. Come closer. I couldn't get that earlier thought of kissing him out of my head. Go away. No, come closer. I blinked.

No, I thought. I don't need another complication in my life.

"I'll scream," I said. "Really I will," and Benjamin excused himself.

～～～

Back then I liked to take walks. Long walks. Whole afternoons when time and circumstance permitted or when things got to be too trying at Little Red. I would put on my coat and hat if it was cold, and I would walk east down Franklin to the river, and there I'd take the paths bordering the Mississippi.

Usually I was so wound up that I would charge along for an hour or two, problems colliding in my head, impossible combinations. Should we cut the breakfast program for those kids who couldn't afford even a subsidized program, or could we do without heat? Or should we go after another sponsor—which would mean *my* finding one. (Stuart, after I used him that night to throw my pitch, had told me, "You do the talking next time.") And what were those suspicious bruises on that kid's legs? And why had the freezer up and quit?

Now, in late November, the afternoon light fading, I was thinking about that freezer. Had the condenser burned out this time? Did it need Freon? Or had the pump motor gone south? I was imagining peering into that dusty mess, a flashlight beam cutting the darkness, when a man of considerable height came striding toward me. He was wearing an old pea coat, a heavy maroon muffler, and a hat that had something of the circus about it—rainbow colors, with odd tufts of fur running along the seams. He walked hunched over, a bit of Charles Laughton as Quasimodo, I thought.

I had on my Confederate-gray ice coat, cobalt wool scarf, and immense mittens. How sexy could that be?

We were still some distance apart; I steeled myself to pass him on the path. Running into someone dangerous, in gray light, when I was by myself, had always been a possibility, and I reached into my coat pocket: bird seed for juncos and sparrows, peanuts for the squirrels, and a sawed-off handle of a baseball bat Peke had given me years before.

I drew the persuader, as Peke had called it, ten inches of Louisville Slugger, from my coat, and had it ready at my side. I had my speech prepared: *Bother me, and I'll beat you to death with this club. Is it a deal?*

Just then I recognized him.

"Little stubby for a walking stick, isn't it?" Benjamin joked, stopping a yard or two short of me.

"Does that hat come with batteries?" I replied. "Or is that glow some kind of radiation?"

We sat at opposite ends of a forest-green bench with a shiny brass plaque set in it. I put my mittens in my coat pockets.

"I should really hate you, you know," I said.

"Ditto," Benjamin agreed.

"Want a peanut?"

Benjamin put out his gloved hand. He couldn't get the peanut out of my mitten. I shucked off my mittens, frustrated at the ridiculousness of it. Benjamin had taken off his gloves. Suddenly our hands were intertwined. We drew back, a little shocked. How . . . *warm*.

We laughed.

"Oh, you laugh, too?" Benjamin said.

I let my head drop back, tut-tutting myself. Oh, the silliness of it all. Smiling. What could be the harm? I sensed it might be complicated, felt a mountain there, between us.

"So how's the school?"

"Fine," I replied. But it was not fine. "How's law?"

"The usual," Ben lied.

We huddled awkwardly on that bench. The wind blew in cold gusts. Birds swooped down and pecked at the seed in the grass. There was an icing of snow, and it glittered.

"Cold."

"Yes, it is," I replied.

A bus rumbled by behind us on River Road. Two squirrels chased up and down an oak, zigzagging, tails like crazed brushes, twitching, waving.

Benjamin tossed them the peanuts.

We were very carefully avoiding looking at each other. A kind of longing rushed up in me, something I hadn't felt in . . . I couldn't think how long.

It hurt, wanting again.

"I've got to go," I said, and like that I strode off down the path.

~~~

He left messages on my machine at home: "This is Benjamin. Call me."

Then at work: "This is Publishers Clearinghouse trying to contact Aja Sharrett-Little. You've won a million dollars and we were wondering when it would be convenient for the Prize Patrol to stop by. Give us a call: 555-9677."

He wrote cryptic letters: "Your cover has been blown. Sec. C17C999./6. Reroute courier to Charley's Dining Exceptionale 0.1800 21/11/87. The microfilm is in the Lobster Bisque disguised as peppercorn. Office: 555-7087."

I was not altogether amused.

Benjamin was all wrong for me, I was thinking. He was on the wrong side, for one thing. A condemnation lawyer? Working for the DNR? Eminent domain cases? And he dressed in those strange clothes. A yak hat? A colleague had given it to him, he'd said. Why do you wear it? I'd asked. It puts things in perspective, he'd said.

I understood that.

He'd worn a bow tie in court. Who wore bow ties anymore? And he drove that peculiar car: a Citroën. Which I'd just spotted up the block from the courthouse now.

Instead of walking my usual lunch route, I'd gone in concentric circles, always larger and farther west, until I reached the Hennepin County Courthouse and found that odd car.

I'm crazy, I thought. After all, he irritates me. He's a bug. He's a head case.

I had a sandwich with me, in waxed paper. Roast beef. Just the right amount of horseradish. Whole-wheat bread. I carefully folded the paper back, intending to take a bite, but didn't. In a bag, beside me, was a big kosher pickle; buying it had made me blush.

I checked my watch. Twelve-fifteen. Benjamin usually ate at the House of Saigon, on Eleventh. On other walks I'd seen him go in; I knew he'd have to pass the bus stop and bench to get there. I flattened down my skirt. The conchas in my belt pinched my waist.

Still, I'd be ready. This was a test of sorts. Sitting on the bench, where he would go by, as if it were coincidence. I'd be businesslike about our meeting. I could do that, I thought. Hadn't I gotten tougher? After all I'd done at Little Red? After all I'd lived through? I would take charge. Put this thing in proper perspective. I wouldn't have Benjamin jeopardizing our case.

"Look here," I practiced saying. "State's interest represents treaties abrogated illegally through Clapp Act forfeitures in the twenties. How can you—"

Benjamin came striding up the sidewalk. Suddenly I found it difficult to swallow. I forced myself to sit with my shoulders squared, which forced my breasts against my jacket. So I slumped. That was no good, either. The proximity of the courthouse seemed to throw things into confusion. Immense, high, serious-looking, glass and fancy tiles. Benjamin had come from inside.

Benjamin smiled, a big, gleaming fifty-kilowatt smile. He was in his professional garb, and looked stunning: polished oxfords, navy-blue coat, gray scarf, a maroon weave running through it.

Suddenly my mind was a blank. I managed to get to my feet. I was saying something, but it got cut in half. I started again and it was no better.

So I handed him the sandwich.

"Eat," I said.

He took a big bite, the corners of his eyes wrinkling with pleasure. The bus hissed to a stop, and I got on. Cavern of fluorescent lights, advertisements for shampoo and radio stations, "KDWB Rocks the Cities!" My heart was flopping around in my chest, like an off-balance wash cycle. The door slapped shut, and I thumped down. Warm orange vinyl seat.

Streetlights slid by and around me. My eyes glassed up. I was furious with myself. God almighty, what is wrong with you? I said to myself. The city was tugged away in the wake of the bus.

My heart was racing, but I'd escaped. Oh, yes! Oh, God, yes! And just barely.

~~~

The everyday things in my life seemed precious suddenly. At Little Red I applied myself to the jobs I'd put off since the school's inception: Standing on a high stepladder, I plastered the gymnasium ceiling and painted it a powder blue, even sponged in clouds. Got the kids to draw pukwanjinini, the little people, Trickster, and nambiza, the underwater panthers, on the walls. I grouted the bad mortar in the boys' bathroom on the second floor. I delighted in doing electrical work, the tape coming off the spool with that sticky peeling sound, which was also now disturbingly sexual.

And at night, in my apartment, I cleaned and polished. The marvels of Mop & Glo! I was a convert! I even rented a buffer, polished the floors to such a sheen that when I first crossed them in my furry leather slippers, I fell, somewhat reminded of learning to skate.

Still, I persevered. Order was necessary. I sucked up the dust bunnies with a secondhand vacuum cleaner. I bought Tupperware containers and made stews and soups, all of which I froze. No more MSG-laden microwave dinners for me.

I was clean. I was cool. I was in control. It was a first. A miracle. A wonder.

I threw my weight around at Little Red. That secondhand-refrigeration dealer? He regretted ever having seen me when I was through with him.

And I needed so little sleep!

Yet when my mother, Nina, visited and said, "What's wrong, Aja?" with that sad, beautiful face of hers, it was as if I'd been harpooned.

"What's *wrong?*" I asked.

"Yes."

"*Wrong?*" Just like that, I was on my feet, hands flying every which direction. Something was pushing in there to get out. "After all these years of looking at my place as if it was a wreck," I shouted, "and now it looks like *this,* and you say, 'What's *wrong?*' I'll tell you what's *wrong!* Why don't you let me know when you're going to visit!"

My voice had risen to a shrill pitch. "And what are you doing wearing your shoes in here? The snow melts and drips all over the place! Did you ever think of that? Huh? And those *stupid* maple candies. I *hate* those *goddamn maple candies!* Did you know that?"

Afterward, when I'd finished whirling through the apartment in a rage, I felt confused, even embarrassed.

"I know it's hard living alone," Nina said, and I gritted my teeth.

∿∿∿

"I'm crazy," I said, calling my aunt Betty.

"Crazy about what?"

"Ah, I don't know." I was very nearly in tears. "There's a kid who needs shoes. Half of them need new clothes. One kid's got bruises on his legs, but I can't do anything about it. And I keep thinking about my brother."

"You don't have a brother," Betty said. "You did have a brother."

"I'm soooo depressed," I said.

"What's his name?"

"What?"

"This heartthrob of yours. What's his name?"

"That isn't it."

"It isn't, is it?" Betty chuckled. "Call me when you want to cut out the b.s. I'm busy now."

"Okay," I said, on the phone to Betty again, nearly two weeks later.

"Let's start with his name."

"Ben."

"That's a good name."

"Grunfeld."

"That's good, too," Betty said. "So what's the problem? Do his eyes glow in the dark, or do his knuckles drag on the ground when he walks, or what?"

"No," I said defensively.

"So what's your problem?" Betty asked, and I tried to tell her.

He pushed my buttons, I told her. And badly. I was afraid he'd mess up my work at Little Red.

"Well, it's about time," Betty nearly shouted.

"He's clever."

"Well, what did you want, smarty-pants, a Neanderthal?"

I said he made me feel confused.

"Uh-huh," Betty said. "And sometimes you'd like to slap his pretty face. And you're afraid he won't fit in up here?"

"Sort of."

"Sort of? Like somebody else we know? Like you?"

"Well, all right."

"Well, maybe you'll have to bring him up and see."

"I don't think so," I said.

~~~

He left me flowers on Pearl Harbor Day. His note read: "Nothing funny this time. I'm crazy about you. I surrender. P.S. Some mornings I walk Loring Park."

On Friday of that week I arrived at Little Red and no one met me in the lot. There was something auspicious in that. Snow on the ground, halos circling the streetlights, I waited. I bit my fingernails, which I hadn't done in years. I was early. Some seriously cold weather was around the corner, and I cringed at the thought of trying to find jackets for the kids. Maybe I should shop, I thought. That's how I could use the time. Go down to the Nicollet Mall for winter jackets. Under my feet was frozen mush. I leaned against the fender of my Rambler and smoked a cigarette.

Any second now someone would come running, I thought, but no one did.

A dog barked, far off.

The lights of the office looked inviting. Yellow, warmish, familiar. Work beckoned, ritual.

I got into my car, started it, and drove out of the parking lot.

Anywhere, I thought.

Which turned out to be Loring Park. I walked around the pond until I got tired. Benjamin was nowhere in sight. I dropped down on a bench, hard wood, patina of bright dew.

Sun lifting over the skyline, blocky buildings, my day began to take shape. I would run uptown, buy those gifts; then, at Ragstock, I'd pick up some winter clothes for the Yellowfeather boys; and back at the office I'd call a few more potential sponsors, try to round up a few more dollars.

I felt suddenly very sad and thought I might cry and be unable to stop myself.

I hadn't really thought I'd run into Benjamin, I told myself. Things in my life were stable enough. I was relieved, yet disappointed. I pressed my hands between my knees. Any second I'd have to go. I'd forgotten my gloves, and my hands were cold. It was better this way, I told myself.

In the pond, geese circled, wet and miserable in the gray light.

I reached into my purse. I had my sandwich, the same stupid

sandwich I'd made for the last two months—cashew butter—and I broke it into bits and tossed them to the geese. I always singled out the smallest one and, diverting the others, tried to get him to feed.

"Come on," I nearly cried, surprised at how choked up I'd become. "You *gotta fight*. Don't let those turkeys run you down."

From the direction of the tall office buildings downtown, now going bright with morning reflection, came a lone figure. His head was bent, his hands thrust in his pockets. He limped slightly, compensating for it by hunching over, and this put me on the outer slat of the bench, poised to defend myself. I thought he might be some flasher, faking me out to get closer.

It's a fact of life, Betty'd told me. A girl as pretty as you is going to be picked at.

And Loring Park? At one time it had been a place of twisted sex intrigues, drug deals, meetings of then furtive homosexuals, and murders. It would be just like me to get whacked in Loring Park, I thought.

"Woman, Looking for Love, Murdered," the headline would read.

And then I recognized the conical hat in rainbow colors.

Benjamin sat on the end of the bench. He glanced at his watch.

"What happened to your leg?" I asked.

"Motorcycle accident a long time ago."

"You didn't do that in court."

"Do what?"

"You know . . ." What was I going to say, *limp?*

"I always wear my leg brace in court. Had it on that day I met you on the path over by the Mississippi."

"Ah," I said.

I handed him what remained of the sandwich, and he tossed bits to the geese. He lobbed a chunk into the center and, while the biggest ones were fighting over it, tossed another, larger piece, off to the side.

"Come on, you," he said to the smallest goose. "*Come on, you!*" he shouted.

Then the sandwich was gone. I rubbed my hands together.

"Take my gloves," Benjamin said.

I did. They were warm and soft.

"I've got this theory," Benjamin said.

"Do you?"

"See," he said, pointing to one of the biggest geese, who was being pecked at. "That one, in a former life, was a CPA with General Motors. Company car, seven-figure salary. Smoked big cigars. Pinky ring. Paid someone named Muffy to give him back rubs."

"Uh-huh," I said.

"That one," Benjamin said, pointing to another goose and squinting, "ran a boutique on France Avenue, liked those Jackie O. hats—you know, pillboxes—and jackets with mother-of-pearl buttons. Read romance novels with shiny purple covers in secret, but it was all Proust on her bookshelves."

I laughed.

"That one was a Hell's Angel. The bull goose biker. And that one . . . that one, he—"

"She," I corrected. "See how the—" I couldn't bring myself to say "breast."

"She . . ." Benjamin made an uncertain hmmm.

"She was married to the king of Finland," I said.

"There is no king of Finland."

"I know," I said.

"But we could create one. He would be like no king of Finland ever before."

"Do you think so?" I said.

The geese, surprised by someone walking by, all fluster and rattle of wings, rushed to the water, where they honked and swung in effortless circles. I pointed to a pair making a slow figure eight.

"Geese mate for life. Did you know that?" I asked.

"Yes," Benjamin said.

"I'm late."

"I'm not yet, but I will be." He stood suddenly, putting out his hand. "Up."

"Why?"

"I want to see something. Up," he said.

I reluctantly stood. There are those moments when the body obeys, whether you—watching, almost as if from a distance—are willing or not. Benjamin took my right hand in his and, holding me at a distance, spun me gracefully around. The snow crunched under our shoes.

"I feel silly," I said.

Benjamin led me in an easy waltz around the bench, spinning me out at the end.

"You're a good dancer," he said.

"You too." I rested my chin on his shoulder. Rough blue wool.

He hummed something, dancing. "You know, I don't really *work* for the DNR."

"Don't you?"

"I'm just a hired gun. I can hire on somewhere else."

"You can?"

"Sure."

I settled against him. "I've got to go," I said. I felt thick and slow and dreamy. I didn't want to go anywhere, moving like that. "I've got work to do."

"I know," Benjamin said. "Would you answer one question for me first?"

"What?"

There was a quiet in the moment. Everything turned now, right here. I felt it.

Something as insignificant-seeming as hello can change the world forever, I remembered Peke saying. *A tiny lever can move mountains,* ninamuch.

"Why did you wait so long . . . you know," Benjamin said, "to turn things upside down like that? You could have done it the day you walked into court. You never told me why."

"This is all impossible," I said.

We kissed.

It was warm. We were not hurried. It felt like falling into something that had been there a long time, a long, long time.

"So?" Benjamin said.

"But you already know the answer."

"I want to hear it."

"All right." I cupped the back of his head in my hand and drew him close.

"I was waiting for you," I whispered.

16

(1993) OF COURSE IT WAS RAINING. IT had to be. Buckets, a downpour, a deluge. My windshield wipers barely cleared the glass. Benjamin, beside me, settled in his seat, silent. Prosper, in back with the baby, sullenly studied Benjamin. When I wasn't pushing my nose right into that space between the windshield and the dashboard, I gave a look-see in my mirror. It was hopeless, thinking I might drive faster. The rain came down without any sign of stopping, turning the windows a glossy silver-gray. Lights on, wipers tocking at full speed, and now the baby begins to cry.

"What should I do with her?" Prosper says.

And after all, since the baby is his sister, I say, "Feed her," which he does, but not until I go rummaging through my bag on the front seat and nearly take us headfirst into an eighteen-wheeler all lights and horns and smoking brakes, headed the opposite direction. Then that car is really quiet. Driving, I chew and pop my gum. I don't often chew gum. Both Benjamin and Prosper know this. I grip the steering wheel, damned and determined to get us there. I don't know why I must do this, but our visiting the reserve has taken on the proportion of some battle. Now I am doing battle with the rain. It hammers on the roof of the car. It clouds the windows. It blinds me. It makes the road slippery.

It is the second week of May, opening weekend for fishing, and I'll be damned if we didn't get very few April showers, and now all of the rain from last month is coming down on us in one shot, as if we aren't meant to do what we're doing, which is going to a kind of christening.

I'm too old to have a baby, Benjamin is too old, but here we are, in our forties, and like Abraham and Sarah, up crops this miracle, and right on his footsteps, my one and only, my son and cross to bear, Prosper, knocks on my door, right out of nowhere, just turned twenty-one, and wanting to know why I abandoned him.

"It was Betty you were meant for," I explain. "I was just the body in there, until now."

I smile. Prosper's eyes narrow.

If there was ever a woman who knew what was hers, it was Betty Stronghold, and Prosper was hers from the moment she laid eyes on him. But this isn't to say I didn't suffer. Not every day, not every hour, not every second. And how do I explain *that* to Prosper?

Ours is a packed car. In the rain, driving, I am assaulted by voices. I can hear them in the drumming of the rain on the roof. Isabel muttering: "God bless it all!" Peke telling me the story of his arrival in Saint Paul: *Aja, I could just see him dancing in that rain. Only this time, blue pants and hat. What a smile. You look out for that Wenebojo. He'll surprise you.* Deborah, Benjamin's mother, running through the house, wailing, heartbroken: "But you *can't* understand."

I bent into the windshield. The world, seen through it, was one big melting wash of blue.

"Do you want me to drive?" Benjamin asks. This is very brave of him.

I grit my teeth, clutching the wheel. I am a woman on fire, but with what I don't know. I am determined. I am going to get us there. I got through that goddamn graduate school, I can sure as hell get us to Ten Chiefs Village and the government docks.

"What's your ETA there, sport," I say, turning to Prosper.

He's rocking the baby. She's moon-faced, ruddy, as yet blue-eyed, an amalgam of Benjamin and me, a real handful and then some.

"When hell freezes over," Prosper says.

"January," I reply.

"Not so long as that," Benjamin offers.

In this 1967 Rambler American, we are: one of the tribes of Israel, Benjamin; one mixed-blood Chippewa (Swedish and Anishinabe), me; one Heinz 57 (Navajo, Chippewa, Swedish, and German), Prosper; and this miracle of mixtures, of all that makes up Benjamin and me, Nodin, our daughter.

Here now, to my relief, is the sign that is so familiar: You Are Entering Tract 28.

That is all the sign says, but I fear I will burst out crying. I get that wheezy breathing and hunch over the wheel, as if trying to see better. I can't see a thing, it is raining so hard. Hundreds of Wenebojos dance on my hood and windshield, enticing me to crash the car. "Just fuck up here—it'll be easier that way," they whisper. In part, I want to do just that. I'm afraid. Not for what I believe, but for what I might be called upon to *do* for what I believe.

The car bumps and shimmies deeper into the reserve.

Suddenly high dark pines rise up in the rain, ominous. I am reminded of the opening of *The Shining*, that tiny car on the hillside, turning this way and that. Nothing good can come of it.

Benjamin rubs my back. His hands are strong and reassuring. I glance into the rearview mirror. There Prosper nearly sneers: I warned him, I did. I told him he might not like his real mother. I couldn't win tobacco-spitting contests, like Betty, I told him, which I couldn't resist, out of pain and jealousy, and out of testing him. After all, I've been his doting auntie for over twenty years. And, too, everything he sees in me now, those weaknesses he shares with me— the deviated septum that gives him a slightly nasal voice, not like Betty's sharp voice at all; the slightly higher right eye; and that rak- ish, sometimes untrustworthy-looking grin—all that he got from me.

So he's studying me real hard as he sits with that baby on his lap, and, seeing how I need Benjamin's touch to be reassured now, he's in a snit.

Because, of course, that is exactly what Prosper is asking from me.

My love.

Oh, God, help us all, I think, there at the wheel.

I am too stubborn to stop, say, All right, Ben, you take the wheel and I'll guide you through. We do not have to be in this damned old car, either, bad tie-rods and ruined shocks, but I insisted: I mean, when you're teaching at a school where your average parent doesn't even have a car, driving a BMW to work just doesn't cut it.

And I'm thinking about that, too.

Little Red. Let the maudlin rain in, let me cry a bit more. I grit my teeth, steer that old Rambler around an off-camber turn. Who banks a right-hander to the left? Brilliant, I think, and just then the car skids, too fast again, until I get it under control.

Benjamin smiles, blinks.

Just last week I get a note from Eckles Realtors. They've decided to turn Little Red—which was, when we got it, an abandoned renovation of a decrepit middle school—into an art gallery of some sort. They have given us a month to come up with an ungodly sum of money or turn the place over to them. I've barely slept in all that time. I haven't paid the heating bills for Little Red. I haven't paid the janitors, who, oddly enough, haven't asked. I haven't paid the teachers. I am terrified. And right in the middle of it, this christening, this whatever-is-going-to-be, this first-of-a-kind thing, this ceremony for Nodin.

And all I've gotten for her to wear is a blouse from Kmart, snatched from a bargain rack at an outlet south of Hinckley, and I am half blank-eyed calm and, just beneath it, so angry with the world that I could kill.

I've been out beating the pavement for a month, have prostrated myself at the feet of Ford Motor Company executives, Honeywell businessmen, 3M trustees. I have argued so long and so hard for our people, for all indigenous peoples, and have gotten so much the same response: "Get with the program. We're entering the twenty-first century."

Even my therapist, otherwise wonderful, said, "Aja, maybe that Indian thing is dead?"

So I did the unthinkable. That's what's really bothering me. I asked Betty to look for Gabriel, put her tentacles out where they might catch something. Some hint, some bit of gossip, and as payment for her efforts, I gave her my problems on a platter, replete with humiliating details, only asking her to swear on a Bible to keep my secrets, and God strike her dead if she broke her promise.

"I can handle that," she said.

But now, with the wipers tocking in my face, I'm not so sure what she meant.

"Mom," somebody says in the car, clear as a bell.

I don't hear it, haven't heard it, because it comes from a voice that doesn't say it.

"You're driving on the left side of the road, Mom," Prosper says.

Benjamin has taken the wheel and gently guides me over onto the shoulder.

"Let me drive, *please*," he says.

I tell him no. It is all I can do not to cry.

So it doesn't altogether surprise me when we pull up in front of the government docks and there's a regular mud wrestling tournament, with some pretty good punches thrown in, going on there, blocking the road down to the lake and boats. I roll down the window a crack, put my head out, wondering what to do. Behind us, in Oshogay's bar, a Pabst sign blinks on and off, looking like a blue-and-red bow tie. The rain has subsided slightly, but still it rakes the windows. In front of the car, those thirty or so men, now with an audience, suddenly get nastier, throw bottles, cans, and whatever else is handy, at each other.

It's opening weekend, and there aren't enough fish in the lake for everybody—that's the gist of it.

Through the window comes the smell of warm dirt and water. And lilacs.

"Get off the lake, you fuckin' timber niggers!" the biggest of the men in front yells.

Not him, I think, but I know it right there: I'm going to tangle with him. The only question is how.

Benjamin sighs. He's thinking litigation, court injunctions, due process of law. That's the way he's been trained. Prosper has his head over the front seat, perched there; the baby's making eager sucking noises.

"What a bunch of assholes," he says.

But, looking at the crazy lot of them, I'm not sure who he means. The cowboys and so-called sportsmen to one side, in pastel down vests and fancy pointed-toe boots; or my family—most of them, anyway—on the other: Hondo, in a duck jacket, standing nearly a head taller than the others; Victor Tahpoway; the Finedays and Dibikamigs, all in green canvas rain gear.

Here is one bunch of wild hair, hands clenched into fists, and a whole lot of name-calling. They're so into this fight that they take one look at us, see it isn't the cops, and get on with their happy Saturday. I check my watch. It's after one. There is no time for us to drive into Farnsworth, just down the road, where I'd hoped to buy an outfit for Nodin.

Already we're an hour late.

And we're late because, driving north, it was sunny, so sunny I was awfully depressed, and we stopped around noon for Chinese in Crosbey.

I knew things had to be looking up, so when we'd finished the kung pao chicken and mushrooms and mung beans and the hot and spicy number 7, I reached into that basket of fortune cookies the waitress stopped by with.

Benjamin smiled, cracking his open. He is handsome, dark, with those big almond eyes.

" 'Get ready! Good fortune comes in bunches,' " he read, smiling.

I turned to Prosper. He is fine-featured, hatchet blades for cheekbones, copper skin. I see the good parts of Myron in him: the expressive, playful hands, the easy chuckle, the abashed way he ducks his head.

"Listen to this," he says, grinning. " 'You will soon gain something you have always wanted.' "

I'm bumping the baby on my lap. Light of my life, miracle, gift. I kiss her forehead, and she gazorgles happily, her fingers entwined in my hair. A bell rings, and our waitress, in cobalt-blue kimono, brunette helmet hair, rushes to another table with a tray of steaming edibles.

I crack open my cookie. "Strong and bitter words indicate a weak cause," my fortune reads. Ben, winking at me, reaches for it, and I fold the narrow strip of paper and jam it into my shirt pocket.

" 'You will travel and come into a fortune,' " I lie, affecting a look of good cheer.

Ben and Prosper exchange a meaningful glance. As if on cue, both grin toothily.

"Wonderful," Ben says.

The contest of sides, in the rain, as we hear it coming through the crack I've opened in my window, now has deteriorated to "Fuck you, timber nigger!" and "No, fuck *you,* cowboy!"

Back and forth it goes, every once in a while somebody embellishing it a bit, showing some spark of intelligence, however small. There is, here and there, a smattering of polysyllabic utterances. I stare dully through the windshield at the rain. That Chinese dinner has sunk to the bottom of my stomach like a hot stone, where it is turning end over end.

Christ! I think. I have dragged my husband and my dispossessed son into this ugly mess, and, worst of all, a year-old baby, bright red cheeks, a big, happy baby, a baby who doesn't cry, who delights in the songs of birds, who likes a shaft of light and points to the dust motes in it; a baby who feeds happily, whose eyes are clear and sharp and awake, who laughs at . . . everything, it seems.

Even at me, though I'm oftentimes overly serious.

In the Cities, I've gotten used to trying to stay cool in the face of what would drive most people crazy—the school always running out of money, our kids getting beat up at home or by life, someone always after me to fix one thing or another. It's gotten so I feel like I've got permanent Ray-Bans on. I'm cool, trouble doesn't bother me, I'm above it, I'm too sophisticated to be moved by difficulty. But now, here, I'm frightened.

I listen to them outside the car. It's that bloody gill-netting thing again. The rain has lightened up and I can see a slogan on a placard:

"Shoot a Timber Nigger, Save a Walleye." I grant that this is an improvement over "The only good Indian's a dead Indian," since these so-called fishermen take their walleye and lake trout seriously. Every blue-eyed, towheaded one of them.

I check my watch again. Twenty minutes have passed.

The baby behind me gurgles, and I take her from Prosper.

"What do you say I take over here?" Benjamin says.

There is a whole world implicit in that question. I know that Father Murphy, who has driven all the way up from Saint Thomas, has taken the east entrance to the reserve, and is almost surely already at Nina's.

Frozen behind the wheel, my name, A'jawac', seems to me a sudden and terrible irony.

Carried across. That's what my name means, and here we are, stuck.

And that's when, baby in my arms, I step out into that light rain. That's it, I think. Period. I can hear the car doors slamming behind me, Benjamin and Prosper's concerned voices, but I'm not listening. I have no idea what I'm doing. I just know that *I've had it.* The rain is light on my face; Nodin looks up at me, trusting. I am a fool, a crazy person, but whatever moves me is me and not me. I am a sleepwalker with a baby, approaching a mob of angry men. My feet carry me, more balanced than I have ever been, more sure. Even when I stumble in the gravel, I am pulled up as if on guide wires. Here is so much red-and-black plaid. Torn jeans. The smell of beer breath and the sound of throaty, angry voices.

First it is Hondo, swaying like a pine in the rain, who grows quiet. I'm like Moses parting the Red Sea; I am right there in the middle of them, that baby in my arms, and of course, the one who doesn't step back has to be the tallest (but for Hondo), angriest man I've ever seen in my life.

That man.

Imagine a demented Paul Bunyan. This guy is six feet six, at least, but he's dark-eyed and dark-haired, and that is to my advantage, since when I set Nodin in his arms, he's all the more shocked, looking down at her and wondering what's up.

The rain has stopped. It's real hushed there.

They're about to start shouting again, I'm sure, but I reach into my pocket for my jackknife. Got it from Peke when I was a little girl. I use that knife to open letters and it's real, real sharp.

I examine the blade, and a lot of people there are wondering what this crazy woman's up to. Paul Bunyan is thinking maybe I'm going to have at him, but even so, he does not drop Nodin, who's got her hand tangled in his beard and, oddly enough, as if on cue, smiles up at him, the most beautiful smile you've ever seen.

I can honestly say I've known only one other moment of grace: when Prosper was named, and Betty took him in her arms.

"What's your name?" I say.

"Jack," the man says.

"Well, Jack," I say, "I want you to see something."

I held out my hand. I drew that blade right up the middle. And does it ever bleed. Runs down my bare arm. Dripped into a puddle.

"What does that look like to you?" I say.

He didn't answer.

"You got any children, Jack?"

He nodded. I stepped closer and leaned over Nodin. She smiled, tossing her arms. I was thinking of Abraham and Isaac in that old Bible story.

"Since you seem to think it's such a good idea for us to disappear, to make things easy for you newcomers, how about I just poke myself in the heart here? Would you like that?"

He recoiled a little, made as if to look for a way to set that baby down.

"Or since you really want all of us to disappear, how about I just go ahead and cut this baby's head off? Stop things right in the making. Got a real sharp knife here."

By that time he'd regained enough of his composure to argue with me. "Now, you know that's nonsense," he said.

I nodded and reached for Nodin, taking her in my arms, blood everywhere. Oh, child, what I'd done, what the universe had done, what I'd said!

I rocked her lightly, my heart hammering against my ribs. That fisherman and I looked at each other.

"I'm glad you understand," I said, and motioned for Benjamin and Prosper to get their things.

Everyone else just sort of drifted off quietly.

∿∿∿

In the boat, on the way over to Big Island, I held my hand under my breasts, wrapped in that dress I'd bought at Kmart. Everywhere, landmarks cropped up, each a portion of submerged memory. Here was Snowbank Island, where Herman had lived, and, further up, what was left of Barney's Ball Lake Resort, which I had been in only after it had gone to ruin, the walls already rotten, the boathouse filled with what at one time had been expensive outboard motors, all of them destroyed by fire. Here Peke had taken Delia Pederson up to see Herman, and here, just minutes east on Turtle Lake, was the old Dibikamig place, high and barn-red on the spire of the south shore. Still green shingles. And between the lake and the path, silver poplar, birch, and a swatch of scrubby blue-green tamarack.

Taking the lake and islands in, I got a lump in my throat the size of Idaho.

For years I'd been yakking this place up: the way the poplars turned in the fall, when whole hillsides would shine gold in the morning sun. How, even when it rained, as it was doing just lightly now, there was something beautiful in it. Then the lakes smelled of pine and cedar and wet stone. Thunder leapfrogged the islands and tumbled over you.

But here, as usual, was some kind of trouble. My hand hurt.

"You'll need stitches," Benjamin said, easing back on the motor.

There was something odd in his face. I could see he didn't know what to say. He was angry, but he had other feelings, too. I had done something outrageous, but then again, I hadn't done anything at all: I wasn't yet sure myself what had carried me out of the car, had pulled that knife from my pocket.

I know one thing: Prosper was looking at me differently.

"I can't *believe* you did that," he said.

"Well, I did," I told him.

We all ducked down under our ponchos. The rain came heavier now, the lake fuzzy with it.

Turtle Lake is a big detour: you enter on the west, because the government dock is on that side, then follow it north and around Horseshoe to the west. Here we were, finally, crossing the last stretch. Nodin, wrapped tight under my jacket, feeding. Right there, the boat bumping gently, Benjamin looking proud and handsome as any Indian at the stern, running the outboard, and my son in the bow, I got this swelling. I felt, just in that moment, that I would gladly die for this, for these people, would lay down my life. But what comes stronger now is something I've learned the hard way: that dying for a cause is *nothing*.

What you've got to do is stand up and stand up and *stand up!* And even when you think you can't do it, not ever again, you stand up anyway, take the blows, and just keep dishing out love.

This place, these islands, tears my heart to pieces.

I am but one infinitesimal speck on a lake, displaced, and returning home, a miracle at my breast, another in the bow—in a way, on loan from Betty for a short while, I know that—and Benjamin, of the same, yet different, tribe, steering us home to a place he has, up to this time, known only in his imagination.

I am terrified he will not understand. So I have to ask.

"What do you think?"

Benjamin smiles. He breathes deeply. He stands, gently guiding the boat up a channel through cattails and lily pads and flowers, yellow and white, with brilliant gold centers.

"Cool," Prosper says.

The spine of the south shore rises, magisterial. Clouds scud by overhead so heavily that for a second I have the impression that the sky, the island, and the cabin are moving, and not us in the boat.

"Use the boathouse," I say.

Benjamin gives the motor a little scoot, and we breeze right in, sudden smell of oil and oak and musty kapok life preservers and gasoline. Prosper, light on his feet, hops out and ties the boat to the dock. There are creaky steps, and I climb them, Benjamin taking our luggage. The boathouse seems not to have changed at all. I have not been in it for nearly twenty years, yet going out, the hillside there daunting, waiting for Benjamin, I freeze. On the doorframe are height marks in pencil, the oldest 1950.

Nodin stirs, and I clutch her more tightly. But it is for me, really, I'll admit it.

Just a letter there: *A*. The horizontal line is barely as high as my hip. Could I ever have been so small? And even with it, is another line: *J.,* 1956. The markings progress up the length of pine. The last is 1960, again, Jerry's. A barn swallow swoops in from the lake. I am astounded. Here, in the same corner, for forty years now, swallows are building nests. When I reach up toward them, a bird darts down, shrieking. As a child, I'd teased these birds mercilessly. Now I understood them.

∿∿∿

Earlier that year, Benjamin, after six years of marriage, risks giving me a bit of advice, and since his work is in the area of negotiation, I listen.

"You're a bull in a china shop," he tells me. "Aren't you ever going to stop fighting people?"

"Was I right?" I ask him. "Or not?"

I had just been on the phone with Northern States Power, who wanted their money, and wanted it *last month*. In the middle of what amounted to a scolding, I'd asked if they would like some free publicity, of the picketing kind, since they'd refused to cut us in on Federal Fuel Aid.

"But that's for indigent families," I was told.

"Give me another week," I said. "With your help we're getting there," and I hung up.

"So?" I ask Benjamin.

"Yes, you were right," he concedes. This he says, pacing in the living room, tugging at his hair.

"So shouldn't I say so?"

"You've got to be more—"

"Diplomatic."

"Yes."

This is why I've lost Little Red.

Again, at the Ford plant, all I'm asking for is a matching contribution. I have already canvassed Edina, Richfield, Burnsville, all of south Minneapolis, walked the soles off my shoes, begging. There, in the general manager's office, I explode when he offers to help us out with five hundred dollars.

"Five hundred dollars!" I nearly shout. "What can I do with *five hundred dollars?*"

"Wasn't there something in the news about your first school?"

"It burned," I tell him matter-of-factly, not wanting to get thrown off my pitch. I am not about to explain about the furnace and the fuel oil. I try to show him the totals I've gotten from individuals. A very hard-won five thousand dollars. But he isn't listening.

"So how about it?" I say.

"We'll mail it," he tells me. "Good luck," he says, ushering me out.

Suddenly I'm tempted to join AIM. I imagine scenarios in which I do Malcolm X proud. This is all sick, I know it, but I am desperate. Benjamin holds me at night, while I shudder and cry. If Gitchi' manido or Yahweh or Allah or the Light and Life of the Universe wants me to do this thing, why am I so bad at it?

I'm a scrapper, not a crooner. Sure, I'm pretty, or was once, but what does the world like less than an attractive woman who's demanding justice? A women who's got a big voice and her hands on her hips, dishing it back.

"It's a game," Benjamin says, caressing me.

He strokes my hair and I cry.

"Doesn't all that Holocaust stuff make you furious sometimes? Doesn't it get to you?"

Benjamin hugs me tighter.

"I'm trying *so hard*," I say.

Benjamin kisses my neck. "I know you are. And so am I," he says.

Our love that night is divine, and I am healed.

But weeks later I'm really sick. I'm doubled over the toilet. I'm getting it into my head that if I keep up the steam-engine pace I've got going, trying to save world by saving Little Red, I'm going to get cancer. So I put off going to the doctor.

I'm paranoid. I'm sure I've got it: ovarian or breast or bowel. Something *really* awful. And to make it worse, I get more and more tired, putting in my hours at Little Red, arguing with teachers over salaries, and I hate myself when I forgo my own salary to pay theirs.

What we should do is close the school.

I'm menopausal, I tell myself. I need something.

I stop, late one afternoon, turning the lights off at Little Red. In the gymnasium, smell of wax and sweat, and the mint dust the janitor uses, I study the walls. Our students, K–12, have painted the world on the back of a turtle, thunderbirds, nambiza—even Mishipishu, the underwater king—pukwanjinini, the little people, and central, on each wall, is Hare, in one depiction, his back aflame, bringing fire to man; in another, dancing; in yet another, leaping over the moon.

All I know is this: some movie star from around Santa Fe wants to start a southwestern art gallery in the Twin Cities and wants to take over Little Red for it.

I am beyond anger.

I reach for the light switch and in one decisive snap throw the room into darkness, finished, maybe for all time.

Which is exactly when I hear a familiar voice, my ersatz nephew's.

Prosper's.

"Hey," he says, looking at me in the dark.

His eyes are glassy, and somehow this darkness and quiet and all the ghosts in the Little Red gymnasium are just the thing for our reunion.

"I turned twenty-one," he says.

Embroiled in keeping Little Red open, I'd forgotten his birthday, I told myself. But that was a lie. I hadn't sent him a card or a gift because I knew he'd be coming. Betty and I had agreed on it, this year of Prosper's life.

When it rains, it pours, right?

"Betty told me," he says.

He is my height now, and even in this dim light I can see he is handsome in the way of his grandfather, Peke. The truth is, a mother is always in love with her son. I sighed.

"Do you hate me now?" I said.

By the red light of the exit sign, I could see him in profile. He had Isabel's fine lashes.

"How could you?" he said, stifling a sob.

I had planned to have Little Red bristling with new desks, new lights, a new roof, endowments, scholarships for brighter students. I'd planned on throwing my arms wide, showing him the lives I'd saved, the edifice I'd erected, the institution I'd lifted out of the ashes.

"Prosper," I said, but he was already gone.

∿∿∿

At my gynecologist's I'm up on the table, suffering yet another indignity. I am so flat broke, so tired, so broken, it makes no difference, I tell myself. I hate that cold speculum but feel next to nothing. I'm nothing more than a slab of meat on the table. My doctor is humming one tune after another from *Magical Mystery Tour.* Somehow it sends shivers up my spine. I'm not ready, I tell myself. I've got things to do.

She takes my chart off the counter behind her, whistling "Strawberry Fields."

"Feel a little swollen?" she asks, prodding my abdomen.

Here it is: the Grim Reaper, Pauguk, in her white coat and stethoscope. But is it the ovaries or the uterus? Or something else down there?

She smiles a little smile.

"You're pregnant," she says, and I nearly leap right up from that table.

∿∿∿

Benjamin is beside himself with joy. Prosper stops by, still surly, to apologize, and that's all he does and is gone. Time passes, and we smooth things out. I balance money, grow as big as a house, go door to door, trying to drum up more funds to buy out that actress, if we can. I'm an administrator, I tell them, from a school called Little Red. Could I talk to them a minute.

I tell them how our government was modeled on the Iroquois League of Nations. I tell them how the kingfisher got that tuft on his head—fooled by nasty old Wenebojo. I touch on how we are trying to be self-sufficient through education and development. I ask them to stop by the school, and a bashful few do just that.

"That baby's gonna be a walker," Benjamin says.

Every day he's off to the government center downtown; he, too, drums up some money for Little Red, and to my surprise, so do Deborah and Saul, Benjamin's parents. That money is so hot in my hands I can barely stand to hold it, even though all of it comes in checks.

Saul is a sweetheart. He tells me good Yiddish jokes, I tell him Chippewa ones.

But still, there are reminders.

Taking the MTC 52K in from the Fair Oaks, a kid a ways back, snickering, jokes with his buddy: "What's yellow and red and screams?"

"A school bus fulla Indians goin' over a cliff," the other laughs. "Har-har-har."

So when that baby is born, when I bear down like I've done only once before, forcing that kid into the new world, I've got mixed feelings. I've got this terrible, terrible desire to protect her.

Truth is, I get a little mentally ill. I very nearly smother her. I tie her up, Chippewa style, in an oblong bundle, do everything but put her on a cradleboard, though it occurred to me to do that, make a cradleboard decorated with dyed porcupine quills and seed beads, blue and ruby and pearl. I am singular in my love. At even the hint of a cry I am up. My breasts ache, always full, as if I have willed them to be this way.

But I realize I'm crazy when I won't let Benjamin hold her. I picture deserts and bombs, and Nodin at some kibbutz, being blown to pieces.

I admit this to him.

"What about those kids on the bus a while back," he said, "those kids you said you could have killed with your bare hands?"

Right there I handed the baby over, Nodin screaming and carrying on.

∿∿∿

But at my mother's now, there is only the bustle of happy preparation. She has moved into Peke and Isabel's house, and oddly enough it suits her. In her own odd fashion she has sewn the most beautiful lily of a dress for Nodin, layer after layer after layer of creamy silk, which shows off the brick tone in her skin. She sews the cut in my palm, two layers, puts on some antiseptic, and that's that.

"Fixed," she says proudly.

I tell her she should have been a surgeon. Prosper touches the nasty-looking welt. Benjamin cups my hand in his and, just like that, kisses my palm.

Nodin, my necklace twisted in her hand, clucks.

The house is all baking smells—cardamom, cinnamon, yeast. My mother has been so hard at work that flour motes hang in the weak light coming through the windows.

Then the front door swings open, and into it all bursts Betty, perfume and her loud voice, Betty, who clutches me to her chest, kisses me, really meaning it, and I squeeze her in return.

She kisses Benjamin, too, and with the greatest of good intentions, reaches for Nodin.

What can I do but offer her up?

Courting Nodin, Betty bobs her head, makes farting noises, hums the Brahms Lullaby, all at the same time, like some one-man band. Betty and I, it occurs to me right there, are just two sides of the same coin: after she lost Henry Junior and I stumbled into the equation of her life, she became a mother again, and, I can see now, with her own degree of difficulty, that she wants to be recognized. Nodin obliges her, finally, by squalling, and Betty gives her back.

"How was the drive?" she says, sneaky like.

Before I can reply, Nina say, "All right," dodging from the kitchen into the living room with a pitcher of watery-looking reddish tea. "Sumac," she tells Benjamin. "Try it, you'll like it." We engage in the usual small talk: weather, the price of groceries, Governor Carlson's BIA policies. Nina reaches for the tray of snacks and sees Betty there, polishing off the last finger sandwich.

Betty's got her radar out, senses something has happened. "So what's up?" she says.

"You ate all the sandwiches," Nina snaps. "That's what's up."

Still, old Betty is eyeing my hand, daintily licking her fingertips, catlike. I wink at her, unable to stop myself. She hates not being in on a secret.

"So, you gonna tell me?" she says.

"Oh, it's *nothing*," I say.

Prosper rolls his eyes.

"How bogus," he says, and we all burst out laughing.

∿∿∿

A short while later, going out to Prosper's van to drive to the service, I lift the lid of my mother's garbage bin to drop in another load of Nodin's diapers.

In the bottom there, wadded against a paper bag, is the canvas pack of my father's parachute, his name stenciled across it: Capt. R. Sharrett, USN.

I finger the rough green material, perplexed, wonder what it's doing there.

"You coming, Aja?" Nina calls.

∿∿∿

A narrow, grassy track between white pines. Picket fence flashing. Up. Down. Then down again, my stomach rising. Wheels thrumming.

"Hey, there, Mario!" I say.

Prosper grins. "It's a shortcut."

He insists on playing a new tape, one of the Ramones, and we're rocking and rolling, Benjamin playing drums on a Tupperware container, Nodin squalling.

Right out of nowhere, here's old Sam Dibikamig kicking up the grassy center line.

"Cut the stereo," I tell Prosper.

He hits the brakes, gravel chuttering under the tires. Sam, taking his time, approaches the driver's side. *"Boju,"* he says, to us all. Hello.

He takes an affectionate slap at Prosper's head, and Prosper punches back. "Old fart," Prosper says, and Sam guffaws. "Punk," Sam says in a wheezy voice.

With a sliding rattle, Benjamin throws the door open.

"Get in," Prosper says.

A few miles up the road, we drop Sam off. Prosper pushes a button, and, stereo blaring, windows open, wind in our hair, we careen up the road in that loose gravel. Footloose and fancy-free, even if a little carsick.

Finally, to our right, down a rutted drive, we approach Our Lady of the Lakes, a squat sandstone church with a high clapboard steeple surrounded by spring-green birches and white and blue lilacs. Off to the north, Turtle Lake sparkles, all diamonds.

I am speechless.

Behind the church are forty or so of my relations, streamers in red, white, and blue, hanging from the trees, mostly poplar. It seems half of White Earth Village is there, and I feel my face heat.

"Mom," I say.

Behind me she breathes deeply. She moistens a finger and tamps back her hair, now silver, ready to field my protestations.

"We thought—"

"*Who* we?"

"Betty and I."

"Ah," I say, and sit back. *Betty.*

My mind races. My heart beats erratically. Benjamin smiles and takes my hand. I want to ask him if he knew about this.

"Family reunion," my mother says. "We figured, since it was close enough to the same time anyway, and we had this little miracle to celebrate, what the hey? You know? Why not make a family get-together of it?"

This is a lie, but what the truth is I'm not sure. I have this sixth sense that something sneaky is in the works. After all, I have told my mother nothing. She can't know anything about my run-in with Northern States Power, or the Actress with a capital *A,* who wants to buy Little Red. Nina and I are very much like tennis friends. I call her once a month, perhaps to let her know I am still breathing, that Saint Paul hasn't fallen off the face of the earth, and that my degrees haven't somehow been taken from me.

Still, something makes me settle.

From the van I watch my relations dancing on the grass: old Bart teasing the kids, big-bellied and chuckling; Josie Kokopence and her boys throwing a baseball; Josie's husband, Cephus, close by, watching, a bit the worse for wear, but happy. In the shade of an elm, Victor Highcloud, with a few others, has the hood of his new Thunderbird up, talking motors and tires. And smack-dab in the middle of it all, at the barbecue pit, is Betty, her hands on her hips, commanding a number of men with a wave of her spatula as if with a scepter.

Folding chairs, warm spring sunlight, smell of charcoal and hickory, the *ffft! ffft!* of soda cans, and now, down on shore, the waxy, glossy cottonwood leaves make that lovely, watery pattering.

I am transfixed.

A mixture of such love and melancholy fills me that I fear I will burst or be torn in two. I'm shocked at how everyone has aged.

"I want out," I tell Prosper. "Now."

The van eases to a stop. Benjamin throws back the sliding door, and we pop out, all five of us, including Nodin, in my mother's arms. Nodin, broad cherub's face, eyes bright with pleasure. Nodin, bundled in blue, feet kicking. Nodin, who is already reaching for the lilacs she cannot eat.

"She's hungry, Mom," I tell her, and that is how I escape them all.

∿∿∿

In the end it is Sam Dibikamig who comes for me. I am skipping stones on the flat glossy water of Turtle Lake, taking it all in. Right here, in 1861, right where I am standing, Hole-in-the-Day, then tribal representative, signed a peace treaty out in front of the first mission. To the north, Peke was struck by lightning. To the south my onetime love, Henry Junior, was killed, and with him went a part of me that afternoon.

I bump Nodin on my hip, melancholy.

I'd thought I wanted to be alone. But what I'd wanted, it occurs to me now, was not to suffer. Which, of course, is causing a good deal of it.

A stone plunks into the lake, making rings in the calm water.

"Achh!" Sam says.

Grizzled gray head, bittersweet chocolate eyes, though now clouded with milky cataracts, he takes my arm, directs me back toward the reunion. He has to tug at me to get me going.

"You know," he says, "we used to call people like you in-betweeners."

"Is that bad?" I ask, genuinely curious.

Sam chuckles. "No. You two are just more honest than most, that's all."

"Who?"

"You and that Mr. Ben," he says.

ᴧᴧᴧ

Suddenly, in the nave of Our Lady of the Lakes, I do not want Nodin baptized after all. That old battle I've had with the Catholic church rears itself like a horned serpent, like old Mishipishu himself, all copper scales and shining eyes. But here we are, surrounded on all sides, and Father Murphy is rambling on endlessly and I am certain I will faint. The windows swim blue and lovely around me. Someone has lighted incense, and I breathe it in, deeply. A stone building, that's all it is, this church, but now it is filled with us, the Dibikamigs, the Finedays and Jacksons, the Sharretts. The White-horses, Sharrett-Thunders, the Morrisons and Strongholds.

I smell patchouli. Lime aftershave. Sharp chemical hair spray. There is the mumble of voices, in English and Ojibwaymowin. Light filters down through cobalt and crimson and emerald stained glass, Chagall-like figures, spirits lifting. I can feel myself rising with them, weightless.

Don't, I think, but Benjamin is there.

It's my hand, I tell myself, picking at the rough stitches. The cut is hot, and it prickles. So I scratch. I cannot stop. Benjamin takes my hand and very, very gently enfolds it in his.

The priest lifts Nodin, her dress, in that blue light, shimmering silk.

On the fourth flounce in, right there on the hem, on all that beautiful cream silk, amid those ribbons, and embroidery, are the words "Property U.S. Navy."

My mouth drops open.

That baby's gown is a parachute, my father's, which brings me to my knees in a swoon, only everyone thinks I'm praying. Which I am. Just make my heart big enough, I pray, through my clenched teeth.

Which it does, long enough for me to stand, dip my fingers in the baptismal font, and drawing a circle on Nodin's face, say loudly: "*Aigwu giwi'wiigo ninamuch.*" We receive you, loved one. And to my surprise, the congregation behind me intones "Amen."

Which cuts that service real short.

∿∿∿

Outside, bright sunlight, Nodin squalling and wanting to be fed, there is trouble again. Father Murphy is after us. He's heavy, real big around the middle, and he's pretty mad and moving fast. He comes storming out of that church like a hobgoblin, arms windmilling. He gets right up in my face, spittle on his lips, back of the barbecue pit, in that white dress and all.

"*What . . . was . . . that?*" he demands.

I think, first, to do what I would normally do, which would be to say, "None of your business, Pops." But instead, I smile, kiss him square on the mouth.

"Thank you," I say, and shake his hand. "*Thank you* for such a *nice* service."

Father Murphy's got one of those whiskey noses, and it turns as red as red gets. He's about to launch into me, give me a couple millennia of nasty Catholic invective, when I pluck a wienie from the grill and poke it into his startled mouth. (A bit of his own medicine, I think.) This really throws that priest's fuses, or is it just that that dog's hot? And in a terrified bluster, he puts on his best the-roof-needs-to-be-fixed smile and rushes back inside.

Benjamin is beaming.

"You know what I like about you?" he says.

"No, what?" I ask.

"You never fail to surprise me."

$$\sim\!\!\sim\!\!\sim$$

At the Dibikamig table, while I'm trying to eat a little fry bread, Bart Kills-in-Sight attaches himself to me, suddenly friendly. Since that afternoon when Henry was killed, he and Betty have been close, and I can smell her now in his every move: the twiddling of his pinky—a big diamond on it, no doubt her idea—his awkward silences, his halting way of getting at something.

"Just spit it out," I tell him.

Bart's roundish face goes through a number of transformations—weasel, mink, otter—and finally he smiles, missing a few teeth. A poker face. "Hear you been havin' a little trouble," he says.

"Trouble?"

Bart's eyes kind of sink into his face. "Oh," he says, as if he's surprised. "Betty had me under the impression—"

And right there I'm catapulted out of my seat.

Betty . . .

But now I can't find her, not in the church, not down on shore, not even at the baseball diamond. Then, in the middle of it all, we have a giveaway, Bart presiding. It's a formality, but still, here are three longish folding tables, junk stacked to toppling on them, and with the shout of a go-ahead, that stuff gets exchanged. Toasters. Pots and pans. A microwave oven. Tire pump. A few quilts. It is all good stuff, and thinking that, I set my watch down, but don't touch a thing.

I *can't*.

And then everything is gone. I tell myself it means nothing, but that isn't true. I'm rankled. Am I of so little value that I can't take part in the giveaway? I can only cut parts of myself off? At least, I tell myself, it's Sam who's got my watch. I hope Benjamin will understand. Diamonds don't come easy, even for lawyers.

So I'm back to searching for Betty.

"She's down by the lake," Loreen Sharrett, my not-so-distant cousin, says, blinking disingenuously. I get the feeling I've got just part of the thread, and pulling hard, I can see all these happy faces beginning to unravel. There's some private joke here.

And where's Prosper? The van, for that matter, is gone. And here, the sun shining warm on my face, the grass wonderful and springy under my bare feet, the crack of bat and ball coming from the diamond, where the boys are playing baseball—"Hey, put some Waboos on that ball, brother!"—amid the iron *clank! clank!* of horseshoes, and the low chuckle of the older men, I am suddenly reminded, all over again, of that dream I have.

Again I am wearing that humiliating crown of turds, only this time I'm covered with it, too.

The joke's on me.

Of course it is Betty's doing, this whole scheme, whatever it is, and when I stop pitying myself, I get that old protective anger, stand with my fists clenched at my sides, building up some steam. Oh, yes, they got me to let my guard down. I was a fool, but I'll get her, I think. Only I'm not sure yet what the joke is. No doubt Betty's told the whole bunch what a failure I am, how my mismanagement has tossed promise to the wind, how their kids, now school age, won't have Little Red to fall back on. *I've* lost it for them. Oh, yes I have.

I did it, but no one says that.

"*Siddown,* Aja. You got ants in your pants?" Old Lady Whitehorse says.

Here Aja Sharrett-Grunfeld has her sad lunch.

Snakelike, I smile. I'll get it out of them. But if there is one thing they have learned, it is when and how to keep their mouths shut. Getting anything out of them now is like trying to get a pearl out of an oyster with a crowbar. The instrument of language isn't fine enough. No, it takes some quiet and some looking in the eyes. But even that doesn't work. There are just too many of them, spread out on their blankets, talking and laughing.

"Where's Prosper?" I ask over at the ballpark, but he isn't there either.

Finally the van, Prosper at the wheel and Betty riding shotgun, rumbles into that picnic area of Our Lady of the Lakes, pulling with it a cloud of dust. A strange silence ensues. Bart, at the grill, doesn't flip so much as another burger. A radio, and its up-tempo rock and roll, goes dead. The ballplayers come in from the field, tall and silent and somber. Benjamin, in the middle of them, rocks Nodin in his arms.

The sun slides out from under a high white cloud, and that van glows, those coats of pearl paint Prosper put on at the VoTec shimmering.

"Come over here," he says slyly.

The door pops open on the side, and that van is full to bursting: typewriters, paper, boxes of pencils, pens and crayons, chalk, cleaning supplies, a microwave, oil, antifreeze, a Singer sewing machine, still in the box, a tool chest full of shiny new Craftsman wrenches, and Apple computers.

That van is riding right on its axle. The tires even look a little flat.

I'm stupefied, don't know what to say.

"It's from *all of us,* for your school," Betty says and, saying it, hands me a shoe box. "Here," she says.

Right there I make a wish.

By nightfall all I can do is lie on my back on the dock with Benjamin and Prosper, Nodin at my breast. After a time, clucking and cooing and wrestling with my hands and trying to put a birchbark charm into her mouth, she sleeps, and as the sun drops like a red curtain, I think to myself, I will never forget this.

Not any of it.

Up in the cabin I can hear Betty and Nina arguing. The windows are a warm yellow, the last of the sunset reflected there.

"Sizing was *not* a big fraud," Betty says.

"You'd have thought so if you'd had to mess with it," my mother counters. "It's synthetics for me; no ironing."

"Don't bring that up again."

"I didn't say anything."

"You didn't have to sew for the VA."

"Didn't I?"

The argument is endless but good-natured, a ritual, really. A breeze carries in off the lake, warm, lifting their voices away from us. Soon the stars are out, fine sharp pinpricks of light.

"What about all these stars?" Benjamin says, taking them all in with a wave of his hand.

"What about them?"

"My mom"—Prosper says—"*Betty* says Peke knew all those stars in the old-time way."

I know this for what it is, a challenge. They want to see if I've got it in me, the old stuff. The new shows all too well: in how I dress, the cut of my hair, the glasses I am forced, through myopia, to wear.

"So?" Benjamin says. "We're waiting."

I have heard it a hundred times at Little Red, which, now, thanks to Gabriel's having leased nearly one thousand acres, is going to float, and for some time. At the picnic he stepped straight out of the thick of it and, with that warm smile of his, shook my hand.

Peke and Isabel's triumph.

"Hey, how ya doin', Aja?" he said.

All those years, he'd been just a few miles north of us, on old Highway 52, with Johnny G., the General Motors dealer. I'd been on his lot, with Peke. Now it made sense that Peke and Isabel had been the only Indians to drive Chieftains and Star Chiefs while everyone else drove twin I-beam Fords.

Why else would they have bought cars off-reserve, and cars with such embarrassing names?

But the lease: It's a trade-off, since it's through some agribusiness, Pfizer DeKalb, which has as its logo a corncob with wings. Betty and Gabriel and the others have given me a seed-corn cap with a green visor, that logo right in front, which I'm wearing, out of gratitude.

Gabriel and Betty and Nina fixed that all up, put the hat in that shoe box with the paperwork.

"Maybe we should think about buying that place?" Gabriel'd said, winking.

Right there, I'd put that hat on. Not turds with a feather stuck in them, exactly, but close enough. There is, it occurs to me, no escaping these ironies in life.

~~~

Now Benjamin tugs at the hat. We are all four of us sprawled across the dock.

"Say, those stars, right *there*," Benjamin says, pointing to the Big Dipper.

"That's Ojeeg Annung," I tell him.

It's quiet; no one says anything.

A loon cries out on the lake, long and wobbly-sounding, echoing, an emissary of the dead. Remember, when you tell something, speak up, Peke told me. I settle my back against the rough boards of the dock, Nodin tucked in the crook of my arm.

"There was this hunter," I begin, but then, somehow, another voice is there, talking.

So I stop, let the other go on.

There was this hunter, Ojeeg, the Fisher, who lived where it was always cold. Peboan, the wind, tore down from the north, raking everything with snow. That wind howled, set trees to quivering. Ojeeg, every day, trudged through the snow, hunting. Peboan, blowing, tried to suck the breath out of him.

Ojeeg had a wife, Osin. And after a while there was a boy, and Ojeeg took him hunting. Peboan tore at that boy, bit at his hands and feet and nose.

Peboan wanted the boy's life, and Ojeeg knew it, but was powerless against him.

Now there happened to be a squirrel in a tree, and it says to the boy one afternoon, Grandchild, tell your father you need summer to come. So the boy did that, crying and carrying on like the squirrel told him to, and Ojeeg decided to look for it.

This summer.

He cut a hole in the ice and dived to the bottom, but it was all just rocks. He wrestled a windigo, but it wouldn't say where summer had gone. He climbed the highest tree, Peboan biting him, so that he lost one of his ears.

From up in that tree, he looked everywhere on earth, but nowhere was summer.

And now they were starving, so he couldn't search any longer.

It was hopeless, Ojeeg thought, but just then he got it into his head that there was one more place to look. He'd try to go through the sky, to see if summer was up there. He got otter, beaver, lynx, and wolverine, whom he'd been trapping, to go with him. If it's so good, this summer, I can fish, he told them.

They climbed the tallest mountain. Peboan clawed and bit them the whole way up. At the top they were half blue with cold and shaking. If they jumped, just a little, they could scratch the sky there.

Otter slid back to the earth. Lynx tumbled, scratching ravines with her claws. Beaver tried to catch himself with his tail and made landslides.

Which left just Ojeeg and wolverine.

So Ojeeg says to wolverine, Since you're so fierce, you give it a try. Which wolverine does, gnawing and snarling, and tearing a hole through the sky.

They both stuck their heads up, through that hole.

I paused there. "You listening?"

Benjamin's eyes shone in the dark. Prosper lit a cigarette. Oh, well, so much for perfection, I thought. Then had to have one myself.

In the above world, I said, *there were fat rainbow trout in sparkling streams. Deer grazed at their green shores. Beavers lived in wide muddy dens. Ducks waddled fat and lazy everywhere.*

But it was in some lodges, bigger than any he had seen, that Ojeeg found the cages.

"Mocuks," Prosper said. "Right?"

"Right," I said.

What did I want to say? I sat up, cradling Nodin. I put my feet in the lake. I felt that old feeling, roots, the water, blood.

"And?" Benjamin asked.

"Finish it," Prosper says.

There were birds of all colors in those cages, green birds, the color of spring, birds the color of water and of sunsets and of corn, of ripe rice, and of sleek new fur, birds the color of blueberries, of gooseberries, of blue jays, of puppies, of children.

And Ojeeg, he breaks all those cages apart. Smashes them, letting out the birds. Big birds, wings furled like summer wind and storms and clouds, birds with tail feathers like sheaves of wheat, birds smelling of lilacs and roses—the whole lot of them escaped right down through that hole, which tough old wolverine was holding open, until the summer world people, like shadows, saw what was happening and started shooting arrows. Wolverine jumped down the hole and back into the world.

But the birds were still flying, and Ojeeg, with his teeth and claws, held open the sky so they could all go down. A porcupine now for all those arrows bristling in him. He wanted all of it, sum-mer, for his wife and boy.

Out of love.

At the last second he tried to dodge down through the hole too, but he got hit in his fatal spot, at the base of his tail. Got stuck up there.

And the hole in the sky snapped shut.

"And that's what you're looking at in Ojeeg's tail. The Fisher Stars. See? The arrow's still there, too."

I point to those stars.

"He's the Summer Maker. That's what the name means. Ojeeg Annung."

In that moment, there on the lake, the cabin quiet behind us, I am struck by something. It is more a feeling than a thought. You'll know the difference, Isabel had said. You'll *feel* it.

The world is *alive!* Peke had said. Even a stone breathes!

I cradled Nodin there in my lap.

The stars turned over us. Prosper was humming. Far to the north a spike of lightning came down blue-white. A cool breeze was blowing.

"You think it'll rain again?" Benjamin asks.

I laughed. "Rain?"

I reared back, tossed that winged cap out as hard as I could. The wind caught it and spun it end over end.

That hat kicked its heels and winked and, just like that, was gone.